DARKNESS UNKNOWN

Beshadowed

Darkness Unknown
Blood Bound
Shadows Awoken
Everdark Cursed

Published by Fairies and Fantasy Pty Ltd 2020
ISBN: 978-1-922390-15-8 (paperback)
ISBN: 978-1-922390-16-5 (hardcover)

www.selinafenech.com

DARKNESS UNKNOWN

SELINA A. FENECH

BOOK ONE OF

BESHADOWED

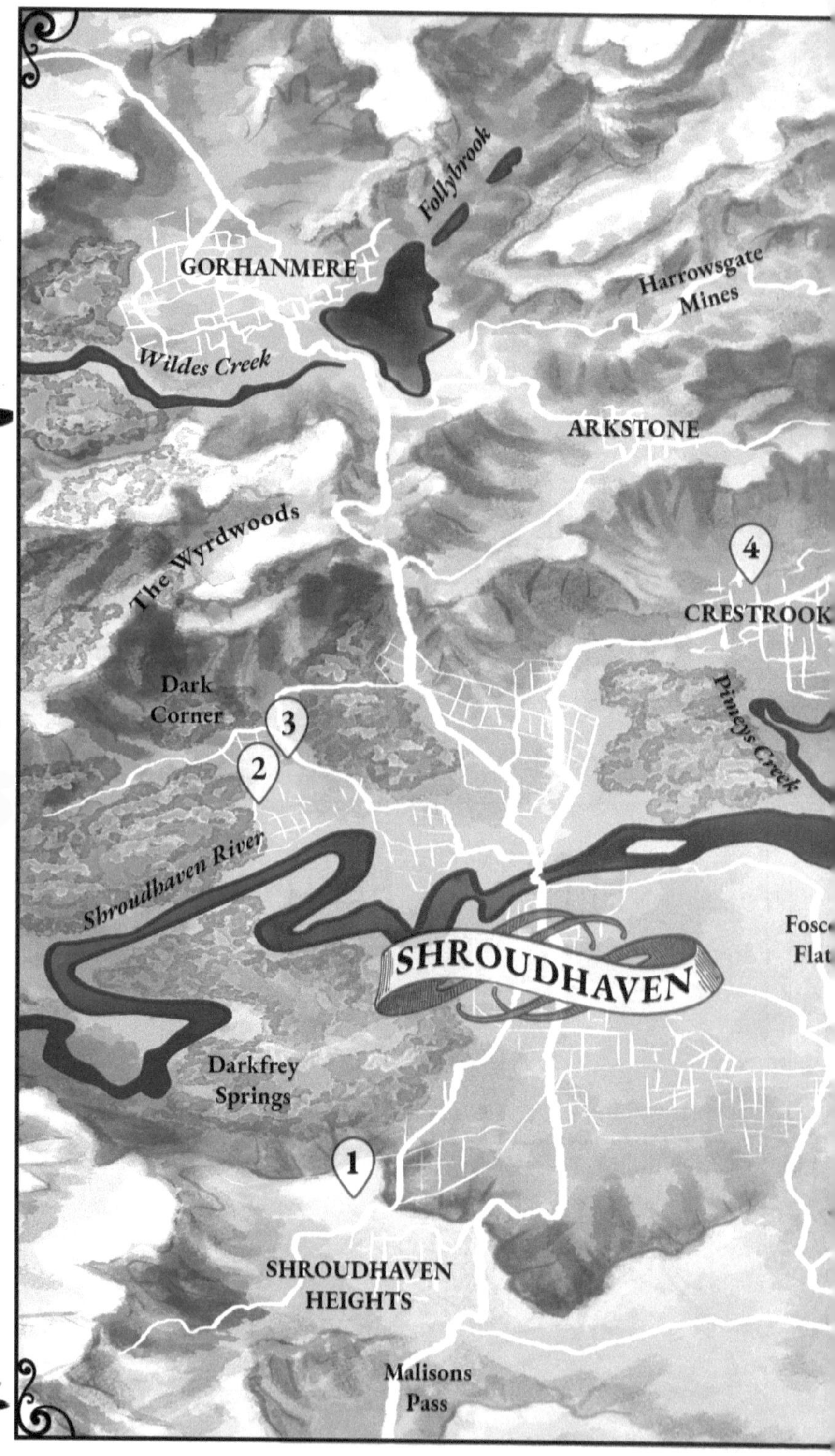

GORHANMERE
Follybrook
Harrowsgate Mines
Wildes Creek
ARKSTONE
The Wyrdwoods
CRESTROOK
4
Dark Corner
Pimey's Creek
3
2
Shroudhaven River
SHROUDHAVEN
Fosce Flat
Darkfrey Springs
1
SHROUDHAVEN HEIGHTS
Malisons Pass

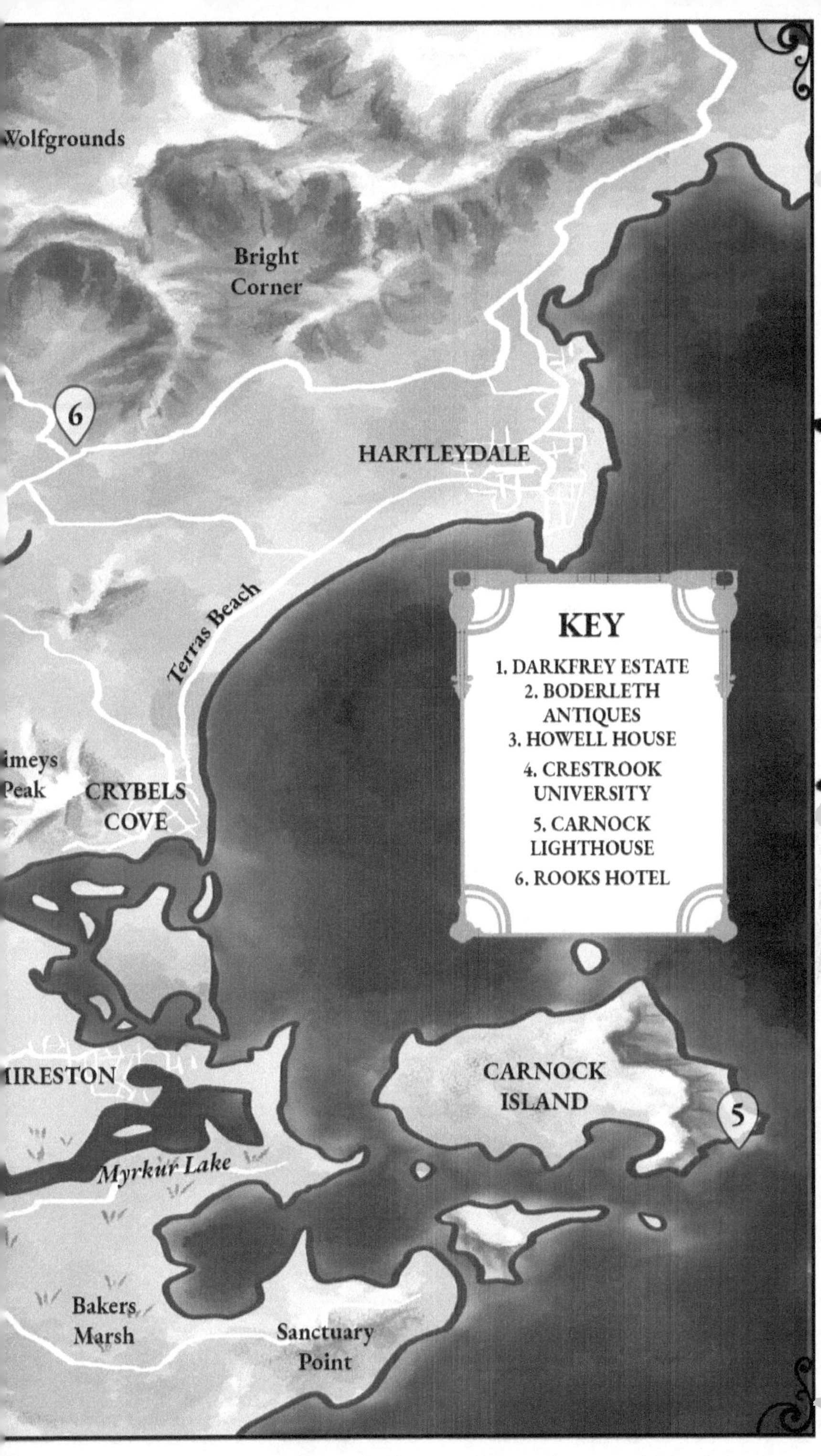

Wolfgrounds
Bright Corner
HARTLEYDALE
Terras Beach
imeys Peak
CRYBELS COVE
KEY
1. DARKFREY ESTATE
2. BODERLETH ANTIQUES
3. HOWELL HOUSE
4. CRESTROOK UNIVERSITY
5. CARNOCK LIGHTHOUSE
6. ROOKS HOTEL
CARNOCK ISLAND
HIRESTON
Myrkur Lake
Bakers Marsh
Sanctuary Point

Chapter One

The white noise hum of anxiety grew in Everly as the man on the phone said, "I regret to inform you that your mother has passed away."

She'd missed his name. He'd introduced himself over the patchy line as the administrator of Janey Boderleth's estate and her brain jolted like touching a hot wire, blanking out the next part.

She fumbled with wet hands to get a better grip on her phone, turning away from the leaky pipe she was unscrewing. Her heart raced. The wrench in her hands dropped, clattering on the concrete floor.

The echoing clang made Harper squeak from across the basement. "Are you trying to scare a girl to death?"

Everly mouthed an apology and bent to retrieve the tool.

Am I going to have to pay for the funeral?

Maybe that shouldn't have been her first reaction to the news of her mother's death, but she couldn't handle any more expenses right now. She was already drowning. Horror struck at the thought her mother may have left her debts.

That's what she wanted to ask, but when she opened her mouth it formed the word, "How?"

The sound of papers shuffling came over the staticky line. "She was found in an alley behind the main street, but no foul play is suspected. All signs indicate it was due to substance abuse. Janey Boderleth had a number of legal and illegal drugs in her system."

No surprises there. And considering Shroudhaven's high unexplained death count, at least her mother kept things simple.

The man breathed heavily over the line. "Ms. Boderleth? Are you still there? I understand this must be very upsetting. I can call back later to discuss the details if you'd like."

"No, it's fine. I'm here." Everly's fingers trembled—a warning sign. She ran through a grounding exercise to make sure her over-enthusiastic adrenal system didn't get set off by the news.

Five things she could see: the bare red-brick walls of the basement, the water-stained concrete floor, her pale, distorted reflection in the chrome of her wrench, the harsh glow of Harper's LED ring light, and her friend, setting up another shot across the room.

"We haven't been able to find any record of a will. It seems your mother never made one."

Lucky, or I'm sure I would have been written out of it.

Four things she could touch: the cold metal pipe, the water wetting her hands, the callous on her finger where the wrench rubbed, and the worn fabric of her red jacket's cuffs.

"And it seems as though you are the only surviving next of kin."

Acutely aware, thanks.

Three things she could hear: the man's sandpaper breaths through her phone, the hum of the water heater, and the click of Harper's camera.

"Making you sole inheritor. Although ... there are no savings."

Shocker.

Two things she could smell: ancient deposits of oil and grime, Harper's vanilla perfume.

"There are also no debts."

Everly released a long sigh of relief and completed the grounding exercise.

One thing she could taste: the blood of her bitten lip.

A bitter pain burned Everly's throat, and her voice

came out child-like. "She's really dead?"

"I'm sorry, *what? Dead?*" Harper froze mid pose change.

Her lacy pink dressing gown was hanging off her shoulders and she flicked it back up, but it did little to cover the rose-gold corset and hotpants beneath that contrasted against her pained expression.

She rushed over on tappy stilettos. Her ankle turned on the broken concrete floor, and she tumbled.

Everly thrust her arms out, catching her. "Careful."

"Sorry. Thank you. *Who's dead?*"

Everly let go of her friend then lifted the wrench and one finger to shush her. Harper's lips pressed into a thin line and she stilled, waiting, as the administrator rattled off a bunch of legal terms.

He ended with, "The only asset to be dispensed with is the house."

Air rushed out of Everly's lungs. The house.

A surge of old memories from that place and her life there made Everly's heart rattle against her ribs. She thought she'd left it all behind.

Everly leaned against the wall as a wave of wooziness hit her. "Actually, I will call you back later if that's okay? I'm in the middle of something."

The moment the phone was tucked away in Everly's pocket, Harper raised the shutter remote in her hand

and thrust it at Everly as though they were dueling. "Did someone *die*?"

"Yeah. My mom."

"Oh no. Oh Ev, I'm so sorry!" Harper pulled Everly into an embrace of flawless brown skin and silky black curls.

"It's okay, really."

There was pain. Everly could identify it, sitting heavy behind her eyes and beneath the curves of her chest. But it was an old pain, a familiar pain. It had been with her since the end of her and her mother's toxic relationship when she'd been kicked out of home four years ago.

She had mourned the loss of her mother since the day she left home, despite the damage the woman had done to Everly. Damage she was still working through.

"How can it be okay? I know you two had problems—"

"Understatement of the century."

"And they were *her* problems, not yours. I'm sorry. But still, your mother!" Harper brushed loose strands of Everly's silver hair away from her face and rubbed a thumb across her cheek as though wiping a tear that wasn't there.

"Honestly, I've been expecting that call forever. I'm surprised she lasted this long, considering her lifestyle."

It was a small mercy that she hadn't died in the house. That place was haunted enough already.

"She *was* still young, though, wasn't she?" Harper pouted, as though the greater tragedy was the lost potential of a late-in-life mother-daughter reconciliation.

Everly held onto no such hopes. "Early forties. Although the life expectancy in Shroudhaven isn't great even for the healthiest townsfolk."

"Sounds like a charming place."

"The charmingest. Gloomy weather, overabundance of deadly mishaps, conspiracy theorists aplenty ... It's a wonder I left."

Everly tried to turn back to the leaking pipe and continue her work, but Harper snatched the wrench from her hand and dropped it roughly into the canvas bag at their feet. Everly winced at the mistreatment of her beloved tools.

Taking both of Everly's hands into hers, Harper said, "What about your dragon? How is it taking the news? Not going to overreact?"

"My anxiety is fine. A little tiffed about having to speak on the phone with a stranger, but no panic attack looming." Everly gave Harper a grateful smile for the check-in.

They'd been roommates long enough now that Harper was used to Everly's anxiety and her codeword for it. The nasty dragon that plagued her emotions and flared up when she least needed it.

"Come on. No more work for the day. Let's go treat ourselves." Harper dropped Everly's hands and started packing up her camera, tripod, and light stands.

"I have to get this finished. It's still leaking, and it's

only going to get worse if I don't fix it." Everly picked up some plumber's tape and her wrench again and worked on the connection.

"These old pipes are always leaking! You're always down here patching them up."

"Kinda my job?" Everly tilted her head to the building superintendent badge clipped over her bomber jacket.

A job I can't risk losing. Not many bosses would overlook my complete lack of qualifications and fake ID. No matter how big of a sleaze-ball the landlord is, and the pocket change he pays.

Harper unclicked a lens from her camera that probably cost a year of Everly's wage. "Let it be someone else's problem. We'll be out of here soon anyway, right?"

"Sure. Soon" Not really a lie.

Everly wanted to get her and Harper out of that building ASAP too.

She knew it could be a matter of life or death. But that didn't help her to have the funds she needed to move. She didn't want Harper, everything-together-Harper, to know, to pity her, to offer to pay her share.

She'd been trying to save but her balance only kept going down. But maybe, maybe her new inheritance could change that. The house could change that. Her thoughts jangled between anxiety and hope and re-awakened trauma as she continued to work on the pipes.

Harper put her hands on her hips. "The landlord should just replace this old water system with something new and be done with it."

"We don't need a replacement. Sometimes broken things just need a little bit of care ..." Everly wiped her work clean and turned the water back on. No leaks. "And ta-da, all fixed."

"Only because you have the magic touch." Harper made kissy lips at Everly.

When it comes to objects, at least.

People? That was something Everly struggled with.

Everly zipped up her tool bag and hefted it up onto her shoulder.

Harper threw on a substantially less see-through robe for the trip back upstairs. "Thanks for letting me tag along and get some good use out of the grungy backdrop. The photos I was getting are fire."

Clicking off her LED, she juggled the mess of tripods and stands in her arms.

"Can I help carry your gear?" Everly asked.

"All good, I'm sure these don't weigh half what you're lugging around."

"Just what kind of baggage are we talking about here?" Everly tried to throw the words out like a joke, but they made Harper give her puppy dog eyes that would put a Basset Hound to shame.

"Whatever you need today, you've got it, okay? I know, I know! You're fine! But you just lost your mom and regardless of your relationship and history, that's huge. It can't be easy having lost both parents."

Everly tried to ignore the tight knot of pain in her sternum as she locked the basement door behind them and they made their way up the dingy stairwell to the lobby.

"I'm not saying it's easy. I'm just saying I did all my boohooing about it years ago. I was barely a toddler when Dad passed, and really, I lost Mom as well at the same time."

Everly didn't know if they'd ever been a happy family. She'd been too young at the point it all fell apart. But there was a time when it had been the three of them, without her mother's substance abuse, hoarding, and addiction to never-ending streams of toxic lovers.

That had all started when Janey Boderleth's husband died, leaving her a young widow and mother to a child she was convinced was the source of all her hardship.

"I am going to hug you *so hard* again once I put down all this junk!" Harper rattled the tripods in her arms.

The lobby was brightly lit with a stream of afternoon sunlight and Everly's work boots squeaked on the tiles. She pushed the elevator button for the top floor—Harper's apartment—so she could drop off her camera gear and get changed.

Despite them living together, they still kept two

apartments. There wasn't enough storage in Everly's smaller rooms for them both, and no way enough room for Harper's wardrobe.

But they both slept at Everly's, for safety.

The elevator dinged and the doors opened to reveal a man inside.

The cheerful gym-bro from floor three. Harper tensed and stepped back. Everly moved closer, standing in front of her friend as she offered the man a polite smile. He seemed to look right through her, giving Harper a long look as he walked away.

Everly was used to it. Silver-haired and plus-sized, she was practically invisible when she was beside the immaculate Harper Bells, or 'Bellsy' to her millions of social media fans. It was hard not to be in awe of someone who looked like they had a beauty filter running on them in real life.

But the kind of attention Harper had attracted recently was nothing to be envied.

A little positive attention in my direction would be appreciated though. Everly was ready for a relationship. Anything to help her get over her unrequited feelings for someone she could never have.

Harper's face scrunched as she stomped into the elevator. "I hate this. I hate jumping at every shadow. We have to get out of here."

Seeing her friend feeling so powerless and being unable to help hurt Everly more than the news of her mother's death. "I'm sorry."

The elevator rattled closed and lifted them to their destination.

"Babe, it's not your fault! Sorry, I'm just venting. I'm not making today about me." Shaking off her frown, Harper's expression returned to one of picture-perfect sympathy. "What needs to be done about your mother? You know, legally?"

Sighing, Everly picked up the end of her long braid and flicked the nearly white hair between her fingers. She wished she could regulate her own emotions so well.

"I'm guessing there will have to be some kind of funeral. And apparently, I now own a house."

A toothy grin split through Harper's sympathy. "Wait, wait, wait. There's a house? Like, are we talking cute little cottage or spooky huge mansion?"

"A bit of both, with a built-in antiques store. It, plus its many riches of whatever my hoarder mother trashed the place with, are all mine. I'll call the administrator back for the details in a minute. I'm sure there's a bunch of paperwork to do to make it all official."

The elevator came to a stop and Everly noticed thinly concealed hesitation and fear on Harper's face as she stepped out.

She glanced up and down the hall twice before unlocking her door. "That's kind of exciting, right? You own a whole, real house! It could be a holiday home!"

"It wasn't in a good state when I still lived there and tried to keep it all together. Who knows how bad it is now. Maybe I can pay someone to burn it down and sell the razed earth."

If only I had enough savings to hire an arsonist.

Everly put her tool bag down and remained near the front door, careful not to touch anything. The living room of Harper's apartment was too white for Everly to move around in comfortably, especially after working. Visions of grease stains on snowy suede made her shudder.

A sickening feeling swelled inside her. Her hands tingled and her pulse thrummed in her ears. Suddenly unsteady, she leaned on the wall and hoped she wasn't smudging dirt on it. Everly counted out her breaths, trying to stay grounded.

Harper disappeared into what was once her bedroom and now all wardrobe storage. "You have to at least go back and visit first."

"Do I though?" *In for seven, hold for four, out for seven.*

Harper called back through the opened door, "For closure. And a trip back home could be good in other ways too. You might run into that boy you've been crushing over your whole life. Things might happen! I'm all for things happening for you!"

Rylan. Everly winced as she fought to force down her panic. "Even if I went back—"

"Which you are!"

"Which I'm not, I can tell you for a fact that nothing romantic is going to happen between me and Rylan. And also, he's not a boy, he's a man. At least he would be by now."

Harper gasped melodramatically. "Look at you defending his honor."

"I'm just being factual about the flow of time and aging." Everly's cheeks heated, and her heartbeat reached an overwhelming pace.

Just breathe, breathe.

Her vision darkened and blurred. She slumped against the wall and fell.

Chapter Two

Everly swore as she landed on the ground. Her whole body shook with her rampant pulse. She focused on pulling herself back together, keeping her dragon contained.

Fluttering back out into the room in a new outfit of lace T-shirt and hot-pink overalls, Harper caught sight of Everly and rushed over to kneel beside her.

She pulled Everly up in a tight hug. "Panic attack?"

"Yeah. It caught up to me after all."

"I'm sorry if this is because I brought up Rylan, on top of everything. It's just that I know you still care about him, boy or not."

Pressed in her friend's embrace, the tangle of pain in Everly's chest seemed to release, spreading out through her body, heating her eyes. She blinked back tears.

Home. Her parents. Shroudhaven. Rylan. Every pain,

everything there she'd left behind seemed to come crashing down onto her like an avalanche of emotional bricks.

But what could she do? The past was the tremendously screwed-up past, and Everly wasn't equipped to revisit it.

"Maybe I do care. But it doesn't matter. I get to see him all the time in my dreams, and the real Rylan has made it clear he never wants to see me again."

"Then you're better off without him. We're both better off without men and what they've put us through." Harper squeezed just a little harder.

Everly's broken heart was nothing compared to what Harper's ex had done. The danger he'd caused. The reason they had to move.

Everly needed money. And to get it, she was going to have to go back home.

Before Everly knew it, she was back in Shroudhaven. She didn't even know how she got there, out on the familiar main street in the gusting wind, staring at Pimey's Diner with its faded red-and-white awnings and candy-cane façade, watching through the window as a monster perched on the counter like a grotesque table ornament.

"Oh, of course." Everly pressed her hands to the glass,

and it rippled beneath her fingers. "This is a dream."

Those words grounded her, making her consciousness fully present.

As haunted by nightmares as Everly was, she'd done a lot of work toward controlling her sleeping mind. Lucid dreaming was the goal she and her therapist spent many sessions working toward, and once she'd cracked it, Everly considered it her small superpower.

She worked to get her bearings and decide whether this was a dream she was willing to partake in or not.

The setting didn't worry her. She was often reeled back to Shroudhaven in her dreamscapes. The next thing she checked for were threats, what challenge her mind would throw at her.

Inside the diner, a few patrons sat in booths, chewing slowly over burgers and fries too yellow to be real. Waitresses in frilly retro aprons slid up and down the room on unmoving feet, too many plates balanced in each hand.

And amid it all, the monster shifted and shivered. It was huge, almost the entire length of the vintage counter that spanned one half of the diner, across from the cozy booths down the other side.

Nobody else appeared to notice it.

Everly squinted at the creature, unafraid. It was a mess of darkness and bad feelings with no real discernable features. Her dreaming brain was really skimping on the detail tonight. All it did was label the void-like blob a *monster* and so Everly knew it was.

The way it was slowly and methodically consuming the body of a waitress was another indicator.

"Well, that's gross." Everly winced away from the view, turning to look for Rylan.

He should be showing up soon.

He always did.

A sparkling brightness caught Everly's eye as her dragon flew past, turning laps in the street behind her. Much like the monster, it was as much feeling as it was form. A creature of light and hunger that shook up Everly's insides just by setting her eyes upon it. A visible manifestation of her anxiety.

She turned her back on it. It was better to ignore the thing.

Down the cobblestone pavement, another group of monsters approached. These four were more clearly drawn than the gurgling shadow in the diner.

They moved together with purpose—humanoid, pale-skinned, with midnight eyes and fangs bared. Vampiric.

"Yawn. Can't we do something a bit fresher?" Everly called out, as though there was anyone else in control of the reoccurring situation than herself.

Not that it was terrible seeing Rylan being all tough and vampy. As one of the four striding down the street toward her, he took the lead ahead of his three other vampire followers, face stern and wide shoulders set.

They all wore black soldierlike pants and tank tops, except for the other man in the group who wore a cardigan.

The moon bobbed full and bright behind Rylan in the starry sky, glittering over his short-cropped hair and bare arms, outlining the muscles there.

He was *bigger* than she ever remembered him being, the cords and curves of his arms and chest wrought vividly on marble-toned flesh.

Everly sighed. It was undeniably hot.

This is some cruel and unusual torture. Seeing him like this, every night, out of reach even in her dreams.

The group of four vampires—Rylan, the cardigan guy, a pointy-faced woman with a sharp blond bob, and a redheaded teen with freckles like a galaxy set bright against her deathly pallor—arrived beside Everly.

"Hey, how's it been?" she asked, expecting no reply. Dream Rylan was as unresponsive as real-life Rylan. "Busy? Yeah, me too. Have lots going on. Exciting stuff too."

Everly wasn't quite sure why she felt the need to lie to this figment of her imagination. Especially when he rarely acknowledged her presence anyway. But whenever she saw him, walls went up.

He stared through the diner window toward the monster inside, speaking in tongues to the others, a stream of fragmented English and indecipherable syllables.

When Everly focused very hard, she could hear comprehensible speech, but it was like trying to read in dreams. None of it made sense even when the words came through with clarity.

"Be careful of all the mouths."

"It's not close to fully beshadowed."

"The vasmire mist has the blivs out."

So much confusing nonsense.

Because this was just a dream. And none of it mattered. Except for how it made Everly feel. And it made her feel a lot.

Especially after the day she'd had, getting the news of her mother's death and working through what that meant for her. Regardless of how she felt about her mother as a person, her death made Everly butt up against deeper questions of mortality and existence. Which made an impetuous audacity flare within her.

She took a deep breath and stood in front of Rylan and said with her full chest, "My mother died. And I miss you. A lot."

Hovering in the sky above her, her dragon shivered, scales scintillating like a tide of stars.

Rylan's brow dropped low over his eyes that didn't look at her but over her head. He placed one hand at his sternum as though easing a pain there and then lifted it again, pointing with two fingers toward the waitress-eating beast.

Everly reached out but didn't touch Rylan. She knew he would feel solid, as solid as anything else in the ever-shifting fluidity of her dream, but it seemed wrong to put her hands on him when he was ignoring her so fully.

"Do you ever think about me? Did I ever matter to you?"

Rylan laughed and cuffed the pretty-freckled vamp on the shoulder like one of the boys. He once used to do that to Everly.

Everly blinked slow, wet eyes, and when she opened them, the four vampires were gone from the street. They were inside the diner now, circling the shadowy monster within. The creature had expanded to fill the space and lashed Rylan's group with tentacles made of darkness.

A mist swirled down the counter and crept across the floor, as though pouring out of the monster itself. Fry cooks worked the grills with blank faces as they overlooked the battle.

"Okay, we're doing this. Fine." Everly stepped up to the diner window and then stepped right through it, taking a seat in a red-and-white vinyl booth.

The squeaky bench seemed both infinitely long and too cramped, and Everly had to keep readjusting her sitting position to account for dream-physics.

With a great strength of will, Everly manifested a tub

of popcorn on the table in front of her and dug in, eyes on the show.

A film grain sputtered over the blur of fighting bodies, all black and white like an old-fashioned movie.

Everly crunched on tasteless clouds as vampire Rylan grappled long tangles of inky shadow. He moved with a vicious, precise elegance, tearing clawlike hands into the living darkness.

A chunk of smoky gore spattered against the jukebox which played the haunting melody of a man singing about his beloved mermaid.

Between Everly's blinks, the scene would jump and change.

The other vampires worked in unison, grasping and pinning the monster.

Waitresses circled with stone-faced smiles, a creepy merry-go-round of aprons and clattering plates.

The creature lurched from the counter, overwhelming the redhead and cardigan guy.

Then they were all back on the counter again, rolling in a mass of limbs and swirling shadows.

The floor of the diner turned red as blood oozed out between the booths, flooding over the checkerboard tiles, vivid against the otherwise black-and-white world.

Everly lifted her feet up onto the bench and wondered whether she should wake herself up. The dream was taking a dark turn, and as much as she knew it couldn't hurt her physically, the emotional toll of her nightmares could shake her up for days when they became too intense.

Normally that meant the ones where she watched Rylan get hurt. Ones that felt too real, as though she was going to receive a call the next day much like the one she'd received about her mother.

Tonight's dream was especially vivid, and the edge of danger and death loomed over everything.

Maybe I'm more shaken up by Mom's death than I want to admit.

She watched for a moment longer, and it seemed as though dream-Rylan and his vampire buddies were getting things under control.

There was a time when Rylan's younger brother made up one of the four monsters she regularly dreamed of, but a while ago, for some unknown reason, her mind had replaced him with the redhead. Much like how at some point it had decided to change Rylan's haircut.

The cardigan guy was often around, but neither Everly nor her therapist had any idea of the significance of this dream personality always wearing a cardigan.

It wasn't something her dad did, or any other man who had been through her life—or woman, for that matter. It was waved off as some symbol of comfort or respectability.

The fact that Rylan almost always appeared in her

dreams as a monster was something her therapist had *a lot* to say about.

"This person from your past caused you great emotional harm, so your psyche is presenting him in monstrous forms as a visible indicator of his capacity to cause harm and your fear of confronting the harm he caused."

Everly had tried to argue that Rylan hadn't hurt her, not on purpose or not in a way that was his fault. All he'd done was end their friendship. Fully and finally and for a reason.

Everly sometimes wondered if she appeared as a monster in his dreams as well.

"If you went back, you could ask him in person." Harper's voice intruded into the chaotic battle, crackling into the music from the jukebox.

"That's assuming I actually want to hear the answer," Everly replied.

"You could ask him in person," the disembodied voice echoed again and then again and again, growing louder.

The sound reverberated throughout the diner, rattling milkshake glasses and shaking color back into the dream with a pop so loud every face turned to stare at Everly.

Including Rylan. His features shifted—vampire, human, vampire—and his eyes flickered from galaxy black to warm green and they were on her, seeing her, in a way this dream form of him never normally managed.

Everly's mouth opened to spill the silent words clogging it but a scream cut her off. The monstrous void of lashing gloom threw the redhead across the room, then reared up behind Rylan and consumed him whole.

CHAPTER THREE

B reaths panting in frantic bursts, Everly fought the
sheet tangling her body.

She thrust it off, eyes snapping open into the darkness of
her room. Her phone lay on the bedside, glowing numbers
informing her it was two in the morning.

Rolling to her side, Everly grasped for the phone and
held it to her chest for a long moment as she breathed
through her nose and worked through redefining what
was real and what was dream.

Rylan is fine. He's fine. There are no monsters.

Still, she unlocked her phone and scrolled down
through her contacts to *R* and stared and stared with
sleep-bleary eyes at his number. A deep, harrowing hollow
had opened up within her, desperate to know that he really
was fine.

She knew he wouldn't answer, even if she did call. Maybe she could text.

What would she write?

Hey, just wanted to know that you're still alive?

Wow, that's one awesome way to come across as a passive-aggressive stalker.

If something did happen to Rylan, or had happened to Rylan, anytime in the years since she'd seen him, would anyone even think to inform her? Would his mother or brother reach out to her?

Did they know about what had happened to Everly's mother? It was a small town. They must. But no messages of condolence had reached her.

Were any of them still there? Did any of them still think of her?

If you went back, you could ask him in person.

All her questions. All the worries and hurt and truths hanging unspoken between them. Maybe she could speak them. Maybe she could get closure.

All she had to do was return to the place where all her nightmares first began.

Rylan pulled a wad of napkins from the dispenser on the counter and wiped the viscous black blood that had splattered on his jaw and neck. It smeared slickly over his skin, refusing to absorb into the thin tissue.

This hunt was an utter mess, in more ways than one.

Annabeth was still sprawled on the floor beside one of the booths. Chunks of oozy flesh hung in her red hair.

"Sorry, I thought I had it under control." She rubbed the back of her head.

"Sorry means nothing to a dead shadyr," Vonny snarled in reply.

She marched around the counter, platinum hair swinging like the blade of a guillotine, and kicked at something that squelched. "Which we almost were thanks to you."

Jasper remained silent, lips thin as he inspected a pinpoint splatter of black on his knitted cardigan.

Even with Annabeth's skin stonelike and pale, Rylan saw the flush that colored her freckled cheeks. The girl was fresh, only part of his brace for the last six months. Rylan wasn't sure she was ready for it, but they needed a fourth when Callan up and deserted them.

Even if she hadn't been ready, six months on the job should have had her up to speed by now.

Callan only took two months from when he got brace duty to being as good as they got. But that was Callan.

His brother was always trying to keep up with Rylan and more. The competitive streak between them was strong.

Damn, I miss hunting with him.

It wasn't that Annabeth was incapable. She just wasn't exceptional. And plenty of Darkfreys found their way to a grisly death from being anything less.

Rylan strode over through the swirling mist and offered her a hand. Tough love was Vonny's way, and for years it had been Rylan's way too, but Callan's decision to abandon this life, and his brother, left Rylan questioning everything.

"You did fine. You're holding form much better. And I think we all got a bit distracted there."

She took his hand, pulling up to her feet, and her blush grew. "Yeah, did you feel that weird pressure in the air?"

Rylan nodded. "Blew my ears out."

"It's no excuse. What do you expect? Beshadowings get weird. You're supposed to expect the unexpected and deal with it." There was more muttering under Vonny's breath, and Rylan could guess how she cursed this team she'd ended up with.

As the oldest of their brace by around two decades, she must feel beset by young people.

"We achieved our objectives and without casualties, so we've met the base criteria for a successful mission." Jasper straightened his cardigan, acting as though he were a few decades older than his young years too.

Not a silky-black hair slicked back on his head was out of place and barely a smudge on his warm-bronze skin.

Rylan glanced around the diner. No casualties except for the one waitress, but she was already gone before they arrived. Two other blivs lay awkwardly, toppled over and unconscious in the mist. At least Rylan's brace arrived in time to save them. It was about as successful as they got.

"Oh, technicalities, how I love thee," Annabeth crooned softly.

She smirked conspiratorially at Rylan, but when he didn't return any hint of humor, she pulled her expression back to soldierly stoic.

"Come on, let's get out of here. Our shift is done." Rylan pulled the door open to the jingling of a bell and held it as his team left the messed-up diner and remains of their hunt, bleeding out over the counter.

Dealing with the cleanup and getting the survivors out was someone else's job.

Annabeth went out first, eyes averted from his and jaw set.

Rylan hadn't rebuffed her to be mean. He had seen her subtle glances and the way she was gravitating to him more and more lately. And Rylan had no interest in pursuing a relationship with her. Or anyone, really.

What he was, what he did ... it wasn't a safe space to bring love into. And he'd already sealed and sent away that part of him long ago. And did his best not to think about it. Not more than once a day. Maybe twice.

It was a good day if he didn't think about Everly at all.

But that history had been stirred up recently, muddying his thoughts like silt churned up from below clear waters. Because Janey Boderleth was found dead.

Her death was looked into by the Darkfreys and turned out to have been as natural as they come in Shroudhaven. Not beshadowing related. Not death by any of the horrors what go bump in the night.

But every protective instinct within Rylan went on full, siren-blasting alert. Death is what happened in Shroudhaven. That could have been Everly. She had to stay away.

Does she know yet?

He tried not to imagine her receiving the news.

The brisk wind out on the street hurried Rylan and his brace into the unmarked Darkfrey van. Rylan took the driver's seat, and the two women climbed into the back. The LED clock shone an eerie cyan over the dash. Not much past two. An early night for them.

Jasper tucked away his phone that he'd been tapping on, then leaned toward Rylan stiffly. "Would you mind detouring by the Crow's Nest so I might disembark there? I ... um ..."

"Sure, no problem." Rylan didn't wait for Jasper to

attempt to conjure an excuse.

Lying was so far out of the tightly wound shadyr's league it was embarrassing to even be close to.

Exactly what Jasper was lying about, Rylan only guessed. But he had a pretty good idea. He turned and gave Jasper a long, knowing look, trying to convey solidarity.

Jasper nodded slowly, eyes on Rylan in return as though gauging just how much Rylan might know or what he might do with that knowledge. It was a look filled with suspicion and terror.

Rylan turned back to the empty nighttime street, leaving the rest unsaid. It was none of his business anyway.

There were far bigger secrets that he was trying to uncover.

After delivering Jasper to the shadyr bar, the rest of them arrived back at Darkfrey Estate, pulling the van into the garage at the same time a cleaning crew was piling into their truck.

"Heading to Pimey's Diner?" Rylan asked as he hopped down from his seat, boots thudding on the concrete.

A black woman taller than Rylan and almost as wide-shouldered pulled the zipper up on her maroon coveralls. "Yup. You lot didn't mess it up too much for us, did you?"

Vonny slammed the sliding door of the van closed behind her. "Watch your tone and know your place, *Cleaner*."

A sparkle crossed the statuesque woman's starry gaze, and she smirked, sucking air through her teeth. "Don't pretend my place has anything to do with who is the better shadyr here. Unless you want to test it."

"I'll report you to Mordan," Vonny hissed.

Rylan casually took a step in front of Vonny, as though simply moving in that direction. "The diner is fine. Just a smallish vasmire. Shouldn't take long."

Three other shadyrs moved in behind the woman who was clearly the boss. She looked over Rylan and his abandoned attempts to remove the splashes of black blood covering his face and sniffed, unconvinced.

"If we're lucky, there won't be a body there to deal with by the time we arrive anyway, the way things have been lately." She slapped the side of the truck and yelled at her hovering team, "Come on, losers, move it! I want to be done and showered before sunrise."

Rylan watched the truck peel off into the night, and Annabeth sighed.

"A shower sounds great right now." She nodded farewell and trudged up the brightly lit pathway to the dorms.

"She's far too soft for this," Vonny muttered to Rylan once the younger woman was out of earshot.

"She's getting better. And she's still a kid. Not even eighteen yet."

Vonny raised an eyebrow at him as though she didn't

think he was either.

"You know Mordan put her with us because he trusts your experience."

"Not as much as he trusts your skills, *brace leader*." Vonny shot him a sharp side-eye filled with indignation.

Rylan knew he could pull rank and discipline Vonny for her tone alone, but he honestly agreed that she was right to be annoyed in being overlooked for the role.

"Anyway, Annabeth will learn. Kids can make dumb mistakes sometimes. Which is all good as long as they make it through the mistakes alive."

The color fled from Vonny's face, and Rylan wanted to swallow his words.

"Shit. Sorry, I didn't mean ..."

Vonny looked him square in the eyes, didn't say a word, and it hit harder than if she'd slapped him across the mouth. She turned and stalked away toward the standalone home she shared with her husband on the estate grounds.

It's been one fantastic night across the board.

Rylan sighed and rubbed the underside of his chin, hoping to scrape away some of the dried ghast blood.

Maybe he could still turn the evening around.

Striding up the path to the main estate building, Rylan passed groups of mid-teen shadyrs moving about the lit grounds, running drills and sparring.

He remembered his early days at Darkfrey Estate,

around that age, trying to stay awake through the long nighttime hours required, in awe of the braces heading out on hunts.

He'd been in awe of a lot of things back then. The castle-like mansion, ornate with crenelations and gargoyles, was impressive even now. But being a Darkfrey had lost some of its luster.

It was hard to feel all the warm, fuzzy team loyalty when there was a traitor in their midst.

And Master Mordan Darkfrey didn't believe Rylan.

The missing bodies of downed ghasts hadn't seemed important at first. Just rumors filtering in from cleaning crews. It was when more disturbing rumors started spreading that Rylan took notice.

When a shadyr grave had been desecrated.

The official explanation was that it was a bliv from in town, some dare taken too far from townies who thought the Darkfreys were all vampires.

And the rest of the Darkfrey shadyrs were fine with that answer and moved on. But Rylan had known the shadyr whose grave had been robbed. A friend he had trained with growing up. And he wanted to make sure no further graves were dug up.

So he spent some time staking out the Darkfrey graveyard. Only to see a shadyr clear out another grave.

Rylan couldn't see who it was, but followed them back

to the main building, only to lose them down one of the narrow hallways in the old section.

It was only later that Rylan remembered his mother once telling him how Darkfrey Estate was riddled with secret tunnels.

He hopped up the steps of the main entrance and squinted until his eyes adjusted to the fully lit interior.

There were a few other shadyrs moving around inside, but the main building was mostly used for classes and administration, and at that time of night shadyrs were either training, hunting, or sleeping.

Rylan wound along the corridors and intersections of the mazelike palace toward the place his target had disappeared. He hoped his second hunt of the night would go smoother than his first. He wasn't entirely sure how he was going to find a secret passage, but at least he knew roughly where to look.

He wished his mother had told him more. He wished she'd told him more about a lot of things. He glowered as he turned the corner to the hallway from the night before.

The dimly lit walls were unassuming. Carved wooden panels painted in maroons and gold on one side were contrasted with ancient bare stone on the other. Gilt-framed portraits of stern-faced shadyr ancestors hung in a line, their eyes seeming to follow Rylan's movements, scolding him for disturbing the silence.

"Now, where would a secret door be?" Rylan ran his hand over the paneling, tapping it a couple of times.

Some sections seemed more hollow than others, but he couldn't work out how to make them open and didn't want to explain the damage if he brute-forced his way in.

There had to be a mechanism, he just had to find it.

Man, Everly would love this.

The thought came unbidden, as did the memories of playing games of imagination and adventure in his backyard as a kid, pretending there was a secret door to another world under the steps of his front porch. The wide-eyed, enraptured expression on Everly's face as she led the way.

A stained-glass window featuring the Darkfrey crest of three skulls cast fractured rainbows on the antique carpet runner beneath Rylan's feet.

He stared at them, willing away thoughts of Everly. What was that, three times today? Four? Back in the diner, he swore for a moment he could almost feel her presence.

He had to get it under control.

That was when he saw it, right next to his boot, a strange join in the skirting board. He gave it an experimental nudge with his toes.

There was a subtle shift beneath his touch, a faint click resonating through the corridor.

A panel popped open, swinging on smooth hinges.

Rylan blew out a breath and smiled, then grew solemn.

He peered into the revealed passageway, wondering what he might face down there. His heartrate picked up the way it always did at the start of a hunt.

Somewhere down in the inky darkness of that tight space, a traitor had taken stolen shadyr bones. Who and where and why were what Rylan wanted to know. He just had to find some proof, then something could be done about it, and Rylan could go back to being the best damn ghast hunter the Darkfrey shadyrs had.

Cold, stale air drifted out of the tunnel, smelling of damp earth and death, like a warning to leave dangerous secrets buried.

Rylan shook off the shiver tracing down his spine and stepped into the darkness.

Chapter Four

Anxiety swirled like a building hurricane in Everly's insides, growing more ominous the closer they drew to Shroudhaven.

The campervan rattled and clanked as it took Everly back to the hometown she'd never wanted to see again. Harper was treating the journey like a fun road trip, but to Everly, they may as well have been driving headlong into the mouth of Hell.

It's just a place. A stupid, small town, filled with memories of trauma. What's the worst that could happen?

She turned to Harper in the driver's seat. It was tempting to beg her friend to turn the vehicle around, but instead, she said, "I owe you big-time for coming all the way out here with me."

"Like I was going to miss this!" Harper gripped the

steering wheel with both hands and swerved to avoid the worst of the potholes.

The seat springs squeaked in protest and a cupboard door flapped loosely as they bumped along the craterous road.

"I could fix that cabinet for you when we get there, to repay you," Everly offered.

"It's fine. I'm not keeping anything in there anyway. And I'm sure you'll have plenty of other things to keep you busy once we arrive."

The picture-perfect baby-blue vintage Volkswagen had been purchased purely for a recent photo shoot. The sleeping area had been stripped out for prop storage, with only an ornamental throw over it to give it the appearance of a bed.

Behind the front seats, most of the space was filled with stacked suitcases, all part of a matching rose-gold set—Harper's. Just one well-stuffed khaki duffel plus a messenger bag and tool bag belonged to Everly.

She didn't need much. They weren't staying long.

The door panel continued to thump rampantly. Everly frowned back at it as though it were a war drum, beating a warning of danger ahead.

"Maybe we could stop right now. Just pull over, I'll get that door sorted, then we can turn around and—"

"We aren't backing out now. It's right around the

corner!" Harper quirked her perfectly glossed lips. "And you don't have to fix everything, you know."

Everly wished she could. For now, though, she wanted to fix the bad feeling that Harper was taking a week out of her busy schedule to drive her across the state to deal with her family dramas.

"If I could just—"

"It's fine. Seriously. I'm just excited that I finally get to visit the infamous Shroudhaven!" Harper panned her hand across in front of her as though reading a billboard headline. "Ghosts! Vampires! Mystery!"

"Trauma, abandonment, and heartbreak!" Everly cheered, her voice thick with sarcasm. "Wooo."

"So you have some bad memories of the place. But it's still your home, right?" Harper asked, tapping shiny chrome fingernails against the steering wheel.

Everly had been to Harper's home once, to have dinner with her parents and siblings, all at one table, a home-cooked roast with all the trimmings in a warmly lit space filled with of laughter and hugs.

She could understand why her friend was having such a hard time reconciling that *home* didn't always equal *good*.

Everly pictured her recently inherited family house. Quaint, narrow, two stories, with a shopfront downstairs, and a swinging sign reading *Boderleth Antiques*. Once painted in a charming lavender and cream color scheme,

Everly mostly remembered it looking gray.

It had been four years since she'd left. It had been longer since it had felt anything like a home.

"I just want to get the place cleared out and fixed up so I can sell it off. Without me around to help look after things, who knows what state my mother left it in when she died."

Harper pursed her lips, silent for a moment. "It sucks that even in death she's making things hard for you. I'm sorry if that sounds harsh, but I want so much better for you."

"You can be as harsh to her as you want. We weren't close."

By a long shot, thought Everly.

She'd never been able to win her mother's love. Getting kicked out at fifteen had been just one of her many failures as a daughter. She was raised to believe if you worked hard enough and lifted yourself up by your own bootstraps, you'd succeed at anything.

And she tried. She got a fake ID and started doing odd repair jobs until she managed to lie her way into a role as a building super despite being underage at the time.

But no matter how hard she tried, she always messed up somehow, was always abandoned.

Harper reached over and patted Everly's knee. "Her loss. I can't understand for a second how anyone couldn't see how incredible you are. And I'm still positive you'll get something good out of this!"

Everly stifled a wry laugh. "If I can sell the house for enough to be able to put in my part toward us moving, that's all I need."

She had looked briefly into Shroudhaven property prices. It wasn't exactly a booming market. And the kind of apartments Harper had been window shopping for them weren't cheap.

"Do you think it's all still there, how you described it? Because I have to say, I'm super stoked to see this antiques store." Harper flashed a bright grin.

Memories of vintage dolls peering down from shelves, stacks of books like magical tomes, and a precious treasure dropped from tiny hands sent a chill through Everly's veins. She pulled her jacket tighter around her.

"I can't guarantee there's anything good in there. It's been sixteen years since anyone has stepped foot in those rooms. It could have all rotted away to dust for all I know. But you can help yourself to whatever remains," Everly said.

Harper's grin, if anything, only grew brighter. "My fans have been loving a bit of grungy vibe lately. And I really don't want to think about what they like so much about seeing me get all dirty. But it makes bank. So even if it is all dust, I'm sure I'll find plenty for some photo shoots."

"I just want this to be worth your time, too."

"It will be! We'll get the place fixed up in no time. Once it's all cleaned out and you've worked your magic on it, you might even decide you don't want to leave."

"Five days from tomorrow, Harper. That's what we agreed, and that's all the leave I could get from work. Five days in and absolutely out again."

They had already passed the small, historic village of Gorhanmere with its sandstone cottages and view over a black-water mountain lake and had come out of the mountains into the darker wooded area that surrounded Shroudhaven.

Along both sides of the road, massive, ebony-trunked trees shot up into the sky. They were so densely packed, it quickly became dark as pitch behind the first few rows, turning the forest into something mysterious and unknowable.

Everly's family home was north of the river—not far now—and the burble of anxiety rose in her the closer they got.

"Shroudhaven isn't a place many people stay by choice. And despite how exciting I may have made it sound, entirely unintentionally, it's honestly just a boring and vaguely creepy small town."

"Come on. There must be some happy memories worth keeping from your old place?"

"I doubt it." Everly's therapist had made it clear that

dwelling on the worst of the memories from her childhood wasn't good for her anxiety, which was currently climbing steeply.

She took a deep breath. *Be present. Be mindful.* Everly looked out the window, away from her friend.

Despite being midday, the sky was dark. Clouds hung low with unspent rain, and a strong wind tossed leaves around along the roadside.

Pretty normal Shroudhaven weather.

The whole world seemed dull and gloomy, making the forest look as sinister as the local legends suggested.

"I mean, this is the place townsfolk honestly believe is run by vampires who hang out in the big spooky estate on the hill. That's the kind of people around here."

"Vampires?" Harper sounded far too excited by the idea.

"No. Not vampires. Nutters who *believe* in vampires. Shroudhaven is where businesses go to die and some mundane tragedy or another manages to befall half the population. How many happy memories do you think I have?"

Harper tilted her head, pity overwhelmed by a sparkle in her bright-green eyes. "Don't judge me, but how cool would it be if there really were vampires?"

"You're thinking sexy, broody vampire boyfriends, aren't you?" Everly chuckled.

"Well, duh. Of course, I want some handsome bloodsucker action!"

Everly's laughter faded quickly. "I used to think the whole vampire thing was a dumb urban legend. Then the boy I loved moved into that estate and he ... changed. I'm not saying there really are vampires, but they turned him, somehow."

Harper made puppy dog eyes. "You mean Rylan?"

Everly gave a beleaguered sigh in return. "Yeah."

"Are you still dreaming about him every night?"

Everly hung her head, her voice small as she said, "Yes. Always. Ugh, it's the worst. I'm so pathetic. I should be over him by now!"

Harper squealed. "No, it's so romantic. I can picture it already, and I love this for you! We are going to do everything we have to do to get you two reunited. This is fate! Soul mates! I can feel it!"

She swung one hand into the air dramatically, keeping the other tight on the steering wheel. "The girl who only ever loved one boy, brought back into his life after years apart to discover that she was the only one he ever wanted too."

"Stop narrating my life. You're getting it wrong."

Harper clutched at her chest. "Their hearts, as one, together in their dreams for all the years they were apart!"

Everly giggled and slapped Harper on the shoulder.

"Okay, enough! Look, it would be nice to see him again—"

"I bet."

"—but so much happened. I don't even know what he's like anymore. I used to think we were meant to be together, but I screwed up ..."

Harper whined, "But you still loooooooove him!"

"I'm trying to say—"

Harper made grossly loud kissing sounds.

"That's it. I'm ignoring you now." Everly crossed her arms and stared out the side window.

There was movement in the distance, a shadow dancing between twisted trunks of trees. She frowned, squinting into the dark woods.

Harper sang, "Everly and Rylan, kissing in the sea. It's gonna happen 'cause it's des-ti-ny!"

"That's not even how it goes."

"I thought you were ignoring me."

The thing Everly had seen move became clearer and looked almost like an old woman, crone-like, flickering in and out between the trees in a hectic dash through the undergrowth.

"What on earth ..."

"What is it?" Harper craned her neck, staring over Everly's shoulder.

But nothing was there. Everly blinked, scolding herself for letting her imagination run wild. It must have been her heightened anxiety playing tricks on her mind.

The Wyrdwoods weren't a place many people went, especially old women.

"Thought I saw something. Never mind."

Everly turned back to face the front and gasped. A sleek, sandy-colored creature stepped out onto the road, right in front of the campervan's path.

Cat! was Everly's first thought. *Big cat!*

Quickly followed by, *Oh no, we're going to hit it.*

"Watch out!" Everly screamed.

Harper was still looking the other way. She flicked her head around. Shrieking, she slammed on the brakes.

Everly reached over, grabbing the steering wheel and trying to turn them away from the animal. The van swerved, wheels squealing as they skidded out.

Something thumped.

The girls were bucked in their seats. Limbs flailed and crashed against the dashboard as the campervan went off the road. Harper's head cracked against the steering wheel. Panic swarmed around Everly like a cloud of humming insects, darkening her vision.

She cried out, and a bright light flashed.

CHAPTER FIVE

Light engulfed Everly's senses.

No! Take control. Breathe. Count. You do not have time for a panic attack right now. You're in control.

The sensation battled to take over. Everly couldn't see, but she could sense Harper beside her. It was almost like the light tried to reach for her.

The light seemed to whip out toward Harper. Every instinct in Everly made her pull back, fight the strange feeling. It redirected, shooting out behind her and then retracting as Everly regained control and the world became clear again.

That was not a normal symptom Everly was used to from her anxiety, but as long as the panic attack had been pushed down, she didn't care. Mid-car accident, she had other things to worry about.

The campervan clattered to a rough stop.

"Ow." Harper groaned. "Are you okay?"

Everly checked herself, feeling around for any parts of her body that were in pain. A couple of minor aches.

"Yeah, I think so."

Harper's voice was a whining cry. "Am *I* okay?"

Everly turned to her friend, who had a hand pressed against her temple where blood ran freely.

"Omigod!" Everly moved quick, grabbing her leather messenger bag from between her legs in the seat well.

"I'm so sorry," she said as she dug through the contents of the bag.

"Did I hit it? Tell me I didn't hit it," Harper moaned.

Everly didn't turn back to look as she opened her mini first aid kit and unwrapped some gauze.

"We have to make sure you're all right first. You're bleeding like crazy."

She gently pried Harper's bloody hand away. Dabbing at the area to clear some blood, Everly winced.

This is all my fault.

Harper whimpered. "Is it terrible? Am I scarred for life?"

Everly pressed the absorbent dressing onto the split in Harper's temple and tried to smile reassuringly. "It's not bad. Only small. Looks like it might bruise a bit, but you probably won't need stitches. Here, hold this."

Harper took over pressing the gauze in place. "I have instant ice packs in my makeup kit."

The luggage had shifted and tumbled into a mess when they'd come to their abrupt stop. Everly spotted the glitzy crate behind their seats and started digging through it. The cut was small, but head wounds could be worse than they looked.

If something happened to Harper because of me ...

"Are you dizzy at all? Faint? Nauseous?"

"No. Just, ouch. And embarrassed. And worried about my sanity. Was that a *lion*?"

"A big cat of some kind, I think. Maybe a cougar?" Everly pictured it clearly, as though a freeze-frame of it was stuck as her mind processed the accident.

It had been small—not small enough to be a domestic cat, but not a fully grown cougar either. But there was no way she was telling Harper it was a *baby*.

"I thought they were only in the US. I know people always talk about panthers and things in the mountains, but they're just conspiracy freaks, right?"

"Aaand welcome to Shroudhaven," Everly muttered, rummaging through the pans of bronzer and eye shadow.

"Try not to break everything in there, please?" Harper pleaded.

"Sorry! Okay, got one." Everly held up the plastic pouch, skimmed the instructions printed on it, then gave it a sharp squeeze. After a quick shake, it became icy cold under her fingers.

"Thanks, babe. Concealer can do wonders, but I'd rather not be all swollen." Harper kept holding the dressing with one hand and took the ice pack with the other before pressing it over the top of the covered wound.

She leaned back in the driver's seat and sighed mournfully. "I can't believe I crashed."

Everly shook her head, wiping her hands clean with a wet wipe she'd also taken from the makeup kit. A few smudges of blood marked the cuffs of her jacket, blending into the dull red and existing stains.

"It's okay. The van seems fine. We're barely in the ditch. And it was my fault. I distracted you, and I saw the cat but didn't warn you fast enough, and you wouldn't even be here if—"

"Stop it. I was the one driving and not watching the road."

Everly just shook her head. She knew whose fault it was. Her fault that they were there at all. Her fault that Harper was hurt. Her fault an animal might be too.

"Stay here. I should go ... and see if ..." She trailed off, mouth gone dry.

She didn't really want to know if the animal was dead. Or worse, mortally injured but *not* dead. Everly shuddered.

Please don't make me be the one who has to put a kitty

out of its misery.

She had failed the creature, and having its death on her hands was too horrific to imagine. But if she didn't check, she would be failing it again.

It could be lying there, needing help. It could survive as long as she got to it in time. Yet she didn't move from her seat. Her heart rate increased as panic tried to take over.

No, dragon, I know what you're trying to do. Not now, Everly told her anxiety firmly.

"If I hurt that poor thing, I will want to die," Harper said, and the blood smeared across her face made it all the more dramatic. "But we should go. We should check. I'll come with you."

Everly and Harper nodded in unison, braced themselves, then got out of the van. Everly took the lead as they followed the black lines of tire marks back along the road.

Harper held the dressing to her forehead and whimpered and squealed quietly the whole way, her eyes half-closed as though to shield herself from what they might see.

Everly peered ahead but couldn't see any telltale lumps on the tarmac that might be an animal. They reached the point where the skid marks began.

Nothing. No animal, no fur, no blood. Everly frowned. Where could it have gone? Was it back even farther?

Harper's expression brightened. "Do you think I missed it?"

"Maybe ..." Everly remembered the thumping sound the van had made as clearly as she did the dark-eyed face of the big cat.

She stepped into the overgrown weeds by the roadside, crunching them under her heavy work boots. She scanned around for any movement or pale-caramel fur.

The cougar could have been knocked off the road or stumbled there after it was hit.

Long tassels of grass swished in the crisp wind, but there were no other signs of life.

"It's not here." Everly tried to feel positive about that.

If the big cat had been badly wounded, surely it couldn't have gotten much farther away on its own. She tried not to imagine it dying alone of its injuries somewhere in the dark woods around them.

"So, it's okay?" Harper beamed, still pressing the first aid supplies to her temple. She stepped beside Everly and wrapped her free arm around her back in a cuddle.

"Yeah, we must have missed it. Can't see a sign of it." Everly matched her smile.

It would be good not to mark her return home with another death. She'd already seen enough death in Shroudhaven.

They wandered back to the van, and Everly gave it a quick exterior check, took the keys from Harper, and tried to get it started as they both held their breath. The engine ticked over and rumbled normally.

"I'll drive the rest of the way. You rest and keep that ice pack on there."

"Thanks, babe. Let's hope that's all the excitement we have on this road trip, hey?"

Everly sure hoped so.

As she rolled the campervan carefully back onto the road, a rustle of motion in the woods caught her eye again, gone before she could identify it.

As they drove closer and closer to the place she'd once called home, memories of death wouldn't leave her mind.

The nurse at the small main street clinic cleaned up Harper's wound and applied a butterfly bandage.

"It's a very clean split. Look at that, closing up nicely. Head wounds often look worse than they are." The matronly woman with bright-red lipstick handed Harper a fresh ice pack and then let her choose a lollipop out of a basket as though she were a toddler in for vaccinations.

Everly breathed a silent sigh of relief that Harper didn't need stitches. Her friend could gloat all she wanted about having the best makeup money could buy, but it was better to not be scarred to start with.

Harper asked the nurse for a photo with her, and since she wasn't busy she agreed, although she was confused when Harper fixed her makeup and pulled her portable set lighting from her handbag.

Everly stood off to the side, holding the high-powered LEDs as Harper and the nurse posed—Harper pouting adorably and the nurse pretending to reapply the bandage.

The nurse was a good sport, with both of them bursting into hysterics in between shots. The older lady even dug out a monstrously sized needle and pretended to terrorize Harper with it, perhaps a little too gleefully.

Everly was invited into the shoot too, but as usual, she declined. She didn't care about her weight, but she knew others could still be unnecessarily cruel, especially online.

The photo shoot ended when the nurse had to go and see to someone who had just come in after an animal attack.

Back on their way again, Everly stopped at the office of the administrator of her mother's estate.

She left the camper running so the heater would keep Harper warm. "Wait here and rest. This shouldn't take long."

Her friend poked at her phone, brow furrowed. "Thanks, babe. Ugh. I can't get my photos to upload. Reception keeps dropping out."

Everly had forgotten that charming part of Shroudhaven life—the dodgy cell phone service. "We'll get you connected again once we're in the house."

Everly was met by the administrator in his office. George Flitchworth. She was pleased to read the nameplate on his desk so she didn't have to keep bluffing that she had heard his name the first time.

He breathed heavily as he showed her where to sign—there, there again, on the reverse, and then he handed over the keys and offered his condolences for perhaps the hundredth time.

As she headed back out onto the footpath, Everly stared at the multitude of keys in her hand, wondering what they would unlock and fighting the tears in her eyes, when she walked face-first into a firm body.

CHAPTER SIX

"Oh, sorry!" Everly stumbled away from the person she'd collided with.

Her eyelids fluttered as she tried to clear her vision.

"Everly?" The male voice, all gravel and growls, was filled with surprise.

Her eyes grew extra wide as his form became clearer. *I'm dreaming* was her first thought.

But as a lucid dreamer, she had ways of knowing if she was dreaming or not. She was awake. And yet the man in front of her looked exactly like he did in her dreams.

"Rylan?" Everly squeaked.

They both stared at each other in silence for a drawn-out minute. In the dim light of the gloomy afternoon, Everly could see that Rylan had changed in the years since she'd left town.

His jaw was more angular, shoulders broader, and the foppish boy-band hair he'd once had was replaced with a soldierly buzz cut. Just like how he appeared in her dreams.

How weird.

She couldn't have known he'd changed his look. He didn't even have any online profiles she could stalk. She'd checked. Embarrassingly often.

The tight black T-shirt he wore stretched across a muscled chest. Over it was a gray-green military-style jacket with the Darkfrey crest embroidered on the pocket and a large hood falling over his shoulders.

He was so different, so much older, sterner, but the sight of him still made her heart patter like it had when she was younger. Like when she saw him in her dreams every night.

Everly scrambled for something to say. This was her lucky chance, could be her only chance, to reconnect with him. To get to know what he was like now. To find out if he'd forgiven her, or ever could.

Rylan spoke first. "I heard ... about your mom. I'm sorry."

His eyes were large pupiled and starry-swirled as though a nebula were caught inside, and his eyebrows furrowed over them. Everly remembered the exact shade of hazel–green they were even though none of that color was visible now in the gloom.

Everly shrugged. Rylan knew exactly what her mother

was like, so she just said, "Yeah. That's why I'm here."

"I figured you weren't coming back when you didn't go to the funeral."

"No. I couldn't get there." Everly hadn't been able to bring herself to attend.

Mr. Flitchworth had organized a very basic burial, and Everly didn't want to see who else might—or might not—have been there. She wondered then if Rylan had gone, but before she could ask, he spoke again.

"Are you staying long?" Rylan's voice was a low, guarded rumble.

"Just this week. I have to sort out the old house." Everly jingled the keys on display.

"Right. Good." Rylan's shoulders dropped, and Everly was desperate to know whether it was in relief or sadness.

And good that she was here for a few days, or good that she'd be leaving soon? Even getting a few syllables out of Rylan was more than she'd had since they split ways, but the inability to decipher them was maddening.

She needed to hear more, say more. Seeing him there, in person, made her whole body hum with a strength of emotion that threatened to overwhelm her.

Everly's heart did some hectic maneuvers. Before she could back down, she took a deep breath and forced the words out. "It's really nice to see you. Maybe we could—"

"I have to go." Rylan lifted his chin, staring down the

street toward nothing Everly could determine.

"Sure. Same. No problem." Everly's cheeks flamed.

He started striding away, then paused, glancing back over his shoulder. "It was ... good ... seeing you, too."

Everly blew out a long breath as she watched him go. "Oookay. Okay, okay, okay. Good. *Good*."

He said it was good. *Good*.

Everly made her way back to the campervan as her heartbeat pounded in her ears and her chest grew tight. She fought the urge to vomit.

"That was quick," Harper said as Everly collapsed into the driver's seat.

Her breathing was short. Her hands trembled, adrenaline uselessly claiming her whole body.

"Panic attack," she managed to say.

Harper, who had been leaning back with her eyes closed, slid up the bench seat to be closer. Taking her still cool ice pack, she pressed it to Everly's neck.

"Deep breaths. You're okay."

Everly counted while she inhaled, held her breath, then exhaled, going through the usual motions. She wanted to laugh and cry.

"I just saw Rylan, out on the street."

"No way!" Harper exclaimed.

She craned her neck around, trying to get a glimpse of the man, but Rylan was long gone. "Is he still gorgeous?"

Yes. Everly didn't answer aloud. She shook her head and did another breathing exercise. "A car crash and I manage, but *he* sets me off."

Her heart beat so fast her chest ached.

You're not dying. It's only panic. Just breathe.

"You know anxiety isn't logical. Remember, it's just your dragon, trying to protect you. But your dragon's a great big dumb-dumb and gets confused about what is actually a real threat."

Everly nodded.

Visualizing her screwed-up adrenal response as a protective-yet-stupid dragon had helped in the past, at least with the shame that often came along with the panic attacks. The shame of how she couldn't even control her own mind and body. Especially when it came to Rylan. Her eyes filled with tears.

If she couldn't even control her own body, how did she think she was going to make things right with Rylan again? Even if he wasn't planning on avoiding her until she left.

I'm such an idiot to have even thought there was a chance.

It didn't matter. Her dreams of fate and soul mates were childish. She was back in Shroudhaven for one job. Clean up the house and leave.

She had five days, then she'd never have to think about this town or the parts of her heart she'd left behind here ever again.

The campervan rattled to a stop and Everly turned off the engine, sitting for a moment to stare at the haunted house she'd once run from.

On the outskirts of town, her old home shared the space with other similar vintage buildings. The tree-lined road was lit by dull, ornamental streetlights, drooping like snowdrop flowers. It was late afternoon and the sun set early, taking away what little light had filtered through the thick storm clouds.

The whole area seemed deserted, with most superstitious locals staying inside as soon as the sun went down.

"There it is," Everly said.

"Wow." Harper breathed the word softly, sounding both impressed and sarcastic at once.

The narrow two-story building loomed in the darkness. Moonlight glinted off the attic windows like ominous eyes.

The carved wooden ornamentation around the porch and windows should have been a nice feature, but was cracked and broken, looking more like giant cobwebs and claws gripping the house.

The picket fence posts were loose and hung askew like jagged teeth.

A brisk wind made the faded Boderleth Antiques sign at

the front gate swing back and forth, creaking and banging. The front garden was an overgrown tapestry of sprawling miniature rosebushes and unpruned hydrangeas strangled by long runners of brown grass. Thistles and dandelions filled all the spaces between.

"Are we going in? Or ..." Harper let the word hang.

"Got any Molotov cocktails on you?"

"Fresh out."

"I guess we have to go in then," Everly said.

They made their way along the weedy front path, using their phones as flashlights, then Everly led them away from the front door, down a narrow side track.

"Ugh!" Harper gasped. "I just took a cobweb to the face!"

Everly quickly inspected her for stray spiders. "You're okay. All clear. That's what you get for being unreasonably tall."

"Why can't we use the front door? You have all the keys, right?"

Everly turned and continued toward the back. "The front door goes right into the antiques store. We go around to get into the living area."

It had been that way as long as Everly remembered— one half of the house sectioned off, closed up, unspoken of. She'd learned to pretend that part of the house didn't even exist.

The backyard was worse than the front. The rusty skeletal remains of a swing set had been smothered by ivy and grass. The porch groaned and gave softly under Everly's weight as she stepped onto it and faced the door.

Home. Or at least, the house she grew up in. A lump of sorrow filled her throat and she swallowed it away, unlocked the door, and flicked the light switch.

Candle-shaped lights lit up the small entry hall and the dull-brown floral wallpaper felt so familiar to Everly it sent her mind spiraling back into childhood. She denied the nostalgia, pushing it down before it could bring the bad memories with it.

"Kitchen and laundry are just through there on the right. That door leads to the basement"—Everly shuddered—"and everything else is upstairs."

Everly glanced toward the final option visible from the entryway—the back door to the antiques store. There was a frosted window in the top half of the door, but over the years it had grown so dusty and grimy, not a thing could be seen through it.

The whole section of the building had been closed since her dad had died when Everly was three years old. It had been everything her father had ever cared about. And then no one had cared, or been allowed to care for it, ever since.

"I have no idea what state everything will be in, sorry." Everly cringed as she eyed the badly stacked piles of crushed-down beer boxes and moldy take-out containers in the hall.

Each step she took waded through rattling beer cans. The aroma was a mix of dry-dirt stale and warmly pungent rot.

A faint scratching sound came from the antiques store. Everly and Harper's eyes met, wide and alert.

"Probably just rats?" Everly offered.

She knew, in theory, rats were clever and generally harmless creatures, but the theory didn't stop them creeping her out. She shivered.

Harper put her arm over Everly's shoulders and squeezed. "Hey, it's going to be all right. We'll do whatever you need to do with this place, okay? Even if that means letting it all burn."

"Thought you were out of Molotovs." Everly's lips quirked up. "But thanks. Let's try to clean it up and sell it first before we resort to arson. I just hope I can fix it enough in the time I have."

"Babe, you can fix anything."

Not anything. If she could fix anything, she wouldn't have had to leave in the first place.

Everly forced a smile. "Come on. Let's sort out somewhere to get you resting, then I'll bring our stuff in, okay?"

Everly placed a foot onto the stairs, and they creaked.

She tested her weight on it a couple of times before progressing farther. Harper followed close behind. When they reached the top, Everly clicked another switch, and a row of more faux candles lit a thin corridor.

"Living room was that way. Mom's bedroom—the main bedroom—was down the other end there. My old room was just across here near the bathroom." Everly paused at the door, where bits of old tape and ripped corners were all that remained of the poster from her favorite cartoon she'd once stuck there.

She turned the knob and pushed the wooden door. It stopped halfway, blocked by something behind it.

Everly put her shoulder into it, but it still wouldn't open fully. She ducked her head through the gap to see what was in the way. Harper, much taller, leaned over her and looked as well.

Piles of musty clothing, old magazines, newspapers, and shoes filled the space. If there was still a bed in there, if anything of Everly's old room was in there, it wasn't even visible under the hoard of trash.

"You didn't like cleaning your room?" Harper whispered.

"This is Mom's stuff," Everly whispered back.

"Why are we whispering?"

"You started it!" Everly sighed, then spoke normally. "I have a skip bin booked for tomorrow, but we're not going to be able to pitch camp in there tonight."

Her voice echoed strangely in the old house, making her want to whisper again.

"I'm sorry about your room." Harper bumped her shoulder against Everly as they walked slowly toward the other bedroom.

"It wasn't my place. Mom could do what she wanted with it."

"Yeah, but it was *your* room. My old room at my parents' hasn't changed since I moved out. It's like this little memory shrine, you know? It feels like that's how it should be, like it's a part of you."

"I guess Mom didn't want any part of me hanging around."

Harper pouted. "Don't forget that your mom being an awful parent was on *her*, not on you."

Everly shrugged and broke eye contact. She pushed ahead and swung open the door to what had been her mother's room. It moved freely but whined all the way.

The stink of stale cigarette smoke smacked Everly in the face, coming from overflowing ashtrays scattered around the room.

She hopscotched across the trash-strewn floor and swung open the two sets of large windows. They squealed on old hinges. Below, the overgrown back yard looked like a shambling swamp monster, slumbering in the dark.

"At least there's a visible bed in here," Harper said, gazing around the space with her nose scrunched up.

The bed was a generous king-size with hand-carved wooden headboard that had additional tally notches literally marked down one side. Beside it stood a shoulder-high pyramid of empty vodka bottles. Everly's mother had enjoyed being brazen about her vices.

Everly's mouth twisted downward. "Shame we can't sleep in the camper."

"This will be fine. I have clean sheets and a heavy-duty mattress protector in the medium-sized suitcase."

"You think of everything."

"Number one tip for traveling to photo shoots—always bring your own linen. It makes all the difference to have a couple of additional clean layers between you and whatever the mattress has seen in the past."

Everly grabbed the car keys. "Things that we won't even think about, or arson will start looking like the best option again."

"It's not so bad. The air is clearing already. And the bed is big enough that we can share, if you want?" Harper offered.

Everly shrugged. "That's okay. You take it. I'll grab the couch for tonight. You need a good rest."

"There's really heaps of room. I promise I don't snore."

"Liar." Everly smirked. "It's no problem. I'll start

bringing things in."

She backed out of the room. That space made her uncomfortable.

She was never allowed in there as a kid. Never allowed to interrupt her mom and her male visitors. She'd learned the hard way the consequences of breaking that rule. No way would she sleep easily in her mom's bed.

Harper sat tentatively on the edge of the old mattress, pointedly ignoring the stains. "Okay, you bring the bags in, and I'll try to order us some pizza. If I can get my phone working for long enough."

Everly chuckled wryly. "Good luck with that. Did I not do an adequate job of describing Shroudhaven to you?"

"I may have thought you were exaggerating."

"Since I wasn't, I brought some chocolate oat bars just in case." Everly dug two out of her bag and tossed them to Harper.

"You are a lifesaver, Ev! First priority tomorrow? Getting us online. First priority right now? Painkillers and a nap."

Everly made a couple of trips to the campervan, bringing in her tool bag and the two suitcases that she thought could have been the 'medium one' Harper had referred to.

After putting her work gloves on, she pulled the old sheets off the bed, then used them like a net to scoop as many of the dirty clothes, ashtrays, and beer cans out of the bedroom as she could. Once the sheet-bag was full, she hauled it out and dumped it outside on the back porch.

Harper was halfway through struggling to get the fitted sheet on when Everly came back in, hurrying to help.

With the bed made, Everly pulled a roll of heavy-duty garbage bags from her kit and ripped one off, clearing up the rest of the bottles and rubbish around the room.

"At least we can move around in here now."

Harper lay down with a groaning sigh. "Yeah, my head was really done with being upright. I'm just going to rest my eyes while these painkillers kick in, okay?"

"No problem." Everly ripped another trash bag off the roll.

Harper opened one long-lashed eye. "Don't go cleaning this entire place up without me!"

"I'll just do a little. Enough to get an idea of what we've gotten ourselves into."

Harper closed her eye again. "That's all?"

"Of course." Everly headed out again and carried the rest of their luggage in.

Once Harper had everything she needed, Everly hovered for a moment in the upstairs hallway. She was way too wired to settle in anywhere herself, and although it was dark out, it was still early.

She took her tools and supplies downstairs where she

wouldn't disturb Harper. The kitchen seemed like the best place to start, since it gave off the most biohazard vibes.

At first, she went slowly, worried she'd throw away some treasure amongst all the trash. But as she excavated through grimy, broken dishes and crinkling snack wrappers, nothing of either nostalgic or fiscal value turned up.

Soon, Everly was piling rubbish into the bags by the armful. Within an hour, she'd filled ten bags and cleared the floor and all flat surfaces of the kitchen, attached dining area, and downstairs hallway.

There wasn't enough space near the back porch to pile all the refuse, so Everly began carrying the bags around to the front yard in anticipation of the skip arriving the next day.

The nearest streetlight flickered, making Everly's naturally bad night vision even worse. She fumbled her way down the side path to the front garden each time more on memory than sight.

Dumping the last bag on the teetering pile, Everly dusted her gloved hands off and stared up at the house that was now hers.

A loud squeak from the swinging Boderleth Antiques sign made her jump out of her skin. She marched up to it accusingly, giving the metal it hung on a jiggle to see how it was holding up. A bit of oil and it should be fine.

She stilled, wondering why she was thinking about

fixing it. This place wouldn't be Boderleth Antiques for much longer. Either she or the new owner would have to take the sign down.

The thought of getting rid of it sent a mournful chill down Everly's body.

It has to be done. And then I can leave this town of ghosts behind for good.

Everly reached for the dangling panel to see what tools she'd need to disassemble it, when a low, rumbling growl emanated from behind her. She spun around, seeking the source of it, squinting into the darkness.

Down the road a dark shape prowled toward her, eyes shining like pale-blue stars in the darkness.

CHAPTER SEVEN

Rylan broke into a sprint, hammering down the street toward Everly's house.

What is that? Some kind of big cat?

Not a ghast. He couldn't sense one around at all. But whatever it was, it was going right for Everly. And without a ghast nearby, Rylan had nothing but his human body to defend her with.

He had the full length of the street to clear, and his legs felt too slow.

It was lucky he was there at all. He sometimes wandered past Everly's old home, even though she hadn't lived there in years. Even though they hadn't spoken for longer. It was his way of remembering her, of feeling close to her no matter how far apart they'd become.

He might not have been there at all tonight if he hadn't

bumped into her on the street earlier. Once he knew she was back in town, he had to make sure she stayed safe until she left again.

He'd planned on just watching from down the road, making sure nothing dangerous was in the vicinity. Then he saw her wander out the front under the dim moonlight. He'd had such a strong longing for her presence that when he saw her, it felt as though he'd conjured her out of his imagination.

And then he saw the creature stalking her.

As he drew close, the feline form turned to him, eyes flashing an unnatural blue, then it skittered off into the darkness. Leaving Rylan skidding to a stop right in front of Everly with nothing to fight.

"Umm ... Hi?" She blinked up at him.

"Are you okay?"

"Fine?" It came out like a question, as though it was so obviously the answer she was confused to be saying it.

"Did you see ...?" She paused and frowned. "I'm not sure ..."

Rylan stared back at her, taking in the curve of her round face and her blue eyes that turned vaguely toward their dark surroundings. She probably didn't see a thing. She always did have trouble seeing in the dark compared to him, even compared to regular humans. All the more reason she shouldn't be out.

"I didn't see anything. I was just ... out for a jog."

"You used to hate running." She half smiled in a way that seemed both happy and sad all at once.

"Things change."

"Yeah, they do." The sadness on her lips took over entirely.

Rylan had to tear his eyes away from them. He swore softly into the blustering night wind. She was more beautiful than he'd remembered.

But he'd distanced himself from her for a reason.

And that reason remained, now more than ever. Rylan's jaw twitched. He'd been on edge already, and Everly's reappearance was at the worst time.

It wasn't just the normal Shroudhaven threats that were a danger right now. Not after what he'd found down that secret passage. Not after the consequence of that.

Somebody was up to something, something dark and terrible.

His heart still raced from the worry at the danger Everly had just been in, and anger bloomed around it.

She shouldn't be here. She should be somewhere safer than Shroudhaven. His need for her to be safe was a painful, soul-deep longing.

"What are you doing out here?" he snapped at her.

She took a step back and pulled her arms up, crossing them defensively. "I was just putting the garbage out."

Rylan took in the mountain of overstuffed black trash bags. "It could have waited. Have you completely forgotten what this place is like? You've forgotten all the rules."

"I know it's not collection day. I have a skip bin coming. And a large amount of confusion surrounding why I'm being interrogated about it."

Rylan turned around, swiping both hands down his face and groaning before returning and trying to calm his voice. "It's not safe to go out in the dark. It can be dangerous."

Everly shifted her hands to her hips. "You did see something! Was it a cougar by any chance?"

She peered over his shoulder, as though she were going to follow the strange-looking big cat and offer it a saucer of milk.

Knowing her, she probably would.

"You're not listening. You shouldn't be out here at night."

"You're the one 'out for a jog.' *Totally believable*," Everly muttered, eyeing his tactical pants and heavy jacket. She waved at the line of the fence beside her. "I literally haven't left my front yard, so maybe quit being so weird and aggressive about it?"

Rylan gaped at her, then clamped his mouth shut. She was right. He was acting very weird and aggressive.

Whether that creature was a close call or not, everything

about Everly being back in Shroudhaven, there in front of him, had the blood in his veins burning.

He inhaled slowly, then locked his eyes with hers. "I'm sorry. It would just make me feel a whole lot better if you stayed in after dark. For me? For old time's sake?"

Everly seemed to chew over her response, a fiery, questioning shine in her eyes. "You're going to need a whole lot more reason than old time's sake if you want to be the boss of my after-dark activities."

Rylan's eyes widened, and he stared for a long moment. Then he cracked, a small chuckle of bewilderment escaping.

Ghast damn it, he'd missed her, almost every day since pushing her away, but seeing her there, hearing her voice ... it was going to be infinitely harder saying goodbye to her again.

"Ry?" A woman's voice came from the darkness down the road. It sounded like Annabeth.

Rylan's eyes were well adapted to the low light—a gift that came along with what he was. He spotted Vonny, Jasper, and Annabeth headed his way. A quick check of his watch and he grunted in frustration. He was meant to have met them an hour ago.

Everly had a strange, intense look on her face as the three of them approached, and her chest was heaving breaths. "It can't be ..."

The shadyrs were equally inspecting the newcomer

Rylan had been found with. He didn't want either of his worlds colliding.

His expression closed up and he growled at Everly, "You shouldn't have come back to Shroudhaven. You should have stayed away for good."

Everly's cheeks turned berry red, as though they'd been slapped.

Vonny reached them first, looking Everly up and down. "Who's this?"

"Nobody."

"Nobody?" Everly gasped the word.

Annabeth spoke over her hushed voice. "Someone new to town? Do you know each other?"

Rylan put his hand on the small of Annabeth's back, guiding her to turn around. Everly watched with narrowed eyes.

"Just a bliv getting herself in trouble for being out in the dark." Rylan gave Everly one final, stone-hard look, then turned his back on her, leading his team away from the Boderleth's house.

Down the street, Rylan chanced a look back, but Everly had disappeared inside.

He wasn't surprised.

I was so rude to her. Rylan rubbed a hand over his shorn hair. Better that way, though. Having his brace show up only complicated things.

"What are you doing in this part of town? It's not our normal beat," Rylan asked.

"We could ask you the same question," Jasper replied with a shrug.

He looked completely harmless in a beige knit cardigan, his black hair neatly combed back. Rylan knew better.

Vonny and Annabeth both had jackets like Rylan's, their hoods up, shadowing their faces. A normal look while on patrol. They would all have Darkfrey body armor on under their street clothes too, just as he did.

"We were looking for you, you dingus," Annabeth said with a bemused smile.

"Thought we'd come and check around your old haunts, see if you'd run off home with your tail between your legs like your little brother, to live with the freaks." Vonny's voice didn't have the same teasing friendliness the other two had.

Her narrow face was even more pinched, as though she'd tasted something sour.

Rylan turned his head in the direction of Howell House. It was only a couple of blocks away. He had considered going there, thinking he should tell them what he saw at the estate, that he could go to them for help.

But he hadn't been home for seven years. Not since his dad was killed, and he'd decided he couldn't live like a normal human anymore when that meant he couldn't protect the people he loved.

He wasn't sure he'd be welcome at Howell House these days. But he was equally unsure who he could still trust.

He eyed the three standing in front of him. "So, you found me. What do you want?"

Annabeth pushed back her hood and tucked her bright-russet hair over one ear. She scrunched up her button nose. "Maybe to understand why you keep running off on your own? We're supposed to be a team. You're part of our brace, and our brace leader."

Annabeth used the term *brace* like it was something magical, still holding on to her youthful enchantment at the honor of being in one. She was the youngest of them by a couple of years. But once you were accepted into a brace, age didn't matter. You worked together, had each other's backs.

At least in theory. Rylan wasn't sure if he could even trust them anymore.

"You've been acting strange lately," Vonny scolded. "We were a good team. And you were, I suppose, a good leader. Until you suddenly decided to be a loner who goes poking his nose into everyone's private business."

"Is this new behavior a result of the the woman who's moved into the Boderleth residence?" Jasper asked, looking back down the street to the golden light shining through the upstairs window.

"An old friend of yours?" Vonny's eyes narrowed. "Is this what the new attitude has been about? You had some history with the Boderleths, didn't you?"

"Yeah, and history is all it is. I just need some time alone at the moment," Rylan said.

He cursed inwardly. He needed a better excuse but wasn't sure what he could tell them.

As kids, playing games and getting into trouble together, Everly had always been the clever one, coming up with stories and excuses. He'd followed her lead. He wondered if she was still like that, how she'd changed since she got away from this town and her mother.

It doesn't matter. Stop thinking about her.

Jasper tilted his head. "Time alone? That's not how this is supposed to work. Four is the optimal number for a brace."

"Look, hopefully this is just ... temporary. I'll be back again soon." Rylan really did hope so. He was letting his team down by not being with them. "Just take the night off, okay? My orders."

"And what should we tell Master Darkfrey about whatever it is you're doing alone that you can't tell us?" Vonny shook her head, making her blond bob swing.

"Can you guys just cover for me for a bit? You know I'd do the same for you." Rylan pointed his words at Jasper.

Jasper frowned for a long moment. Then he turned to

Vonny and Annabeth. "I think we should let him."

Annabeth put her hand on Rylan's arm. "Are you sure you want to do this? I know you're one of the best, but it's not safe to hunt alone. Not for anyone."

Rylan put his hand on hers, gently removing it from his body. "I'll be okay. I'm just ... looking into something."

"Not a beshadowing?" She pouted.

"Nothing like that. It's fine. I'll see you tomorrow."

She let her hand drop from his. "Okay."

"So you're all decided?" Vonny scowled, turning her back and heading off. "Have it your way, brace leader. But this is a bad idea."

Annabeth followed after the older woman.

Jasper shot Rylan a sideways glance. "You would really cover for me? If there were something that required it, of course."

"If there were, yeah, I would."

Jasper held out a hand, and Rylan clasped it briefly in return before Jasper nodded once and left to join the others.

Rylan pulled his hood up to block the cold wind on his neck as his brace walked away. He looked once more toward Everly's home, then once more in the direction of Howell House, and then strode away from them both.

It was how it had to be. He had to do this alone. Even if he felt that he could still trust his team. Regardless of the risk to himself, it was the best way to keep the people around him safe—even if it meant he could never be with them.

Rylan couldn't let the darkness claim the life of anyone else he loved.

Chapter Eight

"I know you're scared. But we have to do this." Harper held both of Everly's hands in hers, her expression grim.

Morning daylight barely reached to the far end of the hall, and the candle-shaped light fitting closest to Everly was missing its globe, leaving her and Harper in a thick gloom.

"Do we have to?" Everly looked at the back door to the antiques section and scrunched her face. "I haven't been in there since the day my dad died."

"So you're going to leave it locked up like a time capsule so it can haunt you forever?"

"Yes."

"No," Harper countered. "We're ripping the Band-Aid off. You need to deal with this. Today. It's just stuff. It can't hurt you."

Everly sighed. Harper was right, but she still wanted to avoid it for as long as she could. Unfortunately, the waste management company had called that morning, apologizing that they couldn't make it today—something about an employee not showing up—promising to bring the bin tomorrow instead.

Everly couldn't keep piling too much garbage in the front yard, so they had to switch up plans.

At least the antiques store wouldn't be filled with her mother's trash.

Still, she stalled. "You just want to see what's in there so you can start planning photo shoots."

"It's one hundred percent the reason I came here with you. Obviously. Chop, chop. Let's see what treasures I have to work with already!" Harper snapped her fingers.

Everly knew she was joking, or at least half joking. Harper had been pushing for Everly to return home since the news of her mother's death. Once Harper found out about the antiques, she'd decided they were going together.

Harper could work from anywhere as long as she could post photos online for her followers and keep in touch with her sponsors. And after the scandal that had brought her and Everly together, she needed a getaway as well.

Everly still wasn't sure coming back had been a good idea. But she owed Harper this much, to make the trip worthwhile for at least one of them.

She pulled the jangling collection of keys from her back pocket and checked through them until she found the old skeleton key she was looking for. "Let's see what sixteen years of abandonment does to a place."

We already know what it does to a person, Everly's brain wryly informed her.

"Seriously, no one went in there? For anything?"

"Nope. Mom locked it up and that was that. It was Dad's passion. Apparently one he was more passionate about than her, and I don't think she ever forgave him for it or for leaving her alone with me."

Everly inserted the key into the lock. It was sticky, needing an extra push and jiggle to go all the way in.

"She would tell me all the time that she was going to have a big yard sale or auction everything off or throw it all straight into the trash where it belonged. But she was never great at follow-through or getting rid of things. We're talking about a woman who couldn't even throw away dirty take-out containers. So it stayed locked up."

"Until now," Harper said ominously.

Everly turned the key and the lock clicked. "Until now."

Everly's memories of the antiques store area of the home were nebulous and dreamlike, too young when experienced to have a firm hold on them. As the door swung inward, those memories came rushing back.

The entry opened behind a dressing screen which was

strung with feathery cobwebs drenched in dust.

Everly suddenly knew the painting on the other side of that screen was of storks flying over a river and red sun, her mind serving up the memory that had been so long buried.

She tried the switch, and the pendant lights slowly bloomed to life, giving off a dull, egg-yolk glow.

The unfamiliar illumination made things skitter away into the shadows.

Everly backed up into Harper. "Rats!"

"Aw, cute," Harper cooed. "Remember they're more scared of you than you are of them."

"Doubt it."

Harper nudged Everly forward, and they stepped out from behind the screen into the first room. Everything looked gray, coated in dust so thick it had stolen color from the world. The room was laid out like a maze, old dressers and desks lined up shoulder to shoulder with only a narrow path between them.

Every surface was cluttered. Lamps, vases, photo frames, trumpets, brownie-box cameras, porcelain poultry, accordions, model ships, and butter churns were piled impossibly on every piece of furniture.

Framed oil paintings of country farmyards and whale hunting expeditions hung on the walls between rusty horseshoes, copper saucepans, ornate crucifixes, and more clocks than one might find through a looking glass. Ropey, tangled cobwebs were strung across the room like bunting.

There were four rooms that made up the store in total, all joining together in one big loop. The front entry room with the counter, and the largest room which they stood in now, both held a mix of all sorts of antiques, big and small.

Another room was dedicated just to dolls and old toys, and the fourth room housed old books, with glass display cabinets tucked between each bookcase, presenting the most prized antiques.

That was the room where her father had died.

Harper gasped and gushed as she beelined from one treasure to the next, her hands turning gray as she brushed them over everything.

Everly bit her tongue and winced at the faded Do Not Touch signs. Her father's rules didn't apply anymore. This was all hers now. But following those rules was a lesson she could never forget.

They made their way around and looked into the room to the left. Everly tried the switch but the light didn't come on. Hundreds of porcelain faces grinned back at them from the dark.

"Nnnope," Harper said.

"It's just stuff. It can't hurt you." Everly echoed Harper's earlier advice.

Harper stuck her tongue out, but followed Everly in. "Just telling you in advance that I don't think being murdered by possessed dolls is a good look for us."

A sharp nostalgia clawed at Everly's insides, excavating memories. They were more feeling than substance. The longing to be close to her father, who had spent all his time with the antiques—selling them, sourcing more, fixing them up, keeping the store clean and well presented.

As a child, it had felt like her father had rooms and rooms of toys he played with all the time without her. Toys she'd wanted to play with too but wasn't allowed. Everly had been haunted by the feeling that playing with them could bring her and her dad closer.

Only a little morning light came in through the dust-covered window, along with what spilled in through the open doorframe from the previous room, but Everly could see enough sweet doll faces and wooden horses to bring back every childhood longing. Longing for toys and longing for a distant father.

She didn't touch anything. She kept her hands to herself.

In one corner the dolls were all toppled over, their lace petticoats puffing out around them, interspersed with shredded paper. The pile shifted and bulged.

Everly felt the blood rush from her face. "Okay, I second your nope now."

"Let's get into our nope-copter and nope out of here. Next room?" Harper offered.

Everly eyed the entrance. The open door framed a rectangle of black. What windows there were in the next room were blocked by bookshelves and cabinets lining every wall, with two more aisles of shelving through the middle of the space.

She reached out, feeling around for the light switch on the wall. When she clicked the toggle, the room illuminated.

"Lights, yes!" Harper exhaled. "Although, I'm kind of digging the horror vibe. I could do a whole spooky series. Oh! I could dress up like a porcelain doll and lie in a pile of creepy toys and let the rats crawl around on me. New viral hit for sure. I knew this would be inspiring!"

Everly's stomach churned at a memory of her own that was far too similar. "Don't ask me for help with that shoot, 'kay?"

"Are we going in or what?" Harper asked, as Everly remained still, blocking the doorway, an even worse memory holding her back.

She nodded slowly, not sure she wanted to enter that space. A tapestry of books patterned the bookshelves, everything from leather-bound tomes to dog-eared bodice-rippers and dated cookbooks. Many had tumbled free from the mismatched shelves, lying tattered in confetti piles of dust and droppings in each corner.

The glass cabinets were clouded with a film of grime, but inside, the precious objects glittered tantalizingly.

However, it was something on the floor in the center of the room that caught Everly's eye.

She felt drawn to it, as she had been when she was three.

In the middle aisle, between looming dark-timber shelves, shards of broken crystal were strewn on the hardwood floorboards.

Everly knelt down in front of them as nausea overwhelmed her.

"No one cleaned it up," she said, her voice harsh and croaky.

Harper squatted beside her, staring at what was nothing but chips and splinters of glass glinting dully in the gloom. "What is it? Or what *was* it?"

It had been so alluring, so sparkly. Abstract spiraling fractals of intricately shaped crystal had danced around an inner form, barely visible through small gaps, like a whole world hidden within. A trick of the light and clever artistry had made it appear to glow.

"Some ornament, one of Dad's favorites. I loved how it looked too, although I wasn't allowed in here when I was a kid. But I used to sneak in and stare at it all the time. I just couldn't resist."

Harper blew a raspberry. "Like any kid has that much self-control."

"I should have. I should have tried harder." Her words echoed her mom's voice in her head. "But I just wanted to play with Dad's favorite toy. One day I came in and the cabinet was open. I just had to hold it. Then I broke it."

"Oops. Did you get in trouble?"

Everly shook her head. "Dad got so angry at me when he saw it broken that he had a heart attack and died ... right here."

Harper smacked Everly hard on the arm. "What? Why didn't you tell me before? Like, I knew this was an emotional place for you, but I didn't realize we were dealing with this level of trauma!"

"Yeah, well, that might explain why my hair has been gray ever since." Everly gingerly touched one of the larger pieces of crystal.

Sickness jolted through her. She gulped it away and rolled backward to sit leaning against a shelf.

Harper reached out for her. "You okay? If you need to vomit, don't hold back on my account."

Everly took in long, shaky breaths to combat the wooziness, inhaling the smell of old paper and books. "I can handle it."

Fragmented recollections of her father's death were knotted together with the explanations and guilt-laden retellings of it from her mother—a blur of fact and constructed memories.

But what remained clear in her mind was the joy of holding something sparkly, the terror of it breaking, the fury on her dad's face. And ...

It was all so distant, and trying to bring it into the foreground only made her heart beat so fast she thought it was going to fail.

"You know it's not your fault, right?" Harper asked her in all seriousness. "I need to know you understand that, because it feels as though you're dealing with some guilt here."

Everly shook her head, her words cutting between short breaths. "How wasn't it my fault? I did the wrong thing and my dad died."

"You were three years old!" Harper yelled.

Everly winced.

"Sorry, but for the love of cookies, girl. You were *three*. You can't be held accountable. Shit just happens."

Everly shook her head. "It happens because people don't do the right thing."

"You can do everything right and bad stuff will still happen. And when you're three, *three*, it's not your job to protect yourself or others from that."

Tears formed in Everly's eyes, stinging them with their presence. "I still did everything wrong. I don't even really remember him, you know? I was so young. When I think *Dad*, I think *antiques*, mostly. But him dying just became such a big part of me that ... can I tell you something else horrible?"

Harper tilted her head. "We're sisters. We can share anything."

Everly raised her knees up and hugged them. "When Rylan's dad died, it was awful. Everyone was so sad, but ... I thought it would mean Rylan and I had something big in common, something we could bond over. We were about thirteen and had been best friends forever, but I was starting to want to be *more*."

Everly could remember how big those emotions were, as she'd started looking at her best friend in a different way. She remembered it vividly because she still felt that way when she saw him, alive or in her dreams.

"I had all these dumb ideas of how helping him get through his grief would help him realize he loved me too. Those feelings ... they ruined everything. I'm sure Rylan could tell what I was thinking, and he realized then how terrible I am. The girl who killed her own father and wanted to use his father's death for her benefit. I think that's why he stopped talking to me."

Harper turned around and leaned against the bookshelf beside Everly. "Kids can have messed-up and confusing feelings, especially at that age. That was also not your fault."

"I wasn't able to help him during his grief. I failed him and lost him because of that. I know you have some romantic idea that he and I will get together, but that's why it won't happen. I don't think he'll ever forgive me."

Seeing Rylan yesterday had left Everly reeling. He'd talked to her, at least. That was more than he'd done in years. But it was mostly to keep warning her away.

And those people he'd met on the street. The cardigan guy, the redhead, the blonde. Everly shivered. They were so similar to the characters in her dreams. How could that be? Did she know them from when she was a kid and it was just a coincidence her mind chose them to dream of too?

Everly rubbed her temples, her head aching and finding no viable answers.

Harper watched her with sad eyes. "I am so upset I didn't get a look at this guy yesterday. I want to see what's so special about him that keeps you dreaming about him. Maybe even give him a talking to."

"Don't you ever, *ever* dare," Everly hissed.

Harper hopped onto her feet, reached for Everly's hands, then pulled her up as well. "Come on. Let's lock this place up again for now and go eat cake for lunch."

"Best plan you've ever come up with." Everly smiled.

"You did good today, but now I'm seeing that you carry more baggage than I literally do, so how about I take over antiques-store duty until we're done here?"

"Yeah. If you're okay with that. I think it would be best. Thank you."

Everly looked back at the floor, scattered with sharp crystal. She wasn't sure she could ever accept that it hadn't been her fault, but it had felt good to face it, to say it out loud.

But another memory flickered, harder than the others to catch, leaving her chilled to her core.

A flash of bright light as her father fell, and a sensation of hunger being sated.

Chapter Nine

"I just need one more night." Rylan worked to keep the desperation from his voice.

"Again, Howell?" Vonny leaned against the side of the van and folded her arms, looking ready to murder him.

Jaw twitching, he nodded.

Last night had been a bust. After separating from his brace, Rylan tried to focus and keep searching for the shadyr who was robbing graves, but he kept finding himself drawn back to Everly's place. He wanted to make sure that creature—cougar or otherwise—wasn't still prowling around. That it couldn't get inside.

He had to know that she was safe. He'd watched her bedroom window, but it remained dark, the only light and movement showing in the living room, until that light went out too.

But even when he was sure she was asleep, he remained, unable to drag himself away.

Tonight, he had to make up for that lapse. It was his last chance to find something. He couldn't keep letting his brace down like this. He couldn't keep giving them nights off, and they shouldn't be out hunting just with the three of them, as good as Vonny and Jasper were.

He worried about Annabeth. She was competent but was far more passionate about the academic side of shadyr culture. She'd been pushed into brace duty by Master Darkfrey when they needed more bodies on the field after losing Callan and Cherry.

"One more night? For what? If you'd just explain what you're doing, maybe I could help out. You can trust me." The crunch of gravel turned Vonny's gaze sideways toward Jasper and Annabeth coming to join them.

Her eyes narrowed slightly, as though she didn't intend her message of trust to encompass the other two from their brace. "Or you could just let it go and get back to doing what you're supposed to do before someone gets hurt."

"It's important. That's all I can say. I can't just let it go." Rylan held her gaze.

Vonny looked away first. "Fine. But this is your last chance."

Jasper and Annabeth arrived beside them, suited up in their Darkfrey body armor.

Vonny turned away from them all and said, "All right, let's go."

Rylan stepped back from the van. "I'll see you tomorrow. Good hunting."

Annabeth paused with her hand on the door. "You're not—"

"No, he's not coming with us," Vonny answered for him.

Rylan turned his back on them so he couldn't see the disappointment in Annabeth's big eyes or the questioning interrogation in Jasper's.

The van doors swung and clunked and Annabeth whispered, not quietly enough, "What's going on with him?"

Vonny grunted. "He's probably just using the time for some secret hookup."

"Do you think that's what it is?" Annabeth rasped, scandalized, and the van rumbled away.

Rylan stalked toward the front entrance of the main building, feeling as though he was failing everyone. He needed to be split in three—hunting with his brace, finding out what was happening with the missing bones, and keeping Everly safe.

But he couldn't function as a good shadyr or properly protect Everly if someone had it in for him.

He still wasn't sure why they didn't outright kill him

in that secret corridor after what he saw. The bump on the back of his head still ached. It could easily have been a killing blow, but instead they left him alive, unconscious, only to wake up with all the evidence he'd just found cleared out and no idea who'd blindsided him.

And he wasn't sure why they hadn't tried to kill him since, which made him all the more anxious to get Mordan's ear on this again, make him listen.

The tiny cage elevator rattled up to the floor with Mordan Darkfrey's office.

The lighting was dimmer up here, the warm glow of a few ornate lamps mounted onto the walls casting pools of light down the corridor.

A hulking figure stood at attention in front of the huge double doors.

"Nilson, is Master Darkfrey in?" Rylan eyed the man, having to turn his head up to do so even from his height.

"He's busy." Nilson barely opened his square jaw to spit the words out. His geometrically precise blond crew cut squared off the top of his head as well.

"It's important."

Nilson leaned forward, looming over Rylan, thick thighs and biceps straining the limits of his clothing. "He's in a meeting with Kole, and that's more important. Did you even get an appointment?"

Rylan smirked. "What, are you his secretary now?"

Nilson's hand shot out and slammed into Rylan's shoulder, pushing him and making him stumble back a few steps. "You can't just go walking in on Master Darkfrey. You should know your place, Howell runt."

Rylan stabilized his stance on the plush rug and rolled his shoulders. All the fire in his veins that had been burning him alive for days left him itching for a fight.

But laying out Nilson right outside of Mordan's office was a sure ticket out of the Darkfrey's for good.

He'd have to go looking for a fight elsewhere. "Fine. Be a good secretary for me and let him know I want to talk to him."

Nilson growled like a feral dog as Rylan strode away. *What was that all about?*

Nilson was the finest specimen of jerk at the best of times, but since when was it his place to be playing guard at Master Darkfrey's door?

Was it on Mordan's orders, or was Nilson specifically trying to keep Rylan away?

Rylan shivered at the thought that Nilson was involved in the dark goings-on.

The man had the bulky build that matched the figure Rylan had seen robbing a grave. And he was strong enough to blindside Rylan like he had been.

But what would Mordan Darkfrey's own son be doing messing around with stolen bones?

No, it didn't make sense. Especially considering Nilson had even less mental capacity for conspiracy than Rylan did.

Rylan took the stairs down, heading back toward the secret tunnel, hoping to find something again there, something that was missed, but his confidence was waning.

Whoever his enemy was, they were clearly certain he couldn't catch them. Otherwise, he wouldn't still be alive.

Maybe they were right. He really wasn't the sneaky investigator type. He was the follow orders, take the hits, take the target down type. His investigation had only gotten as far as it had on luck and perseverance and he wasn't even sure where to look next.

It was all he could do to free some headspace from thinking about Everly and wanting to go to her, to be there, right outside her window, making sure nothing could touch her.

He'd had to satisfy himself by calling in a favor with Lucas's brace. His friend agreed to run an extra patrol or two down Everly's street. And maybe Rylan could check in on Everly himself later in the night.

Rylan gave the skirting board a sharp kick, popping open the wood panel entrance to the secret tunnel. He pulled the door closed behind him, left in almost complete darkness.

As good as his eyesight was in the dark, he pulled out his phone and turned it on for enough extra light to get a better look at every nook and cranny of the clandestine space. There had to be something left behind, something the grave robber had missed when clearing out their lair.

The air was damp and heavy with the smell of the ancient stone lining the path, carved in swirling patterns. The passage led him through the deepest corners of the estate, a maze that must date back thousands of years, back to the earliest shadyrs.

Annabeth would know. She'd probably know what all these carvings mean.

Shadows clung to every corner, a history of long-lost secrets held by every wall that had been built upon and built upon over time to create the labyrinth that Darkfrey Estate was today.

Heading back to the chamber he'd discovered on his last trip, he scoured every step, searching for a single fragment of bone, a footprint, or a stray hair. Were those the sorts of things detectives looked for?

He hoped for something more than that because he had no idea what he'd do with a single hair. Shroudhaven didn't exactly have a well-funded forensics department.

The chamber he'd found last time remained as empty as it was when he had woken up after being blindsided. He stalked around the carved stone boundary, checking every corner.

Nothing.

He was ready to rage-quit when a pale patch on the stone ground caught his eye. Moving closer, the brighter section turned out to be a scrap of yellowed paper, no bigger than a coin, pressed flat onto the ground until it seemed to be part of the stone itself.

One corner was marked by a boot print, as though it had been unknowingly walked in.

He gently pried it up with his fingernails. The boot print was only partial and seemed to be a match to the standard-issue boots all the Darkfreys wore.

On the flip side, only a few legible words remained. *Cast.* A cutoff list of names and characters. And the logo for Rook's Theater.

"Okay, that's something," Rylan muttered, examining the paper in the palm of his hand.

It was like a breadcrumb just waiting to be followed. Rylan's pulse quickened. The lead he needed had finally emerged from the shadows.

Rylan wasted no time making his way through the backstreets of Shroudhaven. He moved fast on foot, not wanting to take a vehicle that could be tracked, but wary of the many dangers of simply being out alone.

Rook's Theater sat on the main street, a mix of faded old-world glamour and rotting neglect. A street artist had once tried to revive the magic of the place, recreating vintage movie posters across the façade with spray paint, but those artworks were long lost under a mess of other vandalism.

The hairs on the back of Rylan's neck stood up. There was definitely something there.

Normally, he could tell what he would be facing, based on the way those sensations pulled his body toward change, but this was different, strange, too many confusing signals. Similar to how the bones he'd found in the secret chamber had made him feel.

This is it. They must have moved their operation here.

The street was windy, a chill slicing through from the nearby river, and Rylan pulled his hood up as he strolled around the side alley to the back entrance.

A heavy industrial metal door blocked the way, a padlock and chain wrapped around the handle. Rylan found a metal bar in the trash nearby, wedged it into the ring of the padlock, and the lock cracked.

Inside the theater was a riot of musty props and costumes and the refuse of decades left by daring teenagers breaking in to hold parties. Rylan stalked past it all, following his nose and the shadyr senses that had his skin trembling.

He was so consumed with the need to find his target, to get the evidence he needed to bring them down and end this, that he didn't realize until too late that his senses were also picking up a nearby ghast.

Rylan stood in the empty theater, staring down the

aisle at the stage where a massive monster stared right back at him.

A harsh clarity broke across his thoughts.

His enemy didn't kill him at the estate because they were setting him up to be killed by something else.

Chapter Ten

Everly's dragon sat in the corner, a shining entity of destructive emotion.

The old couch on which her sleeping bag was rolled out was picture-perfect for real life, the old floral upholstery stained and yellowed. Her sleeping bag crinkled realistically as she shifted, blinking sore eyes at horrors playing out on the screen of the boxy, faux-wood-covered TV.

Nightmares within a nightmare.

"This is a dream."

On the TV, static snow obscured a black-and-white vision of Rylan, vampire fanged and monstrous, chasing after something shadowy, huge, and inscrutable.

Everly groaned, rolling her head around and stretching imaginary muscles.

"Vampires again? Great. Why not?"

At least this time she had a more comfortable viewing arrangement. Her dreams after a hard day were always dark and violent, so she wasn't surprised by the graphic visions on the screen.

She focused, holding on to the semi-lucid state she was used to having in her sleep. A state she could use to nudge the dreams toward being more favorable.

Her half-aware self pushed mentally against the reality of the dream, trying to adjust it.

An ocean of garbage surrounded the couch, and rolled out in a wave then back around her.

Sometimes a more physical approach worked better, so she got up and jiggled the bunny-ear antenna on the vintage set, then crouched in front of the screen and clicked the round channel dial.

The image flickered but wouldn't change away from its driving theme. Rylan and monster. Chasing.

One moment it was Rylan chasing a swirling creature; next it was Rylan tailing a monstrously tall man in a trench coat. But it was always him chasing, chasing. A never-ending chase.

Nightmares were much harder to control than more pleasant dreams.

Been a while since I had any of those.

On the TV, vampire-Rylan caught up to the shadow being. They clashed, a blur of violent limbs. Red blood splattered brightly against the black-and-white world. It sprayed out of the TV and hit Everly's cheek.

She cringed, then stoically wiped it away. Monsters and violence haunting her sleep was normal. She didn't like it, but she was used to it.

The fight ended and the chase resumed. She couldn't quite make out the form of whatever it was Rylan was after. It kept changing, shifting, made of feelings and vapors and dream-stuff too slippery for Everly's semi-lucid brain to lock down.

A cougar appeared, stepping out from behind the old TV, made of the same grainy black and white as the show and partially transparent.

A sudden sense of hunger jolted through Everly, but it wasn't her own. It was the dragon. Its scintillating shape slithered closer, prowling through the floating trash bags toward the cat.

Stop it, she scolded.

The glowing manifestation backed away. Everly wished she could just make the thing leave for good, but the best she managed was keeping it confined to a corner and ignoring it.

It was nice to see the cougar though. She hoped that was what she'd seen last night out on the street as well, that it was okay.

Everly reached out a hand. "Hey, kitty. I'm glad you

weren't hurt."

It moved closer and sniffed at her.

Sparks glittered at the ends of her fingertips.

The cougar was gone. The couch was gone. The room was gone.

Everly and the TV remained, floating on a lightless sea. She balanced on a tiny island of refuse that sank quickly, and she had to hop from one trash-raft to another, over and over, to avoid going under. Things moved around her, a swarming oil slick of inky creatures, as the TV still played its horrible show.

Rylan and the creature, chasing, chasing. Out of the screen, into the darkness around her, small but getting ever closer and more real. Chasing, chasing. Everly's stomach churned.

This dream wasn't playing nice. She'd had enough. *Wake up.*

Everly's tongue felt dry and swollen in her mouth, and she swallowed as she opened tired eyes. "Ugh."

Her sleeping bag rustled as she flopped her cocooned legs off the side of the couch. Her heart rate was up and the squelchy, sick feeling from the dream still filled her throat.

She hated that kind of dream—the stubborn, unchangeable nightmare her mind favored when processing a stressful day.

If she went straight back to sleep, it would only start

up right where it left off. She had to break the connection before trying to get any more rest.

Everly slipped out of the sleeping bag, got up, and shuffled along the aged carpet that reeked of years of absorbed cigarette smoke. The air was chilly on her bare arms and feet as the warmth of the sleeping bag quickly faded, leaving just some leggings and a singlet to protect her against the cold.

She headed slowly down the stairs, trying to avoid any creaking sounds that might disturb Harper's sleep. At the bottom of the steps, she patted the bird sticking out of the broken cuckoo clock and wondered what the time was.

The light in the kitchen flickered and buzzed in a way Everly liked as much as she liked electrical fires, so she turned it off. There was just enough light coming in from the hall for her to find her way the sink.

A small, dark shape darted out from one of the cupboards. Everly swallowed a squeal as the rat jumped off the counter like a sleek dart and sped past Everly's bare toes, too close for comfort. She hopped up and down on the spot a few times to shake off the nerves.

Getting back to sleep is going to be so easy now.

She turned the tap on to wash a glass and a long howling sound startled her. Thinking it was the old pipes, she twisted the faucet off quickly.

But the sound didn't stop.

Crashing, ripping, crackling noises followed. Everly lifted the dusty lace curtain and peered out the window above the sink. She looked over the front yard to the street. The drinking glass fell from her hand.

Vampire-Rylan fought a shadowy beast.

The glass cracked on the floor, smashing beside her bare feet.

"That's okay. It doesn't matter. I'm still dreaming. This is a dream."

She bent down to swipe the glass away, erase the mess from her dream world, but a sharp shard sliced into the palm of her hand.

The pain was vivid, real. *Real.*

Wake up. Wake up. Wake up.

Nothing changed. Her eyes didn't open from sleep.

Instead, they stared, confused, at the blood on her hand and then out the window again. Where a man and a monster of living darkness fought on the street.

This can't be real.

Everly's mind scrambled as her eyes remained locked on the impossible violence occurring outside her window. She tried every self-test she knew to be sure she wasn't dreaming, but found she was more awake and more terrified than she'd ever been.

Have I lost my mind?

It was dark outside and everything moved so fast Everly

struggled to follow what was happening. She couldn't make out many features on the man. But it felt like Rylan. It felt like how she'd just seen him in her dream.

Chasing, chasing.

The creature ... Everly stood paralyzed, mouth hanging open as she tried to process it. From a distance it cut the rough silhouette of a man in a trench coat, but too big. Too misshapen.

Draping shadows and writhing tentacles leaked out, lashing at Rylan. It lurched slowly, crookedly, as though injured.

Their fight moved them closer to a streetlight. The man who might have been Rylan wore the same clothes Rylan had when she'd seen him the night before. But he also seemed different, changed somehow. His jacket was torn and one of his arms dangled as though he had lost the ability to use it.

Everly's throat closed up. *He's hurt.*

He kept attacking the creature anyway, as relentless as he was in her dream. His actions blurred, moving faster than a human should be able to.

The creature slashed tentacles through the air and he dodged effortlessly, leaping high and landing behind it, panther-like.

He launched himself at it, trying to drag it away from Everly's home. The size of the thing dwarfed Rylan, threatened to consume him in its twisting shadows, but somehow he matched its strength, the speed of its dizzying attacks.

He shook out his arms—both seemed to be working again—and caught the largest of the whipping tentacles and wrenched. It tore off, and the thing howled—the same sound Everly had heard before.

Rylan stumbled back as though the effort had taken the last of his energy.

Dark smoke and mist poured from the creature's wound. It seemed to expand in size.

Tumbling and hissing, it flailed its whole body at Rylan, wrapping him entirely. Rylan was caught up in it, wrenching against the tangle of tentacles that enveloped him.

They tumbled together, and Rylan got back on top, but long ropes of the creatures flesh were bound around each of his arms, tight to the shoulder. Rylan cried out as the creature lifted him into the air.

A cracking sound pierced the night as the creature tore his chest open down the middle.

Rylan fell.

CHAPTER ELEVEN

Everly didn't think, *couldn't* think about what she'd seen. She just knew she had to help Rylan. She ran.

She leaped over the broken glass and skidded out of the kitchen, through the back door, around the side of the house, and onto the street.

The street where Rylan had fallen.

Was it really him? It couldn't be. This couldn't be real.

But there lay a body, bloody and broken.

Hesitation froze Everly in place for a moment, staring from the body of the man to the mangled pile of shadows across the road where whatever it was had also slumped to the ground.

Her vision swam, sickness filling her throat. She couldn't deal with whatever *that* was right now.

She dashed across to the human form, breath turning

to sharp spikes in her throat as she saw his face. All too familiar.

It was him.

Everly knelt at Rylan's side, holding one of his hands in hers as tremors raked through her.

"Ev ...? No, no ..." Rylan stared up at her with his galaxy eyes. Blood spattered from his mouth as he gasped out the words. "No. *Go.*"

Everly could only stare back, unable to speak, unable to breathe.

He was Rylan, just Rylan, no vampire or monstrous features of any kind. Just Rylan, torn open and bloody, the last of his life gurgling in his throat.

Everly, who had felt so capable and quick to act with Harper's small cut, now felt utterly at a loss.

I can't. I can't fix this. He's going to die because I can't fix this.

She couldn't put pressure on the wound because there was too much of it. The coppery scent of blood hit her nose. His shirt and some kind of underlayer of thicker metallic fabric was shredded, blood gushing around it.

She didn't know how he was still alive.

This can't be happening.

Everly hoped that her mind had broken with reality, that this was some kind of hallucination. She'd rather be insane than this be real, when this reality was enough to drive her insane.

I didn't see what I thought I saw. My night vision is terrible. Rylan is just Rylan and the other thing was probably some animal. But what animal could have done this?

The answer was it didn't even matter if the result was the same. If Rylan was going to die.

Rylan managed to raise an arm and touch her face. It was wet, the blood on his fingers painting her cheek.

He held her gaze intensely and pleaded, *"Go."*

Everly nodded, her voice still trapped in her throat. She should go, get her phone, call for help, call out to anyone for help.

Then Rylan's arm dropped, and his gaze held still, and his rattling breath stopped. His skin grew cold, pale, and hard beneath her hands.

She grasped at his face, lifting his head into her lap. "Rylan?"

There was no response. A rasping cry broke from Everly's mouth.

No, no, no.

Believing that she and Rylan would one day find each other again, that they were meant to be together, had once been her greatest dream.

Now that dream lay dead on the ground in front of her, and she'd give it all up, every chance at romance or love in her life forever, if it meant Rylan could live. Her face contorted as painful tears burst free.

A shadow grew over Everly as she cradled Rylan's head, screams wheezing silently from her mouth.

A cracking, slithering sound lifted Everly's eyes away from Rylan. The ghastly mound was no longer where she'd last seen it.

Whatever it was, it wasn't dead.

Whatever it was, it was right behind her.

She turned her head and found herself face-to-face with an uncountable number of gray tentacles—tentacles made of tentacles, bulbous and misshapen, sliding over each other, covered in teeth and eyes and dripping shadows.

Panic roared through her body. Adrenaline scorched her heart, lungs, and brain. She scrambled to stand. Bare feet skidding in blood, she ran.

A tentacle lashed out at her, smashing into her back with a force that lifted her from the ground.

She flew across the footpath and into her front yard.

She crashed into something spiky and brittle, some kind of sculpture left there among the weeds. It broke under her as she tumbled into it. The sound was lost under her heartbeat pounding in her ears.

Beneath her were what looked like black bones.

Tentacles slithered into view. A sickly gas oozed from them.

Everly choked on it and it made her dizzy, sleepy,

clashing with her body that raged in adrenaline-fueled overdrive.

Every part of her was a knife's edge of nerves and frantic energy and she couldn't contain it.

She lost all control over her panic. Her mind snapped.

It felt as though her whole body exploded.

Wispy tendrils of bright light and sparkles filled her vision, searing her flesh. She lifted off the ground, hovering as the blinding bright threads lashed out at the tentacle creature. Caught in the web of light, the creature writhed, consumed within the blaze.

Everly's overworked heart was set to burst, and she almost embraced it, because how could she go on? If Rylan was gone ...

But years of pulling herself back from the brink kicked in, automatically fighting back, trying to return to still and calm and control.

The light went out.

Everly fell into the overgrown garden. She gagged on the lingering vapors that swirled amongst the weeds. They fogged over her already failing consciousness.

She didn't know what was happening, what was real. Had she been hit by lightning? Was she dying?

She lay tangled in the rosebush, unable to move, to even cry out, as her consciousness faded. Through a small gap in the bushes, she could see Rylan's body, motionless on the pavement.

She tried to reach for him, stretch herself out to hold him, protect him, give anything she could to bring him back to life.

Some other form moved in the distance. A person, hobbling slowly up the street. Everly's eyelids drooped, fighting against her will to stay awake.

Save us. Save Rylan. Please.

Everly couldn't get the words out. Darkness edged in all around her.

The figure moved strangely. Silhouetted, hunchbacked, human-shaped but wrong. Dragging something. Coming closer.

"Everly!" Rylan rushed over to her as she sat up from the rosebush.

"Rylan? How?" Everly stumbled forward, clinging unashamedly to him.

His chest was firm and unbroken, his shirt whole and dry, his lips free of blood. Tears of relief hung in her eyes.

He grabbed her too, holding her briefly before he checked her over, brushing his hands along her face and arms. "Are you okay?"

Light crackled and glittered between her and Rylan where they touched. The roses didn't scratch her as she stood within them. She could see clearly, despite it still being night.

Her dragon swam through the air nearby, swallowing, smacking its jaws.

No ... Oh, no.

Everly's hands dropped and she stepped back, her heart aching.

He frowned. "What? What is it? Are you hurt?"

She stared up at him, his unmarred skin, untorn clothes. Her voice came out wan and lifeless. "I'm dreaming."

His lips twisted into a wry smile. "What? What do you mean you're dreaming?"

"I mean, dreaming." Everly waved a hand and daylight sparkled on the white miniature roses that surrounded them, fields and fields of them stretching on forever.

In the center of each tiny rose as a toothy mouth, dripping in blood.

Rylan jolted back, circling around to take in their surroundings. "What in the Everdark just happened?"

The nonsense words, as usual. Everly's shoulders slumped, and she didn't bother to answer. What was the point in explaining anything to a dream? But she didn't go anywhere, didn't try to rouse herself, too worried about what she might wake up to.

Maybe it was all a dream. But what if it wasn't?

"I don't know what's going on, but I'm not asleep—at least I don't feel like I am." Rylan stared at his surroundings, then his own hands, then Everly through narrowed eyes, as though suspicious of everything. "Are we caught in a beshadowing of some kind?"

"A what? No, never mind. Look, you can feel however you want to feel because this is my dream and you're a figment, saying whatever my sleepy brain decides it wants you to say. The real Rylan is ..." Everly choked on the words.

Was he dead? Had it all been real?

Her memory of it was so confused, with too many not-everyday-reality moments taking place to make sense of anything. Maybe she'd never woken up, never gone downstairs. Maybe she was still dreaming on the couch, more vividly than she ever had.

Or maybe she and Rylan were both dead.

Rylan had grown pale, forehead furrowed in thought. "The real Rylan is *what*?"

Everly clamped her mouth shut.

Tendrils of light swayed over the tops of the rosebushes as her dragon swam sharklike through them. It seemed bigger than usual. Everly wasn't surprised, given her recent anxiety-fueling experiences.

The dragon slithered closer, hungry. Everly stood between it and Rylan.

Go away!

The glowing, fractal-shaped creature caught Rylan's attention. He tensed. "What is that?"

"That's just my anxiety."

"Your *what*?" Rylan raised his eyebrows.

He rubbed a hand over his mouth and muttered something about maybe dreaming after all.

Her dragon pushed against her will in a way it didn't usually, and Everly pushed back until it cowered and shimmered away.

Everly remembered the similar tendrils of light that had surrounded her in the front yard. Only it couldn't have happened. Not if she was awake. Maybe she hadn't been.

"What do you remember?" she asked.

Rylan grunted, rubbing his temple. "I remember ... what was I doing? I was chasing a ..."

Chasing, chasing.

Everly swallowed away the sick sensation of the echoing words. "Chasing a what?"

Rylan looked at her from under low brows. "Nothing."

Everly tried to nudge him with her mind, to make him answer or change to a different subject. Nothing happened. It was strange that he was even there, talking to her, looking at her the way he was.

"You're not like how you normally are in my dreams."

Rylan pressed his lips together and made a quiet

humming sound. "I'm ... normally in your dreams?"

"Maybe. Sometimes. It doesn't matter." Everly swallowed, growing flustered under the intense stare of his warm green eyes.

"What am I normally like in your dreams?" Rylan smirked, keeping her fixed in his gaze.

"Just, you know, *dreamy*."

Rylan's eyebrows shot up.

Her cheeks flamed.

She rambled on. "I mean, the way dreams are, not *dreamy* dreamy. More nightmarish dreamy if anything. For example, the dream I just had where you were a vampire chasing a big, weird, shadow tentacle thing."

Rylan's eyes grew wide, then were quickly schooled back into place. "That's one crazy dream."

"So you're not a vampire?"

"Of course not. There's no such thing as vampires."

Everly took in a long, frustrated breath. "Then what did I see? Tell me, in the frame of things that do exist, what did I see?"

Rylan turned away, staring out over the sea of roses as though there might be an exit in sight. "You said you were dreaming."

The dam broke and tears poured over Everly's cheeks. "What if I wasn't? What if you're really dead?"

"Dead?" The word dropped roughly from Rylan's

mouth and he turned back.

Everly wiped her eyes on the backs of her forearms. "I saw you die. And if you're not some kind of immortal vampire, if that can't be real along with every other crazy thing I saw, then it means you're really dead."

Rylan stared at his hands for a long moment, saying nothing.

"I used to like dreaming about you every night."

Rylan looked up at her, a sadness on his face that was heartbreaking. "Every night?"

"But if you're gone, if you only exist in my dreams ..." Everly sobbed.

Rylan reached out for her, but she backed away. She didn't want to be comforted by her dream. She didn't deserve it.

"I'm not a vampire," Rylan said, his voice soft. "What happened, what you saw, it's not what you think. You have no idea what goes on in Shroudhaven."

"Then tell me. Tell me so I can do something for you."

Rylan shook his head, locking her in his gaze again in a way Everly thought could burn right through her heart. "When you wake up, no matter what happened to me, you have to leave and never come back."

CHAPTER TWELVE

Everly rocked back and forth. Shaken roughly by unseen hands, she roused from the clutches of deep sleep.

"Oh my gosh. Please, wake up!" It was Harper's voice.

Everly's eyelids snapped open, and her hands shot out so fast it made Harper squeak. "Are you *trying* to give me a heart attack?"

Everly's eyes darted around, trying to take in reality. The night-shrouded front yard was lit by Harper's phone lying beside them. A light rain fell, cold and tingly on Everly's bare skin. Her clothes were soaked through.

Harper had a blanket draped over her head, which gave them both some cover as she leaned over Everly, her mouth and eyes both wide.

"I'm so glad you woke up. I was freaking out. I got up to go to the bathroom, and you were *gone*. I found you here, completely out of it. I tried to call an ambulance but the reception is still dodgy. What are you doing outside?"

"I'm not sure." Everly rubbed her temple, but she was aching all over.

"Well, you look like you've been sleepwalking and picked a fight with a rosebush."

Is this real? The rain felt real. Harper's hands on her shoulders felt real. The sharp twigs and brambles sticking into her back felt real. Everly blinked once, twice, then sat bolt upright out of the weedy patch she'd fallen into.

"Whoa, slow down."

"Where's Rylan? Is he okay?" Everly scrambled to stand up.

Harper grabbed her arms, pulling her free of the overgrowth and onto the somewhat clearer path. "Rylan? There's no one else here."

"He was. He was right over there." Everly careened along the path and out onto the street where she had last seen Rylan, last seen his body.

The surface of the road was black and glistening in the rain. She couldn't see any sign of him, of blood, of the terrible fight she'd witnessed. Of his body, alive or …

"It sounds kind of like you've been sleepwalking and dreaming about him. Look, I knew you had it bad for this guy, but wow." Harper smiled and elbowed Everly gently.

Everly shook her head. "No, I know when I'm dreaming.

I was dreaming, but then I was awake ...”

And then dreaming again. Or was I never awake?

She looked down at herself—pajamas spotted in washed-out blood, arms scratched by thorns, wet leaves and grass plastered all over her.

She remembered the creature throwing her into the garden—but maybe she'd tripped into it in her sleep? She remembered light coming out of her, destroying the shadowy thing—or had it just been her dragon in the dream?

“I don't know what's going on,” she whispered. “It felt so real.”

“Tell me what happened,” Harper coaxed.

“Rylan was ... a vampire. And he was ... fighting a tentacle creature, but it killed him.” Everly choked out a wry chuckle. “Wow, yeah. Okay. Now that I'm saying it out loud, it couldn't be real, could it? Ugh. I'm sorry for being such a head case.”

“No wonder you decided to go toe to toe with the rosebush. Sounds like one exciting dream. Shame the rosebush looks like it won.”

“It was less exciting and more mortal-terror-inducing.”

Harper wrapped Everly in the blanket, her arm around her shoulders, guiding her away from the road.

“Come on. Let's get back inside. It's five in the morning, and I doubt I'm getting back to sleep after all this. We'll get you cleaned up, get some of the world's strongest coffee brewing, and pretend like we're actually morning people who want to be awake."

Everly nodded. She glanced back one more time at the road, needing to confirm again that it hadn't been real. Wind gusted, blowing the rain sideways. It sparkled under the streetlight, like the way the glowing tendrils had.

Anxiety churned within her, and she counted out some long, deep breaths.

She'd only ever seen light like that once before. So long ago it felt like a dream, like the confused memories of an infant.

And it had to have been a dream. Because if it was real, Everly didn't want to face what it meant.

Everly couldn't shake the feeling she'd seen Rylan die. But with everything pointing toward it only being a vivid dream, she worked hard to shut off the parts of her mind that replayed the horrific scene.

She and Harper sat together on the back step, warming their noses over mugs of black instant coffee. After some half-hearted rummaging through the kitchen cupboards, it was the best they could do.

They hadn't even found any sugar and had only bought cake when they shopped the day before. Harper added a proper grocery run to the list of priorities for the day.

The sound of clanging metal and rattling chains came from around the front, and they went to watch as the truck dropped off the skip bin.

Everly's breath stuttered from her throat as the bin was placed right beside where she'd seen Rylan die the night before.

No. It was just a dream.

"Time to get to work." Harper yawned.

"I'll keep going with the cleanup. You really don't have to get into the dirty work too." Everly had already changed out of her thorn-scratched pajamas into her regular outfit.

Harper was still in her satin nightgown and fluffy slippers.

"Any luck yesterday getting the house's internet connection going?" Everly asked.

"No. Might need a new router." Harper took a sip of coffee and grimaced. "I *neeeed* that wired connection. I can barely get online on my phone long enough to reply to a single comment. Being offline so long is making me physically itchy."

Everly patted her friend on the shoulder then left to get to work.

She had cleared the bulk of the rubbish out of the main

living areas except her old bedroom the day before. The state of disrepair beneath the mess had become apparent then. Mostly cosmetic fixes, with the bones of the building remaining strong.

Everly lugged her tool bag from room to room, focusing on some quick and easy tasks—puttying small holes in the drywall, replacing a washer in a leaky tap, and screwing down some loose flooring. It felt good to work on things she could fix.

Deep cleaning was going to take a bit longer, but she figured she'd leave that until after repairs that would only add to the cleanup.

She unscrewed the switches and light fittings in the kitchen and found their loose connection before fixing them so the lights didn't flicker and buzz. As she turned them on again, testing her work, she froze for a moment.

It was when she'd woken up in the night that she noticed the fault. Right before she'd seen ...

No. She must have noticed it earlier. She'd probably forgotten, gotten confused, merged it into her dream.

It was just. A. Dream.

Harper had hooked up her modem, then sat on her bed, laptop and phone both at hand, tapping, muttering, and growling at the spotty reception.

"This is ridiculous! I'm going round in circles. How can I do two-factor identification if the internet isn't working but I need to do that so I can make the internet work! I give up! I'm going to have a shower!"

"I haven't finished cleaning the bathroom yet," Everly called back down the hall apologetically.

Years worth of spent shampoo bottles and moldy towels had been shoveled out the day before, but the space was far from clean. They'd both skipped showers the day before, worried they'd only come out of the space dirtier than they went in.

Harper stomped a foot petulantly and started grabbing bottles out of the cleaning bucket, piling them into her arms. "Then I'll hose down the whole room while I'm in there. This is all going to work out!"

It was an hour before she emerged again in a puff of steam, looking glamorous as ever, with the jade-toned bathroom tiles and matching bath behind her glistening and gleaming. It was the cleanest Everly had ever seen it.

While she'd lived at home, she tried to keep her own spaces and shared spaces like the kitchen and bathroom clean. But it had been a constant battle against her mother.

A mix of substance abuse, hoarder tendencies, and generally not giving a damn had meant the house was always filthy. The kind of men she'd brought home in a never-ending stream didn't seem to care about the mess either.

"Okay. I've calmed down, and I have a plan. I can't

get through to the telecom to get the connection switched on here. I'm going to head into town, find some better reception, and better coffee," Harper said, jingling her keys on her way out the door. "Want me to bring you back anything?"

"No, thanks. I'm okay," Everly said.

Her eyes were gritty and lack of sleep made her body beg for some proper caffeine. But she couldn't impose.

She gave Harper directions for the best places to go, then had a drink of water and the last oat bar from her bag before getting back to work.

There was still a little room left in the skip bin, so Everly decided she needed to get the trash out of her old bedroom one way or another.

She propped the door ajar with her pry bar and began filling bags with whatever she could extract through the gap. Once she'd cleared enough refuse to open the door properly, she stepped inside.

Like an archaeologist unearthing lost ruins, it surprised her to find her original single bed under the layers of filth. As she sifted down through the mounds of garbage, that seemed to be all that remained of the bedroom she'd once known.

Digging her fingers under a pile of rotting clothing, something sharp poked her thumb, almost piercing through the thick work gloves. Scraping the rubbish away revealed a broken picture frame. The glass sat shattered within silver art nouveau edging. Everly shook the shards off into the trash bag and stared at the faded, scratched photo beneath.

Her dad and her mom were smiling in front of the brand-new Boderleth Antiques sign, holding a puffy pink baby with a gurgling grin.

Everly touched the photo and the surface peeled away under her rough glove, as though she'd taken a bite out of her father's shoulder. She inhaled sharply, then sighed.

This might be my one happy memory I find here, and it's ruined.

She considered just throwing it into the trash as well. Was it really worth holding on to, this token of a family she didn't even remember?

All she knew was a life of only herself, her mom, and the men her mother brought home—none of whom ever stayed long enough to even come close to earning a *dad* title.

The closest she'd had to a family, the only time she learned what a family was meant to be, was with the Howells. When she'd become friends with Rylan as a kid, his mom, dad, and brother all welcomed her in and showed her what love meant.

Everly's heart still hurt with the feeling that Rylan was somehow *gone*.

She wandered downstairs, put the photo away in a kitchen drawer, got out her phone, and stared at it.

I should try to call him, just in case.

Skimming through her contacts, she found Rylan's number—the last number she had for him anyway. She'd called it from time to time, and it had never been disconnected.

It never got answered, either. She gave herself a countdown so she couldn't back out and dialed.

It rang. And rang. And rang. No voicemail. No answer.

Everly sighed and continued her cleanup.

It was late afternoon by the time she'd gotten most of the main rooms into what passed as a livable level of cleanliness. She hadn't yet unlocked the attic or basement and wasn't in any hurry to.

One rat nest had already been uncovered in the corner of the laundry and Everly had to spend a while standing on a chair as the rats relocated themselves. Probably into the attic or basement.

Everly tied up and lugged her latest bag of rubbish out to the skip.

On her way along the garden path, she looked over at the crushed rosebush. There was nothing strange there—no black bones, no weird light.

It was just a dream.

She grunted with the effort of hauling the heavy bag over the edge of the large metal bin. It clanged and echoed as it landed among the others.

She paused there, staring at the black road under her feet.

It was right here. Right here when I held him as he bled, then went still.

It had felt so real.

Frowning, she took off one glove, knelt down, and ran her fingers over the asphalt.

Her skin came away a rusty, blood red.

Chapter Thirteen

Everly gasped, standing quickly and backing away from the dark patch on the ground.

She stood there shaking as Harper pulled up in her campervan.

Harper hopped out of the driver's seat, balancing two takeaway cups from Pimey's Diner in one hand and holding a brown paper bag in the other. "Hey, are you all right? You've gone a weird shade of green."

Everly turned her reddened hand around to show her friend.

Harper ducked her face down and stared over the top of her sunglasses. "Oh no! Did you cut yourself?"

"No. No, I think it's Rylan's blood. It's from the ground ... there." Everly grabbed the rag hanging from her back pocket and wiped her hand mostly clean.

"What if it was real? I'm not saying vampire-and-tentacle-beast real ... but what if I saw *something* bad and real, and my sleepy, panicked brain processed it as a nightmare? What if it was an animal attack and Rylan really was hurt, is hurt?"

Harper pushed one of the coffee cups into Everly's hands. "I guess it's not completely unlikely. We did see a flippin' cougar on our way into town. I mean, how is there even a cougar here?"

"Keeping menageries was the done thing for rich people around Shroudhaven in the good old days. A bunch of animals got out over the years and have been spotted in the Wyrdwoods ever since. There was also the old zoo that closed down a while back under weird circumstances."

"You're telling me *anything* could be running around out here? No wonder no one goes out into the woods." Harper looked over at the spot near the skip that Everly was staring at.

"I feel like I need to do something," Everly said. "Tell someone. Just in case."

"Okay."

"Okay?"

"Yeah, let's head in and report it at the police station. Maybe they can look into it for you, make sure everything's all right." Harper waved her toward the campervan. "Just got to unload some groceries first."

"Thanks," Everly said. She looked down at the coffee cup warming her fingers.

The red-and-white Pimey's logo caused a rush of homesickness to flow through her. "For this too. I told you I didn't need anything."

"You always say you don't need anything." Harper jiggled the paper bag in front of Everly and tossed it to her before grabbing one of the canvas tote bags full of supplies. "So I got donuts too. 'Cause I'm the best friend ever."

Everly returned a faint smile. Harper's support made it seem possible that last night's events weren't just a dream.

But that was the last thing Everly wanted.

"**O**h, another *animal attack*, is it?" The police officer leaned over the front counter, sipping slowly from a mug that said *Boss Bitch*. She tapped it with long red fingernails in time to the tune playing softly on the radio in the background.

Everly remembered all the words to the folksy "There's a Mermaid in My Lighthouse" song that played. She'd heard it more times than she could count while growing up.

The officer called over her shoulder, "Hey, Holt! There's been another animal attack."

The balding man at the desk behind her didn't even look up. He coughed a laugh and muttered, "Do we look like bloomin' animal control?"

Everly stuttered, "Umm. Do you know Boderleth Antiques? It was right out the front there. Last night."

"Sure, sure." The officer rustled some papers around behind the counter but didn't appear to be taking any notes. She eyed the minor scratches on Everly's hands. "And you're the victim? Was it a Persian or a pug?"

Holt laughed again and Everly pulled her red jacket cuffs over her hands. "Not me. It was Rylan Howell, and he seemed really badly hurt."

"Really? One of the Howell boys? We didn't hear anything about that, did we? Nothing from the hospital?" Officer Eccleston, as her name badge identified her, directed the comment at Holt, who shook his head.

Everly looked to Harper for support, and she nodded her encouragement.

"That's the thing—he's missing. We were hoping you'd look into it."

"Missing? Just what is your relationship to the Howell boy?"

"Nothing. I just ... witnessed ... something." An ugly heat rose around Everly's neck and ears.

Eccleston seemed to size up Everly through her dark-rimmed glasses and smacked her bright-red lips. "Well, we haven't heard anything from anyone who *does* have a relationship with him. Did you check around? See if he's home? Talk to friends or family? No? Maybe think about starting there instead of wasting our time."

"I ... tried to call him, but he didn't answer. I saw—"

"I don't know what game you're playing, sweetheart, but getting the police involved isn't the way to track down a guy who's ghosted you. Go hire a private investigator to stalk the Howell boy for you."

"Like anyone would take *that* job." Holt chuckled under his breath.

"Go on. Out. We have our hands full with real troubles." Eccleston took a long, slow sip of her coffee.

"But this—"

Eccleston raised a sharp eyebrow.

Everly and Harper backed out of the station, the bell dinging above the door on their way out.

"So, that was utterly mortifying." Everly's shoulders slumped.

"Hey, you tried, right?"

"I think I need more donuts," Everly groaned.

The police station was on a side road from the main street of Shroudhaven, north of the river. Everly wondered about going to the estate and asking there, but it was south of the river in Shroudhaven Heights, the fancier part of town, and it was already late.

The sun, which had been barely visible behind rain clouds, had just dropped completely below the horizon.

Rylan had practically begged me not to go out at night. Everly worried why more than ever.

Down on the main street, half the shops were closed and boarded up. Especially the larger franchises and chain stores that had tried and failed to get a footing in the area.

The oddball collection of remaining shops had vintage frontages with weathered awnings and hand-painted signage. Pimey's Diner, Pimey's Grocery Store, and The Boutique All—a strange, labyrinthine bargain basement shop that had just about one of everything—were visible from the police station.

On the corner stood Cardboard Box Barry. Everly winced as the name they'd called him as kids popped into her head so quickly. To her more grown-up self, it felt so unsympathetic.

The wispy-white-haired, slim-as-a-whip homeless man with a braided beard stood alongside his large, blanket-covered cardboard box. He was as much of a town legend as the mermaid song. It seemed like no matter what part of Shroudhaven you were in, you'd see him.

There weren't many people out on the streets now that night bore down on them—Mr. Flitchworth chatted to a waitress in the doorway of the diner, an old woman in a muddy coat carried a large paper bag out of the pharmacy, and a young man loped on long legs down the opposite footpath to Barry. A young man who looked startlingly familiar.

Everly gestured to Harper to follow her and jogged down the street toward him.

"Callan?" she called out.

He turned, and when he saw her, his face broke into a broad smile. "Everly? No way! It's so good to see you!"

Callan was a year younger but towered over her. He caught her in a hug before she could awkward her way out of it. His dark hair was much longer than she remembered, as though he'd let it grow the whole time she'd been gone. It fell feathery and wavy around his shoulders.

"Yeah, I'm back, for a bit." Her voice was muffled by his chest.

He stepped out of their embrace and grimaced. "I heard about your mom. That totally sucks. I know how things were, but still."

"Yeah."

Callan's intensity made Everly gulp. He was so much more grown up now, but still had his familiar boyish charm and ever-present smile.

Harper cleared her throat during the lengthening silence.

Everly waved a hand at her. "Umm, this is Harper."

Callan turned his attention to the Amazonian goddess

who matched him in height and froze for a split second as he took her in. "Harper? Not ... Harper Bells? Holy shit. *Bellsy?* Shit, sorry, I mean ... *shit.*"

Harper laughed and extended a hand to shake. "Not the worst greeting I've ever had, promise you. You follow me?"

She acted slightly surprised, but despite the fashion and makeup content of her business, she knew precisely how large a percentage of her audience were men.

"No ... sort of. I mean, there's a guy I know, he's a huge fan, kind of introduced us all to you."

Harper nodded knowingly, then indicated Everly with her thumb. "How do you guys know each other?"

"This is Rylan's brother," Everly said.

"Reeeeeally?" Harper drawled.

She raised her eyebrows at Everly as though silently asking, 'Do the looks run in the family?'

Apart from the hair length, and the friendly smile, Callan so resembled his brother it made Everly shiver. But they were also so different, in so many ways.

Callan was having a hard time ending his handshake with Harper, which Harper clearly found highly amusing.

His other hand roamed about, straightening his pale-blue shirt and smoothing down his hair. "What about you two? How do you two know each other?"

"Long story," Harper and Everly said almost in unison. They both laughed wryly.

Harper extracted her hand and nudged Everly. "You should ask him."

"Yeah." Everly cleared her throat. "I don't suppose you've seen Rylan today? Or heard from him?"

Callan's eyes didn't leave Harper. "Nope. Don't really see him much anymore. Not since I moved home about six months back."

"Home? Not a Darkfrey Estate boy anymore?" Everly was shocked.

Rylan and Callan had been inseparable. She was even more shocked about how much the timing lined up to her dreams, when Callan stopped showing up in them.

"Nah," he said, looking like he had a lot more he wanted to say.

Everly still remembered the day Rylan and Callan packed up and moved into the estate. It had felt like they'd been accepted into an enchanted academy without her.

She didn't know much about what happened at Darkfrey Estate or why they accepted some kids and not others. She'd never made it past the front gates.

"Look, this is going to sound a bit crazy, but I think I saw something last night, something weird, with Rylan fighting ... something."

Callan finally returned his gaze to Everly. "Something?"

"I'm not sure. Maybe a big animal?"

"There may have been tentacles," Harper added.

Everly shot her a glare, letting her know the comment wasn't at all helpful.

Callan frowned for a moment, studying her face. He dragged two of his fingers down his chin as though thinking, waited, then frowned again.

"I think he might have been hurt." Everly pushed the words out, feeling ridiculous. "Do you think you could check on him for me? Give him a call?"

"Yeah, okay. I mean, I'm sure it's nothing. Don't worry. I'll look into it." Callan's smile seemed forced.

His hazel eyes, sparkling in the dim light, were so similar to Rylan's it made Everly's heart clench.

"Thanks. It's probably nothing. I just wanted to make sure."

Callan frowned, looking along the street, then returning his gaze to her. "I can give you his number if you want?"

"Has he changed it?"

"No."

"That's okay, then." Everly's eyes sought her feet.

All the times she'd tried to call. All the times she never got through. Each one felt like a gut punch.

Callan pulled his phone out of his pocket. "Is yours still the same?"

Everly nodded, socked in the stomach again.

He put his phone away again, tilting his head bashfully. "Sorry we ... sorry I never kept in touch. Really."

Everly shrugged. "No worries."

Harper thumb-pointed at the bargain shop across the road. "Does everyone else realize that shop's name sounds like The Booty Call?"

Callan's attention turned to her again, his expression brightening. "I know they say never meet your heroes, but this hasn't been disappointing in the slightest."

"Shucks."

"I'm not going to be weird and ask for a selfie. Yet." Callan grinned and started backing away.

He waved to Everly. "Don't worry. I'm sure Rylan's fine. I'll let you know as soon as I hear anything. You two better get home—it's late."

Harper lifted both hands in the air. "It's barely five o'clock!"

"That's Shroudhaven for you," Everly muttered.

A light mist had descended over them, glowing around the infrequent streetlights. There was no one else out on the street anymore, making it feel like a ghost town. Even Barry and his box were gone.

"Can you see yet why I'm keen to get out of this town as soon as possible?"

"Callan was nice, though. And he didn't seem worried about Rylan. Maybe we'll find him safe and sound, and then you'll change your mind?"

Callan had once felt almost like a younger brother to

Everly. She and Rylan had been thick as thieves and Callan would chase them around, trying to be included too. Until everything fell apart.

Rylan had been the one good thing about her life in Shroudhaven. And whether real or in her dreams, he only wanted her gone.

Everly exhaled a puff of air that merged with the mist around them. "I don't think there's a happy ending for me here."

Chapter Fourteen

Everly shuffled along a crumbling path, partway up the sheer side of a deep, muddy ravine. Dry clay crumbled under one foot and dropped away from underneath her.

Rylan's arm shot out. He caught her around the waist then pulled her close to him.

"Careful," he growled.

"It's okay. It's just a dream," she gasped, her heart racing from the feeling of his arms around her more than the threat of the fall.

Chunks of rock and dirt splashed into clear water more than three stories below.

"Right," Rylan said, shaking his head and letting go of her. "Just a dream. But is it your dream or my dream?"

"Mine. I thought I'd made that clear," Everly said, continuing along the ledge, clinging to brittle exposed tree roots to avoid tumbling off the narrow ledge.

"And why exactly are we doing this?" Rylan asked as she led the way.

"We're going to the day spa in that grass hut up ahead," Everly answered. "This is the only way there."

"Day spa," Rylan confirmed flatly.

"Yup."

"Don't you think it's weird a day spa would have such a treacherous entrance?"

"I mean, if it were real, sure. But this isn't real. Obviously." Everly wasn't surprised by the strange journey and wouldn't be if they had to go back and forth a few times either, just because. Dreams liked repetition and challenge. Better to just go along with it.

But she was surprised by Rylan's clarity and curiosity.

"Still feels real to me, Boderleth." Rylan checked his footing as a loose rock tumbled free. "Way too real."

Real like the way Rylan called her by her last name like he used to when they were friends.

"This is probably just a side effect of seeing you in person again," Everly said, more to herself than him. "My head's just all messed up."

"You think your head is messed up? I have no idea what's going on. I feel like I've been asleep," Rylan said, his husky voice echoing in the ravine around them. "But now that I'm awake again, everything is like a dream."

"Yes. My dream."

Rylan reached out and grabbed Everly's arm, and she could feel a slight tremble in the firm grip. "It would really help me out if you stopped treating me like I wasn't real. This has to be some kind of beshadowing. Or ... I've been thinking about what you said, about what might have happened to me."

"You remember the last dream I had?" Everly stopped walking, but the grass hut still grew steadily closer regardless.

"Yeah, with the roses and scary anxiety dragon and telling me I might be dead? How could I forget?"

That hasn't ever happened before. Rylan acknowledging the entire dreamscape existence and previous dreams in a very meta way was a new development that Everly struggled to process.

"I was probably wrong about that anyway. When I woke up from that dream, you weren't even there." *But blood was.* Although Everly thought the words, they came out clear for everyone to hear.

"Well, whatever happened, whatever this is, this isn't being alive."

Everly turned to look at him, desperate to comfort him somehow, yet unsure if she'd only be comforting a dream. He shifted his eyes away from hers as though ashamed.

She reached for him but held back at the last moment. "Come on. Let's get somewhere more comfortable."

They were close to the end of the ledge now, and she could see a fruit stand outside the grass hut, but when she looked a second time, the colorful melons had become round, fluffy creatures. Her dragon appeared behind them, chasing and tearing into them ravenously.

Everly stepped off the end of the path and sat down beside a wide pool of still, aqua water at the base of the ravine, far below the grass hut and carnage above.

Rylan peered up at the cliff behind them, then at the water. "I can't get used to this dream logic. I feel awake and real. How do I convince you I'm not a dream?"

"Even the fact you're trying to convince me is just making me feel like this is just an especially weird trauma dream. I mean, you're here, in my dream; therefore, you are part of the dream."

"What about things only you and I know about?" Rylan persisted, taking a seat next to her on the lush green grass.

"Like?"

"Like that time we went fishing together and you were so excited, but when you actually caught a fish you cried the entire time I was getting the hook out and throwing it back? Or when you got your head stuck in the banister and I found you there hours later, you tried to pretend it was all part of a cops and robbers game?"

"So your plan is to bring up only the memories that

humiliate me?"

Rylan shook his head, thinking some more. "What about when we first met? Do you remember that? What you said to me?"

On the surface of the still pool, a memory drifted up, playing out in front of them.

Everly, her ashy-white hair tied in twin plaits, scruffy with snagged sticks and leaves, lay curled up on the ground under ancient trees, hugging a ratty, purple plush lion. Rylan, teary and angry and confused, approached.

Everly remembered running away from one of her mom's boyfriends. She got lost, was hurt, weak. It was just luck, or fate, that Rylan found her, also having run away. He never told her why he'd run, only that he felt like a monster.

"You're not a monster." Everly's five-year-old voice was high yet decided.

"Is that how you remember it?" Rylan asked from beside her at the water's edge.

"Pretty much. I was so young, though, and kind of out of it. I must have been seriously dehydrated at that point."

"You don't remember me looking ... *different*?"

"Different how?"

Rylan shook his head. "I remember finding you, helping you get home. I was amazed how strong you were, how quick you got better. I know we were young, but I remember it the same way, mostly."

"Yeah, but these are all things we *both* know. So this could easily be my sleeping brain feeding me information from my own memories."

Everly watched as their younger selves faded away from the surface of the water. A miniature fishing boat cruised by, throwing a net across their past.

"It is weird, though. I hadn't known you cut your hair but have been dreaming about you looking like this for a while, even before seeing you again. But you were always still dreamy, distant. Not full-on tangible inquisition-Rylan like you are now."

He thought for a moment, brows furrowed. "What if there are other parts of me that have changed, that you couldn't have known about? What if I could show you something new?"

Before she could answer, he stripped off his jacket and lifted his T-shirt up over his head. Everly flushed hot. Her jaw dropped, but she didn't look away. Rylan had invited the looking, after all.

"What exactly are you planning on showing me?" Everly's voice cracked.

Under his T-shirt was another layer, an unusual formfitting woven fabric sectioned into plates across his chest and shoulders, joined together with a sinewy elastic. Then he took it off too.

"Oookay. Yes. This is new."

"You never dreamed of me naked?" Rylan teased as he threw the garment onto the grass nearby.

Everly shook her head vehemently. Whenever she dreamed of Rylan, he was always distant, out of reach, doing his own thing—an elusive being she longed for but couldn't have. Just like in real life.

"You can admit it if you have. It's a pretty normal kind of dream."

"I really haven't. Normal? Wait ... *have you*—?"

"This is actually what I meant by new." Rylan turned his bare chest toward Everly, revealing a tattoo she'd never seen before—a coat of arms with the Darkfrey Estate crest.

But his skin was also a patchwork of scars. Some faded white hairlines, and others still puffy and red, drawn across his muscles in parallel lines like claw marks.

"What happened to you?" Everly whispered. She reached a hand out but didn't touch him.

"Nothing." He looked away from her, snatching his shirt and shrugging back into it. "Dog attack."

Everly dropped her hand and raised her eyebrows. "Dog attack? Really? Have you been employed training vicious guard dogs or something? Run an illegal dogfighting ring? Is that what goes on up at the estate? 'Cause that was a whole lot more than one dog attack."

"Forget about that." Rylan's jaw clenched. "I meant

for you to see the tattoo. It is new, isn't it? Something you didn't know?"

"I didn't know there was a grass-hut day spa at the top of a muddy trail either, and yet here we are. Brains create weird things in dreams." Everly sighed and put her toes into the water which had risen closer to them.

Her head spun. Was he real or wasn't he? Did the scars mean anything or not? Unless she could see his real body out in the real world, she couldn't confirm anything.

"But ... something does feel different. About my dreams, since I saw you. You feel different."

Rylan nodded solemnly. "And if I'm not a dream, then I'm guessing I must be dead."

"Don't say that."

He raised exasperated hands to indicate the rising water and strange slant of the ravine around them and dragon flying high in the purple sky above. "I can't think of any other explanation for how I'm trapped in all this, not one that doesn't mean I'm dead either way."

Trapped. He thought being there with her was a trap.

Is that what he was? A ghost, forced to haunt the dreams of the person he only ever wanted to get away from.

Everly's dragon approached, still hungry after its decimation of the animals above, and she shook off the dark thoughts.

"There's no proof. I saw Callan today, and he didn't

seem worried. The police didn't seem worried. And whatever happened, you're missing—not there at all. You probably just left, and these dreams are me dealing with that. Or it has all been a dream."

Everly stood up again as the ground she sat on narrowed and the pool dropped away. She was back on the clay ledge, heading to the grass hut. Always moving toward a destination she knew she'd never reach.

Rylan took hold of her arm, stopping her futile march forward. "I'll find a way to prove to you I'm real."

Because she was pretty sure he was a dream, Everly had the courage to say, "I used to think we were fated to be together. Whatever is happening, it's just proof I've been wrong my whole life."

Rylan bent toward her, and for a moment it seemed like he would kiss her. She froze, her breath caught in her throat as he stared at her in a way that could have cracked her heart into pieces.

"You never know what you're fated for until you reach the end of your story. I think my story has ended."

CHAPTER FIFTEEN

*H*e's dead. He's dead.
There was blood.
Was it blood? Was it his blood?
It all felt so real.
It couldn't have been.
Where is he?
Was any of it real?
Please ... Rylan, please be okay.

Everly was scrubbing the linoleum in the kitchen when Harper stood in the doorway and made puppy-dog eyes and kawaii poses at her until Everly couldn't ignore her any longer.

"Do you need something?" Everly asked brightly.

"You're the one who clearly needs something. You've been scrubbing that same spot for forty-five minutes. You're going to wear a hole through the floor."

"Oh." Everly stared at the one wet patch in front of her, scrunched up her face, and dropped the scrubbing brush into the bucket beside her. "I may be a bit distracted."

Harper raised one shoulder. "Seeing the love of your life get brutally attacked and then go missing might do that to you."

"There's no part of that sentence that's necessarily true." Everly stood up and gave the bucket a gentle kick with her boot. The sudsy water blooped in a little splash.

"The whole vibe I've been getting from you ever since makes me feel like it is. You deal with anxiety and panic attacks every day, but this, this is different. Something is going on."

Everly pulled her work gloves off, tossing them on the counter. "I just need to clear my head. My dreams have been wild lately, and weirdly accurate."

"All the more reason we need to find Rylan. I believe that you saw something the other night. Whether it was a vampire, a prank, or an escaped wild animal, I don't know, but you need to find out."

Everly turned to the kitchen window, imagining again what she'd seen through it. "Animal attacks really are pretty common around here. That's actually how Rylan's dad died."

"That's a great big yikes." Harper folded her arms over

the shell-pink pirate shirt she'd paired with pinstriped dress pants.

"That's Shroudhaven for you."

Harper shook her head. "If my horror movie addiction has taught me anything, it's that an *animal attack* is never just an animal attack. Also, if that *is* all it was, how much of a jerk is Rylan if he got up and left without saying anything to you? What kind of guy gets mauled and leaves before you wake up, right?"

Everly couldn't contain a chuckle. "Thank you. For everything."

"I'm just getting started. By the time we're done in this crazy-ass town, there's going to be a whole new, less traumatized you. Starting with some closure on this Rylan business." Harper turned and swept out into the hallway, as though expecting Everly to follow.

Everly remained planted, calling after her friend, "We should just leave it. We only have a couple of days left and so much more cleaning to do. And I haven't heard anything from Callan. He said he'd handle it."

Harper leaned back into the doorframe, grinning impishly. "And you're really going to leave it up to him? I think it's time we paid him a visit. We're going to find out what's really going on around here."

Howell House sat in the middle of some fields like a slumped wedding cake, faded ivory wrought iron wrapping the all-around veranda like frosting. The veranda Everly and Rylan used to race laps around as children—races Rylan had let her win.

Everly and Harper walked up the lane leading to the aged homestead, lined with birch trees and lilies, their white blossoms glowing in the light of sunset ribboning through the trunks.

It was only a couple of blocks away from the Boderleth residence. Everly hadn't been able to get through on the phone to Callan, and she felt weird about showing up unannounced.

Her nerves were trying hard to get the best of her, make her turn back, but Harper urged her up the gravel drive.

Fields of long grass and blackberry brambles bordered the lane on each side. So much of it was just how Everly remembered it from her childhood.

Long late summer days when she and Rylan would hide away together in their cave of thorned canes, gorging themselves on the fruit, faces and fingers covered in dust and sticky juice.

She looked into the brambles, hopeful to spot some of the dark, juicy berries, but it was the wrong season.

Instead, something glinted, two reflective eyes piercing through the foliage.

Harper reached out and grasped Everly's wrist sharply, making her gasp.

"Do you think they'd let me do a photo shoot here?" she asked.

Everly returned her gaze to the field, but if there had been eyes there, they were gone.

"Yeah, maybe. Rylan's mom, Lian, was always really nice," she replied as the house came closer into view.

It was much how Everly remembered it, but in a worse state of repair. Lian was a Pimey by birth—one of the older families of Shroudhaven that held claim over the naming rights of a hill, creek, and number of businesses.

It was only after she'd married that the homestead took on the name Howell House.

The front garden area was a mix of well-tended yet dated ornamental plants with white-washed garden edging. An unfamiliar, run-down RV was parked crookedly on one side between the house and the garage.

An equally unfamiliar small figure sat on the porch swing, all in black, cuddling their knees and shadowed by an oversized hood.

"If Lian even still lives here," Everly added, then called out, her voice timid and cracking, "Hello?"

The girl looked up slowly. She had a shaved head, pale skin, and the face of a doll—a doll that clearly hated the world. She unfolded hands that were stained as black as ink.

Her eyes stuck to Everly and Harper as they reached the front steps but she didn't reply.

The front door swung open, the screen door clattering and drawing Everly's attention away from the goth girl to a middle-aged man sporting a stained brown T-shirt and uneven blond beard.

"Hoooooly shiiit!" he sang like a crude game show host. He punctuated it by cracking the tab on a beer can and taking a swig.

"Uh, hi?" Everly began.

The man pushed past her to Harper. "It really is Bellsy! Callan said he saw you yesterday in town, but I didn't believe him. He also said you were as good-looking as your feed, and I didn't believe that either."

The goth girl grunted in disgust, but when Everly looked over, the girl was gone, as though she'd vanished into thin air.

"Always nice to meet a fan," Harper said, sounding almost like she meant it.

"Been following you forever! Callan wouldn't even know you if it weren't for me. When you got doxed, I considered coming to visit you—that's how big of a fan I am." He smiled beatifically as though providing the highest compliment.

The look on Harper's face was one of utter horror. "Please don't ever. Ever."

"Yeah, that is not okay. Look, is Callan around?" Everly asked.

"Probably." He shrugged like he couldn't offer anything more helpful. "I'm Denny, Denny Sketchman. You can call me Sketch; all my friends do."

He reached out for Harper's hand to shake, and when she didn't immediately extend hers, he reached farther and took it anyway.

"Ew," Harper squeaked.

"There are precisely zero people who call you Sketch." A tall woman with a tidy bun of salt-and-pepper hair appeared behind him.

She carried a tiny dog under one arm and a broom in the other, looking like she wanted to beat Denny with it. "How many times do I have to kick you out of here?"

"Come on, Mama Howell. You know you love me." He put on a charming smile, swiping his curly blond hair back.

"Is that my beer?"

"Busted." He winked at Harper and took another long swig.

"Out, now! Or you and your RV can go find somewhere else to park." Lian exclaimed, stamping the broom handle against the hardwood floor.

The dog, fluffy-haired and dim-eyed from age, started barking.

Holding up his beer can with his middle finger sticking

out prominently, he trotted straight through a garden bed toward the motor home. All three women grunted in disgust at the same time.

"Sorry about that." Lian turned her attention to Everly. "I heard you were back in town. It's been a while. You look well."

Everly brushed a hand along her braided hair nervously. "You too. Is that Birdie?"

Lian left the broom leaning beside the doorframe and ruffled the white curls on the dog's head. "Yep, still with us. You here for a visit? I can put some tea on."

"That's okay. We were just hoping to see if Callan had found out anything."

"You just missed him. He went up to the Darkfreys to see his brother. Found out anything about what?"

"He didn't say?" Everly frowned at Harper.

Everly wasn't sure why Lian didn't know about Rylan's possible missing status, but felt that if Callan hadn't mentioned it, she probably shouldn't either.

"It was nothing really. Just about ... where we could get, umm, a weed trimmer, for cleaning up my old place."

"I have one in the back shed," Lian said, waving them both inside, her floor-length gray knitted coat swinging behind her as she led the way. "The boy would know that if he ever helped out in the yard. Hey, Rushelle?"

A broad-shouldered woman with outrageous curves

and white-gold hair piled on top of her head stepped into view at the end of the hall. She wore a marching band jacket over a sunflower-yellow leather corset.

"This is Everly and ..."

"Harper," Everly answered.

Rushelle beamed. "Are they—?"

"Old friends, from *out* of town," Lian said, and handed Birdie over to Harper. "Look after my guard dog for me. I'll go get that weed trimmer for you."

Birdie yapped once, then worked on licking every inch of the underside of Harper's chin.

"Great to meet you two! Let me pop the kettle on." Rushelle smiled cheerily and led Everly and Harper to the kitchen.

Everly breathed in deeply and the familiar scent of the home, one of laundry soap and baked vegetables, filled her chest with warm memories.

Everly was slightly heartbroken that the kitchen had been renovated, changed from the one she'd had some of her few happy memories in with the family that wasn't even hers.

Some parts of the original design were still present though—a unique mosaic backsplash and the historic farmhouse table, so thick and solid it probably couldn't be relocated if they tried. As familiar as the home was to her, it felt strange to find it crawling with strangers.

Rushelle bustled about cheerily, pulling cups from the cupboard.

What is going on here?

"Do you live here too?" Everly asked.

"No honey, I'm just a regular. Come by whenever I can to help out Ms. Howell. Just a sec—let me save my writing." She tapped briefly on a yellow laptop covered in rhinestone mermaid stickers that sat on the kitchen counter. "Tammy and Cherry are the only live-ins at the moment, and Callan's back now too. And Denny, albeit entirely unwelcome."

Harper shuddered and cuddled Birdie closer.

"You met him?" Rushelle barked a laugh. "That guy is *the worst*."

"Spoke to him for a whole of a few seconds and have to agree completely." Harper made a gagging sound. "What are you writing?"

"Fantasy romance satire mostly. The Far King series is my main one. *Taken for the Far King, A Virgin for the Far King, Hunted for the Far King*, and *A Bride for the Far King*." She ticked each title off on her fingers. "It's a good little side hustle."

Harper laughed and patted Birdie. "I will absolutely be checking those out."

Rushelle winked. "Thanks, little duck."

"Is Lian renting rooms?" Everly asked.

She turned her head upward, as though magnetically drawn in the direction of Rylan's old room, hoping it hadn't been renovated or changed—or used as a hoarder's trash pile.

"No, she's an old softy, that marvelous woman. Brings in those who have nowhere else to go." Rushelle filled the vintage-style kettle and put it on the stainless-steel gas range. "What do you girls want? We have all the beverage basics covered. Hit me with your requests."

"We're fine, really. We'll just grab the weed trimmer and head off." Everly felt awkward enough already.

She didn't want to prolong the small talk. But she was curious about a few things. "Callan said he moved home six months ago. Does Rylan visit sometimes, too?"

"Not in years." Lian pushed the back door to the kitchen open from outside.

The sun had set and insects zoomed about in the porch light behind Lian as she kicked off her boots on the way in.

She thrust the weed trimmer out to Everly, who tried to take it, but Lian didn't loosen her grip. She put her other hand on Everly's shoulder. "But you know you could have always come by, if you needed anything, even after the boys left."

"Sorry I didn't visit you after ... everything." Everly's face heated.

The funeral for Rylan's dad was the last time she'd

really seen the Howell family together. Rylan was already not talking to her at that point, and Everly never thought she'd still be welcome in their home.

Had Everly abandoned Lian just as thoroughly as her sons had? Her childhood errors were so much clearer through grown-up hindsight.

"I'll try to stop in again soon, when we can stay for a proper chat, while I'm still in town." The offer felt hollow, knowing she only had two more days, but she had to offer something.

"That would be lovely." Lian let go of the garden tool and took Birdie back from Harper. "Now, you know you shouldn't be out so late. You need someone to walk you home?"

Harper looked at her watch and raised her eyebrows at Everly.

"I'm sure we'll be fine. It's not far." Everly gave Lian a stilted hug and thanked her for the loan.

On their way down the front steps, Lian called out from the front door, "Sorry about your mother."

Everly nodded, a pang of guilt passing over her. Lian had been more of a mother to her than her own ever had.

Should I tell her about Rylan?

It didn't seem worth it until she had some proof. She rested the weed trimmer over one shoulder, getting a strong whiff of cut grass and gas, and waved goodbye.

As they reached the end of the lane and headed past the row of houses on the main block, Everly said, "You think Callan thought what I said about Rylan was so ridiculous it wasn't even worth mentioning …?"

"Or did he think it was so serious he didn't want to worry anyone yet?" Harper finished the thought. "I mean, it could really go either way."

"He is looking into it if he's gone to the estate to try to see Rylan." Which made Everly think he must be taking it seriously, and that made her anxiety churn her insides into curds and whey. "I know it's late, but can I borrow the van to drive over to Shroudhaven Heights?"

"It's barely past six o'clock!" Harper laughed. "And no. I'll drive. I'm coming too, because if there's any chance of seeing a vampire tonight, I'm in."

Everly eyed the dimming sky and shivered. Rylan had begged her not to go out after dark. She wanted to laugh at Harper's joke, but the longer they remained in Shroudhaven, the more worried she became that they might really stumble across a vampire, or something far worse.

Chapter Sixteen

Everly squinted through the windscreen into the darkness, only able to make out four smudgy dark figures in the dim light. "Is that Callan? Who's he with?"

Harper spoke out of the corner of her mouth as though telling a joke. "A cute Asian guy with bright-red hair, a mean looking blond woman, and a guy in a cardigan? All walk into a bar—"

"Pull over."

"Huh? Why?"

"Pull over here!"

Harper brought the campervan to a lurching halt against the curb, down the street from the intimidating silhouette of the Darkfrey gates.

"Did they see us?" Everly asked, reaching over to turn the headlights off herself.

"They don't seem to be paying any attention our way. What's going on?"

Now that they were a little closer, Everly used Harper's description to clarify the vague shapes she was seeing. Callan and someone else on the footpath, and the blond woman and cardigan guy inside the gates.

The people from her dream again. They were Darkfreys?

"On our first night here, I saw Rylan again, after you fell asleep."

Harper swung around, resting an arm on the steering wheel and staring at Everly with high eyebrows. "Please, do tell."

"Not like that! Just out front while I was taking out garbage. I talked to him for maybe a minute before a couple of those people showed up, and he went all cold and rude, even more than usual."

"You think they have something to do with what's going on?"

Everly wasn't ready to tell Harper that she'd been dreaming of those people too, or how much it was starting to feel like her dreams were a lot more real than they should be.

She winced and shrugged. "Maybe? I don't know about the other guy with bright-red hair. Who did Rushelle say was living with them? Cherry?"

"It would fit. So what do we do? Wait for them to go

before we talk to Callan?"

Everly chewed her lip, eyeing the couple of cars parked along the street near the gates. "I kind of want to hear what they are saying."

Harper's mouth dropped open and then broke into a wide grin. "Secret spy-like eavesdropping? Yes! Let's do this."

Climbing out of the van, Everly and Harper closed their doors softly, then ducked behind the parked car in front of them.

A whipping wind swirled through the leaves of tall trees lining the fenced-off Darkfrey grounds across from them, covering their footsteps as they scurried up to the next car, then the next, until Callan's voice reached them.

"Jasper, this could be serious. Just let us in."

Everly tilted her face to peer over the hood of the car she crouched behind.

Through the gate, the cardigan guy—Jasper—fidgeted with one of his buttons. "You can't come in. Sorry."

"You should be." Cherry shoved both hands aggressively into the pockets of his red-and-white racer jacket.

A brisk wind whipped his bright-scarlet hair into his face, and he scowled.

Callan leaned against the gate, but it didn't move, firmly barred.

A high-tech keypad and monitor to one side were in

stark contrast to the ornate black twisted metal of the gate and the word Darkfrey lettered across the top in a curling script, entwined with sculpted bats.

Through the bars, past the dark wooded surrounds and up the long drive, Everly could barely see the massive mansion that sprawled on the cliffside in the distance. The glow from the windows was as small as fireflies from down at the gate, mere pinpricks of light lining the horizon.

She'd often imagined what it was like for Rylan and Callan, growing up behind that barred gate. She jealously pictured castles and feasts and secret passages and fancy boarding school uniforms.

Callan spoke again, the words cut off in a gust of wind before growing clear. "—see Rylan. Could you send him down since you're not letting us in and he's not answering his phone?"

The blond woman folded her arms. "He's not here."

"Then do you know where he is?"

"We haven't seen him for two days, since he chose to venture out alone," Jasper said.

Two days?

That lined up with when his body disappeared from Everly's street. Everly's heart jumped into her throat and she and Harper locked wide eyes.

The blond woman rasped, "Don't tell the Howell runts that. They aren't with us anymore. They don't need to know our business."

"It's his brother—he should know," Jasper said flatly.

There was a rattle of metal as Callan grasped the gate with both hands. "Vonny, you have to tell me what you know. Have you been looking for him?"

"Where would we look? Besides, Mordan's been on our asses about him being gone, blaming us for splitting up, losing his golden boy. He's grounded our brace. Like it's our fault your brother has been playing loner and running off doing his own weird shit," Vonny replied.

Everly's mind was stuck in a loop. *Two days. Two days. He really was missing.*

Callan shook the gate roughly, as though trying to push it open. "You're telling me he's been gone two days and you have no idea where?"

"If he was hurt, he'd have shown up back here. If it was worse, a cleaning crew would have found him."

Harper whispered, "*What the ...*"

"Who's there?" Callan yelled.

Harper's eyes widened. In an even quieter whisper, she swore. "Sorry! How did he hear that?"

Footsteps approached.

Everly raised herself to standing, giving a sheepish smile. "Umm, hi?"

"Her again? What's she doing here?" Vonny's nose wrinkled as though she were seeing something unpleasant.

Callan glanced between her and the gates. "Everly? What are you—?"

"Found it!" Harper popped up from behind the car too and pretended to put something away into a small case she pulled from her pocket. "Missing contact lens. What's going on?"

Everly half smiled at her. She wasn't sure it was even slightly convincing, but any excuse seemed better than nothing.

Everly moved closer to Callan. "We were hoping to catch you here."

Harper followed, arching her neck to take in the scene. "Wow, look at that gate! Gorgeous. Gothic. One hundred percent uninviting. I totally get the vampire stories now."

"Ugh, blivs," Vonny snarled.

"Gesundheit?" said Harper.

"Is Rylan here?" Everly asked, pretending she hadn't heard any of the conversation before being exposed.

"I was just checking in on him, like you asked." Callan smiled, but there was a dark gleam in his eye and a twitch in his jaw.

She looked at him expectantly, prompting him to continue.

Vonny glared at all of them. Jasper and Cherry stared at each other, wordlessly communicating through a series of eye motions and tilted chins.

"And?" Harper sang into the silence.

"He's up in his room but doesn't want to see any of you," Vonny spoke over Callan.

"That's not what you said a minute ago," Cherry teased.

Jasper gave him a warning look.

Vonny eyed them all through the gate. "A minute ago I was ready to beat your runt asses. Do you really want to go back to a minute ago?"

A lean pole of a man cleared his throat from behind Vonny, and she turned around.

"In for it now," she whispered and ducked to the side away from him.

The figure stepped up to the gate, the satin lapels of his black and maroon suit shimmering in the lamplight. His arrival had been so silent it startled everyone. He lifted a goateed chin and stared down his nose at those outside the gate.

He addressed Callan but shot glances toward the two inside the gate as well. "I know why you're here. But unless you're joining us again, Callan, you are no longer privy to estate business. Your former peers should know this as well."

"Of course, Master Darkfrey." Vonny nodded and shot a spiteful look at Jasper. "That's exactly what *I* was saying."

Master Darkfrey ... as in head of the whole Darkfrey Estate? Everly tried to get a better look at the older man, and his eyes sparkled as they passed over her and Harper as though they were nothing.

Callan's jaw worked and his tone was flat. "No, I won't be joining you again."

"Then we're done here." Master Darkfrey turned and strode away so quickly, he seemed to vanish into the darkness.

Vonny threw those outside the gate one last sneer and chased after him.

Jasper turned as well and took a step away before hesitating. He tilted his head back, glancing at Cherry, then Callan. "Sorry."

"Don't be sorry, be helpful," Cherry snapped.

Jasper's eyes flicked from side to side a couple of times, then he moved toward the gate. Cherry and Callan stepped close, and he whispered to them, out of earshot of Everly. All she could catch was something about cleanup crews again.

Then Jasper nodded once, ignoring Everly and Harper, and strode away up the hill.

Callan and Cherry stared at each other, locked in some silent understanding.

"Well, that was *something*," Harper said, a nervous giggle in her voice. "If that old guy isn't a vampire, then I'm a bunny on a unicycle."

Cherry extended a hand. "Hi, bunny on a unicycle.

I'm Cherry. Nice to meet you. Love your work."

Harper laughed and shook his hand.

"His introduction beat yours," she told Callan.

Callan only half smiled.

Everly could tell he was worried, really worried, as much or more than her.

She folded her arms and asked, "So is Rylan in his room like *Vonny* said, or is he missing like *Jasper* said earlier?"

"Shit, you heard that?"

She nodded shakily. "Glad we did too, since it's clear you weren't planning on telling us."

Callan put his hand on her shoulder and directed her away from the pool of light around the Darkfrey gate. His eyes flickered with thought and when they stopped in the shadows, he ran his hands through his hair and opened his mouth, then closed it again three times without managing to say a thing.

"If something's going on, you can tell me," Everly said. "I know you're worried too."

Callan leaned against the Darkfrey fence and groaned softly in defeat. "Yeah. I am. Rylan is missing, but the estate lot are being their usual closed-off selves about it all."

"It really seems to be their way." Everly pulled her jacket closer around her. She coaxed, "But you seem to have gotten out?"

Callan shrugged, looking back at his punk-hair-colored

friend. "The estate was always where Rylan wanted to be. After a while, I disagreed too much with ... their policies. I figured Rylan didn't really need his little brother tagging along anymore, watching his back."

Callan swallowed visibly, and Everly felt the weight of his statement.

They both hoped he hadn't figured wrong.

"The estate, are they up to something shady?" Everly asked softly.

The corner of Callan's lip quirked up, but without any real humor. "What exactly did you see the other night?"

Everly felt the blood rush from her face as she tried to process things that didn't seem real, that were too terrifying to be real, but were starting to be confirmed. She was just getting Callan on her side; she didn't want to scare him off by sounding unbelievable.

"I'm not sure what I saw. It all sounds so wild."

"It's vampires. Vampires with tentacles," Harper said, joining them.

Callan raised an eyebrow at Everly and she sighed in return.

"There's no such thing as vampires," Cherry said, trailing after.

"You're obviously part of the cover-up, so you have zero credibility," Harper sassed.

Everly said, "Look, I can give you all the details, as

weird as they are. If you think it would help find Rylan ... I don't mind sounding crazy."

"All right, let's hear it," Callan said.

Everly had just opened her mouth, starting with an explanation of the dream she'd had leading into the fight on the street, when Callan and Cherry shared a sharp, wide-eyed look.

"Uh, Call?" Cherry cleared his throat. "I really need to go."

Callan turned back to Everly, smile wide and patently fake. "You know what, on second thought, what if we pick this up again another time?"

"Wow, do I really sound that ridiculous?" Everly frowned.

Callan waved nonchalantly, backing away down the street. "No, no, not at all. Just, you know, it's late ..."

"Well, do you guys need a lift?" Harper offered, pointing to the campervan with her thumb.

"All good. We parked around the corner," Callan said as he and Cherry picked up their pace, heading for the darker shadows on the other side of the street.

A strange, soupy, sickness filled Everly's chest. The same nebulous emotion she often had in her dreams when watching the dark, unknowable creatures that populated her nightmares, indistinct in form but clear in their presence.

The feeling she was looking at a monster.

It's just Callan. He's just the boy you've known most of your life.

Everly shook herself and called out, "What about Rylan?"

Callan's retreat faltered. "Do you know anything else you can tell me that might help find him?"

Everly thought for a moment. "Maybe. It's a bit of a long shot, but I might be able to find something out tonight."

"Don't do anything dangerous," Callan warned. "Just leave it, okay? For tonight. I'll come round tomorrow morning, and we can work it out then."

"Bye. Nice to meet you!" Cherry called from the shadows far ahead.

Everly and Harper stared in confusion as the two men vanished into the dark.

"What got into them?" Harper muttered.

Everly pressed her lips into a thin line. "I don't know. But there's definitely something they aren't telling us."

Chapter Seventeen

A harsh, nightmarish stretch of shore and sea solidified as Everly fell deeper into slumber.

When the dream scenery began to settle, she spoke her words, taking control. *I'm asleep. This is a dream. Oh no ... Not this one. Not again.*

Sand shifted under her toes, and she looked out at an endless, troubled ocean. The water twisted and turned, black and peacock green, flashes of white foam dancing across the high peaks of thunderous waves.

The scenery felt familiar, and Everly's brain labeled it as a beach up in Hartleydale, just north of Shroudhaven, despite it looking nothing like the real thing.

The coastline stretched too long, out to infinity, the horizon line lifting too high into the starry sky. Rolling sand dunes of sparkling silver, bare of trees or scrub, rocks or shells flowed into the dark, turbulent water.

Everly gave the waves an anxious look, knowing what was coming.

The dragon chased the shadow of a cougar up and down the argent hills, nipping at the big cat's heels. Toying with it.

Everly turned in a three-sixty, trying to find Rylan, hoping he'd be there again, and found him walking along the beach toward her.

Despite knowing it was a dream, a rush of relief filled Everly at the sight of him. If he went missing from her dreams as well, she didn't know what she'd do.

She held on to her plan, hoping that it wasn't ridiculous, that even having hope wasn't ridiculous.

"I saw Callan again tonight," she told him once he was within earshot. "You're definitely missing in the real world. Even he's worried."

Rylan just frowned, looking out at the water and the receding tide.

"There's something going on, isn't there? Something you know about, and Callan knows, and I don't know who else."

It felt like everyone she met was in on it. Callan's friend, Cherry, had the same dilated galaxy eyes that the Howell brothers had at night, and with his K-Pop idol features, he clearly wasn't related to them, so that didn't explain the resemblance.

Plus, both of them and the people from the estate had been giving off really vampy vibes. It was as though she'd almost been able to sense their teeth *growing.*

"If you'd just tell me, maybe I could—"

"No. There's nothing going on that you need to do anything about," Rylan snapped. Having glowered at the ocean long enough, he turned his frown on her. "Where are you now? If you saw Callan, you're still in Shroudhaven, aren't you? I told you to go."

Everly stood firm. "I know you want me gone, but I still have two days to finish up getting the house in order and a heap of work that needs to be done, so I'm not going anywhere until I run out of time."

The tide drew out farther and farther until the waves disappeared over the horizon and fish and crabs lay bare and flopping on exposed rocks, slick with writhing kelp.

Everly warily watched the bare sea floor. "And I need to work out what *this* is, this version of you here in my dreams and where you are in the real world. I don't know if leaving Shroudhaven will stop these dreams or whether you're ..."

Rylan growled, "It doesn't matter. About the dreams or me. You need to leave so you can be safe."

"From what? What's going on?"

Rylan didn't answer, his attention locked on the ocean.

The water returned, a wall of it in the distance, higher than a mountain peak and swiftly rolling toward them.

Rylan stared at it in horror. "Is that going to be a problem?"

"Come on," Everly said, jogging away from the beach.

Over the sand dune, a parking lot was filled with panicking tourists, screaming and running in all directions. Everly spotted Harper's campervan and led Rylan behind it. She pressed her back to the van, bracing for the wave to hit.

Rylan looked at the rushing water crashing toward them. "Are you crazy? The tsunami will smash this van to bits. This isn't going to work."

"Trust me, it will. I know it doesn't make much sense, but it's a dream, remember? Physics work differently here, if at all. Just keep close behind the van and hold your breath."

The tsunami broke over them. It hit the van and split, pouring past Everly and Rylan on either side in churning waves, only a small gap of air left around them. The protective rift within the tide closed, water pushing in closer and closer to Rylan and Everly. She held her breath as they were submerged.

For a few moments she was breathless, water lifting and smashing around her, trying to drag her with it. Then the wave dispersed, her head emerged again above the salty liquid, and she could breathe.

As the tide drained away as fast as it arrived, she found

herself pressed against the van with one of Rylan's arms around her soft torso, holding her safe.

Rylan drew a deep breath and let her go. Water dripped from his eyelashes and chin. He scrubbed it from his short hair.

"I can't believe that worked."

Everly's pulse quickened, her heart calling out to be held again. "Yeah. This is a recurring dream for me, so I know all the tricks. Just be ready—it will probably happen again."

Rylan wiped his face and watched the beach. "It all feels so real to me. I keep having to remind myself where I am. Are your dreams always so perilous?"

He hasn't seen the worst of it.

This was nothing. Her dreams could get much darker. She shrugged her lips.

"My therapist says that dreams are like our brain's way of testing us with challenges in a safe environment. Like hypothetical training for real-world problems."

"You have a therapist?"

"You don't?"

He shook his head, watching the receding water swirl around their ankles.

Everly looked him up and down. He still wore the same T-shirt, jeans, and jacket she'd seen him in the night everything went crazy, although now saturated.

In past dreams, he'd always been different. He'd be

one of the actors in whatever play her sleep theater was putting on for the night, or sometimes just doing his own thing in the distance, ghostly, like the cougar. He didn't have this consistency, dream to dream—this level of awareness—that he did now.

Now, he seemed as real as he could be.

Maybe her long-shot plan could work.

"You said you wanted to prove you're real. Now's the time," she told him.

"How?"

"Tell me something you know that I *don't* know. But something I can confirm tomorrow when I'm awake." She could see as much turmoil in his expression as she had in the ocean.

"Like what?" he asked, guarded.

"Like about all the vampire weirdness going on, obviously!"

Rylan laughed through his nose. "There's no such thing—"

"As vampires. Yeah, yeah. So everyone keeps telling me. If it's not that, what is it? Give me *something*. Something that could help find out where you are."

A new wave approached, rumbling like a stampede of animals toward them, swallowing up everything in its path.

Rylan frowned at it, and his arms lifted to hold Everly. "I don't know what to tell you. I don't know where I am, and I can't tell you anything else."

"Can't or won't?"

His grip on her shoulders tightened. "I *can't* let you get caught up in something dangerous."

The water hit, rushing past on either side of them in deafening torrents as they looked into each other's eyes.

"And I can't watch you die and just go back to normal as though nothing happened!"

Rylan grunted through clenched teeth, then shouted over the swirling gush of water. "Okay. Fine. Tell Callan … tell him to check the old Rook's Theater. It's where I was before …"

Before you died? Everly's arms lifted as well, holding Rylan in return.

The wave closed in around them, rushing upward to submerge them entirely.

Rylan yelled, "Just tell Callan. Don't go yourself."

As they held their breaths and went under again, Everly already knew she wasn't going to follow Rylan's orders.

Everly couldn't hold on to the dream any longer and woke up gasping for breath. She could still feel Rylan's arms where they'd pressed against her, holding her safe within the raging tide, and felt an even deeper yearning for it to have been real.

But if he's real in there, does that mean he's dead out here?

She shivered into a sitting position, cuddling her sleeping bag tight around herself on the couch.

It would be better if none of it was real, if all of it was just her messed-up head. Better if dream-Rylan was imaginary, the violent death was just a hallucination, and Rylan wasn't missing, but just avoiding her completely. That had to be better than the alternative.

But she had to know. And now she had a lead—something that might offer proof. And she was going, regardless of what Rylan had told her.

She had to see what was happening for herself. She had to know. It was her second to last day of leave from work. There wasn't much time left to find out.

It was still early, so Everly sent Callan a text message to let him know she had a clue to look into, whenever he was ready. She half expected not to see him again until the sun set.

Am I really considering that Callan could be a vampire? What has my reality even become?

Still, she had only seen him after dark since she'd been back.

She shook her head. No, it was ridiculous.

After a strong coffee, Everly got to work doing some

maintenance around her old home, making use of the early hours. It helped take her mind off her worries, and she had to get as much done as she could.

Her leave from her apartment-superintendent job was unpaid and she was watching her budget carefully. She'd just do what she could to improve the place in the five days she had, then hope for the best with a sale.

When planning the trip, Harper had offered, as she had numerous times since they'd first met, to bring Everly on as her paid assistant. Everly had done small construction jobs on some of Harper's photo shoots in the past but refused to be paid for it.

She was helping out her best friend. And she felt like perfect Harper's pet fixer-upper project at times already, without taking handouts from her as well.

Everly was in the kitchen, refitting a couple of cupboard doors that were loose, when Harper shuffled in on slippered feet.

She poked at the coffee maker that had been bought on one of her grocery trips and smiled sleepily. She'd been up late the night before catching up on work now that they had the internet connected.

"This place is coming along beautifully. Maybe I'll buy it off you and move in."

"I wouldn't let you do that to yourself." Everly tightened the last screw, then began clearing away her tools.

The side of Harper's mouth twisted cheekily. "No, really. I can picture it now. I'll marry Callan, settle down, and raise some cute little vampire babies."

Everly huffed a laugh. "I also noticed the way he was looking at you. A blind turnip would notice the way he was looking at you."

Harper picked up her mug and sipped the fresh coffee. "Pretty sure all turnips are blind, babe."

Everly kept reorganizing her tool bag even though everything was squared away. "Would you really? Go out with Callan?"

"He seems nice enough. But so did Bryce when I first met him. And we know how that turned out." The mention of her ex made all of Harper's cheekiness fade. She tossed back the rest of her coffee, shrugged, then set a bright smile on her face. "I'm just happy being man-free at the moment."

Everly smiled in support. What had gone down with Bryce had been not just ugly, but dangerous. As much as Harper loved to flirt, Everly couldn't miss the underlying vulnerability and fear hidden beneath it—scars left by Bryce's betrayal.

Everly said, "Hey, we've missed a couple of days of yoga. I think there's enough room out on the back porch. Might be a good start to the day?"

Harper left her mug in the sink. "Sounds like just

what we need."

It was midmorning by the time Harper rolled out her custom-designed yoga mat and Everly laid out a towel over the worn gray timber of the back porch.

The long ribbons of grass and weeds that filled the backyard swayed back and forth along with the two women as they went through their usual routine together.

It reminded Everly of the waves in her dream, raising anxiety within her that she squashed beneath the peace and feeling of being present that the yoga brought with it.

Everly hadn't checked her phone since waking up, so she was surprised when Callan and Cherry wandered into the backyard in front of them.

"Wow, doesn't this place bring back memories." Callan stepped onto the porch, his voice holding the awe of nostalgia and an edge of sadness.

Everly and Harper both straightened up from their warrior three poses.

There goes the vampire theory. At least for them.

Everly studied Callan, who stood before her in the bright morning sunlight.

The feeling of something monstrous about him that she'd had the night before was gone. He was just Callan, the cute goofball who was like her younger brother. She must have imagined it. Unsurprising, with everything else setting her nerves on edge.

"Bellsy!" Cherry moved in and gave Harper a kiss on both cheeks, then he turned and extended a hand to Everly. "And Everly. We didn't really meet properly last night, but I've heard lots about you, too."

"Really?" Everly shook his hand with one of hers and tugged the hem of her tight tank top with the other, pulling it down over the bare roll of her stomach, feeling self-conscious.

"I might have forced Callan to give me the whole juicy story last night, under the threat of death. I love a good tale of crushes and—"

"So you said you had a lead?" Callan stepped in front of Cherry, looking somewhat pinker. "Ready to look into it?"

"Um, yes to the lead, no to being ready. Sorry, I missed your message. I figured it'd be later before you showed up."

"Why?"

It was Everly's turn to blush, glancing at the bright daylight around them.

"Oh ... oh right!" Callan turned his face toward the sun, shielded it with one arm. "Oh no. It burns. My fragile undead vampire flesh burns."

Everly punched him gently. "Fine, I get it! No vampires."

Callan smirked but didn't laugh. His eyes remained sad.

"Honestly so disappointing," Harper murmured. "I'm going to go and change, if all you non-vampires are okay without me for a minute."

Everly nodded, then watched Callan as he watched Harper go into the house. Cherry watched Everly watching Callan watch Harper, and when she noticed, he gave her a subtle wink and eye roll directed at Callan.

Callan returned to the present and cleared his throat. "You said in your message you might have somewhere to start looking?"

Everly remembered Rylan's arms around her as the water swirled, his voice calling above the waves. "Right. Yeah. I want to check out the old Rook's Theater."

Callan's face screwed up in confusion. "Really? Why?"

"Just ... I can't explain it yet. And I'm not even sure if there will be anything there. But we have to at least check. Can you please just trust me, for now?"

Callan's eyes softened, and he nodded. "I think that's fair."

The back door swung open and Harper appeared, looking stunning in vintage overalls and a sheer lace blouse. Callan gulped like a cartoon character.

"Anyone want a hot brew before we head out to whatever plans you've planned?"

Cherry nodded, slipping past her to step inside. "I've always wanted to see what the inside of this place was like."

Everly urged Callan in next, then followed. "You guys sort out some coffee to go while I clean up. I'd like to get moving ASAP."

Harper herded them toward the kitchen as Everly bounded upstairs.

"Can I see the antiques store?" Cherry asked.

"No," Harper and Callan said in unison.

Leaving them to it, Everly changed into a clean set of her usual clothes. She didn't want to push any matchmaking but figured giving Harper and Callan some opportunities to get to know each other was okay.

Callan had been a good kid growing up. She hoped he was still a good guy now. Harper deserved at least one good person in her life.

Everly packed her phone, a couple of tools, and her mini first aid kit into the pockets of her navy work pants. She wasn't sure what she should be taking to prepare for where they were going.

Who knew what they would find, or if they'd even get in. Would they be literally breaking and entering? It would be trespassing at least.

Maybe we shouldn't. Maybe we should try to get permission from someone.

Excuses tried to take over. She already had threads of anxiety laying over her like a net, trying to hold her back. But there wasn't any time to get permission or let panic take over.

She only had two days, and if Rylan was hurt, who knows how much time he had. It scared her to follow this clue, but she had to know.

She had to know if Rylan was alive, at least in her dreams.

Chapter Eighteen

Everly stared at the aged façade of Rook's Theater. The place that could provide answers—answers she wasn't sure she wanted.

If they found something it could prove that the Rylan in her dreams was real.

But what if that meant he was dead?

What if that's what I find here today? What if I find his body? What if he'd come back here, injured, and I was too slow to find him in time to help?

"This place is pure grunge coolness." Harper stared at the building in awe.

The theater was beautiful in its own decrepit way. Boarded-up doors and windows had decades worth of vandalism scrawled over the surface, a mess of scribbled tags making the faux columns and art deco frontage took on a look of black lacework, as though the whole building wore a mourning veil.

Everly swallowed down her rising heartrate.

The street they were on was a steep wind tunnel running all the way from the river, and an icy gust blasted by them, lifting scraps of paper and dry leaves around their feet, whistling and moaning like the ghosts of the past.

"Seen what you need to see, or are we going in?" Cherry asked.

"I think we need to go in," Everly replied, unsure she should even be suggesting it.

"We can probably find an entrance around the back," Callan said.

"What, you don't want to break into the place through the front door, right here on the main street? You're no fun," Harper teased.

"And you sound like you are." Cherry smirked back.

Everly looked over her shoulder. They were only a few blocks and around a corner from the Shroudhaven police station. "We don't really have to break in, do we? Or at least, anyone who wants to opt out should do so now. We don't need all of us becoming criminals in one hit. We should pace ourselves."

"If you think you're going to caper without me—you better think again. I want in on capers." Harper whistled innocently and headed off down the narrow side alley.

Everly, Callan, and Cherry followed. Around the back, the building had been covered in so many fragmented posters, stickers, and trash it was like the view through a kaleidoscope had been projected over the walls.

The establishment had been closed for decades after a prank gone terribly wrong killed more than a dozen people.

The story was that someone had yelled 'fire' on a busy night, then locked the emergency exit door. They hadn't accounted for the steep stairs leading down to that door and how people tumbled and were crushed in the stampede.

That was the official story, but this was Shroudhaven, so there were a dozen other conspiracy theories about what had really happened.

That it had been vampires who had torn through the crowd. Or a giant satanic hound. Survivors' tales were mixed and wild with trauma and sensation.

Everly had always brushed them off, thinking that the simplest explanation was generally the correct one. But now, she wasn't so sure. Now she wondered how many dark mysteries that her hometown had shared as whispers were true all along.

Callan stepped up to the industrial-style solid metal door and nudged it with a foot. It swung open freely. "There we go. No breaking necessary, only entering."

A long, dark corridor faced them. Everly clicked on the flashlight on her phone.

"Sooo ... what are the odds we're walking into a crack den?" Harper asked.

"You can wait out here, both of you, while Cherry and I check it out. We should probably have someone as a lookout," Callan offered.

Everly grounded herself, locking down the creeping rise of anxiety. "No, I need to see what's in there."

Harper tapped a finger on her chin. "Stand around in a *boring* creepy old alley on my own, or go into an *interesting* creepy old building with you guys? Feels like a no-brainer to me too."

"I really don't know what could be in there," Everly said. Rylan had warned her not to go, and that warning should no doubt extend to her friend.

Harper pouted. "Aw. Don't worry. I'll protect you."

Callan's mouth twisted in a weird way, then he gave Cherry a worried look and took the lead into the theater.

Everly followed, trying to shine her light forward so they could all benefit from it. But Callan and Cherry moved confidently through the dark, and behind them Harper tripped on the randomly located furniture and debris.

Everly stepped back to walk with her, shining the flashlight where their feet fell and hoping not to see anything move in that beam of light.

Cherry jerked to a stop in front of them, grunting softly.

Callan put his hand up for a second and they all

waited. He whispered into Cherry's ear, and Cherry hissed something back.

"Is that ... I don't know if ..."

"It's not ... I think it's okay."

"What's going on? Are you feeling all right?" Everly asked.

Cherry smiled up from under a flop of bloodred hair. "No problem. Just a weird feeling. Probably something I ate."

Callan turned his gaze over all of them, his eyes starry and dark. "Maybe I should check this place out on my own?"

"Then if you go missing too, what am I going to tell your mom?" Everly tried to make it sound like a quip but failed.

Cherry nodded, slapping Callan on the back. "We stick together, tough guy."

Callan stared at him for a long moment, then shrugged. "Come on, then."

The back hallways led them through storage areas where the remains of stage sets and props had been piled in monstrous tangles.

The theater had put on a mix of movie screenings and live shows, mostly smaller local productions. A broken gargoyle watched them from the corner of a papier-mâché castle wall, leaning on a hand-painted swamp backdrop.

Dressmaker mannequins, half-stripped of their tattered costumes, cut creepy, headless silhouettes in the dusty gloom.

They pushed through to the main foyer area, where excess furniture had clearly been stacked, then toppled over, creating a sea of upturned chairs and cobwebs. A dank, nauseating stench floated around with the specks of disturbed dust.

"This place is wild," Harper said, flicking through a pile of old posters on the counter. They crumbled in her hands. "Anything in particular that we're looking for?"

"I don't really know." Everly shone her phone at the faded red velvet curtains leading off to the theater room.

The light fell on a statue of a cheerful round-capped usher with bulging, twitching eyes.

Did it just move?

She held the light on it, and despite the sculpture being terrifying in its own way, it didn't move at all. Fear was playing games with her imagination.

"Maybe there's nothing here."

"There's something," Callan muttered. He frowned deeply. "I mean, maybe. You two should keep looking in here. Cherry and I will go and check out the main stage."

Everly jogged over to meet him at the curtained entrance. "What have I said about splitting up? Not going to happen."

Callan's jaw clenched like he wanted to argue, but he didn't. Harper and Cherry caught up to them and they walked closely together through the short corridor toward the main theater room.

Statues of trumpeting angels lined the walls. The floorboards beneath them whined a sighing song in musical concert.

The angels moved. Everyone else froze.

The statues swayed slowly at first, a gentle dance to the sighing song—such small motions, Everly wasn't sure what she was seeing, but from the looks on their faces, she was sure the others were seeing it too. Then the angels all spun in a jerky and hideously twisted pirouette and were still again.

"What the actual ghost just happened?" Harper squealed.

"We all saw that, right?" Everly said.

Callan had turned very pale. He approached one of the statues. "It's just ... just dated animatronics."

"Yep, definitely *animatronics*." Cherry raised his eyebrows at Callan. "I always hated animatronics."

"Why would they still be powered?" Everly asked.

Callan rubbed the back of his head. "I really don't know but *anyway*, nothing to worry about! There doesn't seem to be anything here, so we should probably be heading off now."

He walked toward them, as though trying to herd everyone back the way they'd come.

"Are you in a hurry to get out of here so you can go get your eyes checked?" Harper stood her ground, folding her arms. "Because those statues did not move like animatronics."

Everly nodded in mute agreement. She reached out and touched one of the angels, and it felt hard as stone.

Are Callan and Cherry lying?

Something was happening here. Something Everly couldn't explain. But whatever was going on with the statues, they didn't give her any clues about Rylan or why he'd wanted someone to come here.

And if Callan had answers, she wasn't going to let him hide it from her. "We're not leaving yet. I want to see what's in the main stage room."

Harper nodded, and they both pushed past Callan and Cherry.

Muttering and swearing at each other behind them, the two men caught up as they left the rows of statues. Everly kept an eye on the angels just in case, but there was no more movement.

"Do you guys smell that?" she asked. The rotting stench from before grew stronger. Everly's stomach turned in on itself, swallowing her heart in the process.

What if the thing we find here is a dead body? What if

that body is Rylan's?

"Yeah, weird smell," Cherry agreed.

"Like a cat vomited out an old diaper," Harped said.

"That's exactly how I'd describe it too!" Cherry replied.

Callan just continued frowning. "I really think we should go now."

"Why?" Everly demanded. "Do you have something to tell us?"

Callan winced and his voice came out high-pitched. "No?"

Everly turned on Cherry.

He held up his hands. "I'm just here in a support capacity."

"Then we keep going." Everly continued on, following her nose.

She had smelled dead things before. It wasn't the normal smell of death. She held on to that thought as they stepped into the main theater.

Holes in the ceiling allowed a few beams of light through, offering enough illumination to see the area in front of them. The folding chairs cascaded toward a shattered stage.

Through the center of the seating, a wide swath had been smashed, as though a boulder had rolled over them, crashing into the stage at the bottom. Splintered planks jutted out at all angles like crooked teeth.

"What happened here?" Harper whispered.

"This isn't from the stampede, is it?" Everly asked.

"No, I don't think so," Callan said, eyebrows low.

Cherry pushed out one of the folding seats and dropped into it. "Cal? That weird feeling is back. I think I'm just going to wait here, okay?"

Callan nodded. "We won't go far."

They stepped gingerly into the mess of the room. Part of the upper-balcony seating had also been broken away, and they moved quickly from under the structurally unsound section.

Harper picked her way over to the stage area, and Everly continued along the side of the room. She headed toward a small alcove off the side of one of the aisles. She wasn't sure why, but she felt drawn there, like a chilling thread of darkness reeled her in.

The alcove was surrounded by broken statuary of Shakespearean characters—not moving, Everly checked— and unlit neon-light tubing above it that read Snacks.

It no longer held snacks.

Bones, black as midnight and *rippling*, were strung together in a symbol that made Everly feel faint as she looked upon them. She stumbled away, gripping the aisle railing for support.

"What is that?"

Callan appeared beside her, looking in on what she'd

discovered. He froze, staring.

"Are those bones real?" she asked.

Callan nodded.

"Are those bones ... human?"

Callan hesitated. His lip twitched ... in anger? "This is ... it's ..."

Everly wasn't sure why he'd be angry, but he seemed furious.

"Do you know what this is?" Everly tried to look at it again and her vision swam. "I've seen black bones like that before. Why are they black? Why are they *moving*?"

Callan either didn't have any answers for her, or he refused to give them.

All he said was, "We have to go."

Was this it? Was this what Rylan had meant for them to find? It was certainly *something*.

Something Everly couldn't have possibly known to find here herself. Which meant the Rylan in her dreams had known something she didn't.

It's real. He's real.

Before Everly could process that fully, Harper called out from near the stage, "Uh ... guys?"

She stood there with her hand over her mouth, staring down into the orchestra pit.

On their way to join her, Callan kept shaking his head. "It was probably just ... some idiot's idea of an art installation or something."

Everly narrowed her eyes at him. "Not even slightly convincing. What do we have to see to get you to admit weird shit is going on?"

"How about this?" Harper choked out the words, as though her voice was fighting with bile for the chance to get out of her mouth.

When Everly looked into the orchestra pit, she was glad she gasped, as the sharp intake of air helped stop anything else from rising out of her throat.

She had no idea what she was looking at, only that it was dead, that it wasn't human, that it wasn't any animal she knew of, that it was huge, and that it had been dead for a while.

The ripped and shredded carcass swam in a pool of smoky haze, as though it smoldered slowly in a lightless, decomposing fire. Everly couldn't identify body parts. There was no clear head or arm or leg.

Just *flesh*. A rotten avalanche of oozing, wrong-colored flesh.

"How do you explain that?" Harper demanded.

"Good question," Callan huffed.

He didn't seem surprised, but rather confused. His body shuddered and he muttered a string of swear words.

Harper pointed, as though any of them had missed the sight. "*That's* a dead monster if I ever saw one. Which

I haven't and never expected to. But I will eat my own foot if that's not a dead monster."

Everly grabbed Callan's arm. "You know what that is, don't you?"

He groaned and wiped his hand over his mouth. "You guys shouldn't be seeing this. You shouldn't know."

Everly tightened her grip gently. "But we have seen it."

"And we'd like to be told, please, what exactly we're seeing and knowing before our brains break, okay?" Harper added.

Callan's shoulders slumped. "That's ... yeah, that's a monster. Monsters are real. Happy now?"

"No," Everly and Harper replied in unison.

Everly didn't really want monsters to be real, but she wanted answers. "What about vampires?"

"Still not real."

"But it's more than just this *thing*, isn't it?" Everly watched Callan carefully. "Could Rylan have done this?"

"Killed it? Maybe. It looks like it's been dead a few days, so the timing lines up. But it doesn't make sense. You said he disappeared from your place."

Everly considered how much of her dreams about Rylan she could share now without sounding crazy. Rylan had told her this was where he was before he fought the thing at her place. Before he had possibly died at her place.

"You're expecting to find sense here?" Harper giggled

madly and ran her hands into her hair. She froze, her face screwed up. "Are there any more monsters? Are there any more monsters *here*?"

Callan stared back up the rows of seating where Cherry was looking remarkably pale and waving to get his attention, then back at the grotesque corpse. He shook his head once before he paused, gasping in a sharp breath.

"We have to leave."

Harper chuckled as though he was having a go at her, but his expression had turned grim. He grabbed each of them and started dragging them up the middle aisle.

"What is it? What's the hurry?" Everly shone her light around but couldn't see any movement. "There's nothing else here."

"There is—there's something coming. Just ... believe me. You have to get out of here." Callan groaned and let go of them. His skin changed, wavered.

Cherry was on his feet too, coming back their way. "Is it what I think it is?"

"Yes!" Callan snarled. "I didn't notice at first because of the ... dead one ... it's too close now ..."

Cherry put a hand over his mouth. "Oh no. We can't—"

"I know!"

In the dim light, Everly thought she saw wisps of black smoke surrounding Callan. "Are you okay?"

Harper and Everly stopped, and he thrust both arms

at them, pushing them away. "I'm fine. Keep going!"

"No splitting up," Everly said. "Just tell us what's happening."

Callan groaned again, jaw set in determination, sweat beading on his forehead. His skin crackled and distorted, obscured beneath a mix of sparking glow and living shadow, like lightning within black storm clouds.

His voice changed, growing deeper, growling. "Don't worry about me. You have to *run*."

Callan was engulfed in darkness.

Snapping, stretching, sickening sounds emerged. Shadows and sparks swirled and grew larger, then faded away.

Where Callan had been standing, now a hairy beast loomed over them. Thick, powerful arms ended in razor-sharp claws. It stood upright on hind legs, barely covered in the remains of Callan's torn clothing.

The face was more wolf than human.

It opened its snout like mouth, baring vicious fangs, and growled, "Run!"

Chapter Nineteen

A roar came from behind Everly and Harper, spinning them around together. Another lupine form stretched and growled, dropping a red-and-white jacket from clawed hands.

"Callan?" Everly squeaked. "Cherry?"

Harper grabbed Everly's hand, her acrylic nails digging in. "Are they *werewolves*? I thought you said it was vampires!"

"I don't know!"

"Are they going to eat us?"

"I don't know!"

Callan looked like he wanted to eat them. Saliva glistened over his sharp teeth.

They should do what he'd told them to do. *Run*.

But Everly was more confused than ever. Was Callan really a monster? Nothing she'd seen in the last ten minutes felt real. It was all too much for her to take in at once and her body refused to act while her mind was in turmoil.

Werewolf-Callan lifted his head to the ceiling and howled, flexing massive, fur-covered muscles at the same time. Cherry howled in reply.

Everly ran. She pulled Harper with her, their hands still locked together, barging past the creature that had been Cherry.

Her heart raced and stuttered, feral, trying to punch its way free of her chest. Her body flushed and chilled, her thoughts swam. Every symptom of a panic attack flooded over her at once, threatening to incapacitate her.

This is too much.

Everly clutched at her chest and wooziness made her stumble, bringing both her and Harper smacking down onto the floor. Coughing out dust, Everly twisted around and looked back.

Callan and Cherry were right on their heels.

And something *else* was right behind them.

Something so big it was twice the height of werewolf-Callan. It had a vague wolfishness about it too, but in a way that was more from a feeling than from any visual cues, except the wicked grin of its mouth.

It was black all over. A black so dark and deep and slimy, it was hard to make out the forms and shapes, like looking into a living oil slick.

There were at least six legs but they were wrong and slithery, the joints bending in disturbing ways, boneless and deadly silent. There were no feet, each limb tapering to impossibly thin points that it balanced on.

It prowled toward them, its movements confusing and sickening, with no face or eyes to ground it as anything familiar.

But it did have a mouth. It opened slowly, slobbering, a strange green glow emanating from within as it kept opening wider and wider—so large it seemed half of the creature's body had split apart.

Everly stared, jaw slack, head aching from the sheer incomprehension of what was in front of her.

Callan let out another roar, but it sounded more frustrated, almost scared. He turned away from the fallen girls to face the nightmare.

Everly was sure she heard werewolf-Cherry mutter a colorful string of curses as he joined Callan at his side.

"Come on." Harper climbed back to her feet, pulling at Everly.

Everly forced herself up, despite the hitched, panting breaths that didn't draw in enough oxygen and the tremors in her legs.

Callan leaped onto the creature's back, tearing into it with his claws. As soon as he made contact with the slimy black being, there was a sizzle and the scent of burning hair. Callan wrenched one of his tree-trunk arms back and a slick coating of darkness covered his hand, burning patches in his fur like acid.

A spatter of ooze landed on Everly's hand, stinging and fizzing.

She gasped and wiped it away. "Watch out!"

Harper squealed, swatting at her bare arms. She dodged another spray of the slime and huddled behind the closest seat.

The creature swung around, smashing through the room with each step, spattering acid like rain and Everly ducked to the other side.

Cherry charged the creature, wolflike feet pounding down the aisle. He jumped and was struck midair by one of the dark mass's long legs. It flicked him, sending him flying over Everly's head.

He hit the crumbling upper balcony, smacking through the broken barrier and into the chairs above. Broken timbers and plaster shards exploded through the air.

Everly was on her feet again, staring up where wolf-Cherry landed, rubble still spilling down around her. She shielded her face from the pattering dust.

Was he ... could he survive that?

She wasn't sure what Cherry was, what Callan was, but she didn't want either of them to be hurt.

Harper screamed as a solid beam landed across the row

of seating she'd taken cover in.

Her scream turned to a groan as she twisted on the spot. "My leg! My leg is stuck."

Callan tore into the back of the monster, and it didn't even seem to notice. Its boneless limbs flew upward, swatting and cracking against Callan, landing with bone-crunching thuds.

It's not enough. He's not enough. The monster is going to win.

It felt like watching Rylan die all over again—a memory that now felt horrifyingly real. She had entangled everyone in her curse, doomed to witness those she loved die. Again and again.

Everly stood frozen in place. Should she go and try to help Cherry? But she couldn't leave Callan to die alone. But if she didn't help Harper get out, Harper could die too. She was going to fail them all. She couldn't think through the pounding in her head.

The creature trapped Callan in one of its appendages and reeled him in, closer and closer to its glowing maw.

"Help!" Harper cried, tugging at her trapped leg.

"I can't. I don't know what to do. I can't fix this." Everly gasped out the words.

I'm going to get everyone killed.

Panic closed around her like a vise. She tried to move closer to Harper but crumpled under the pressure.

"You can fix anything. Don't let your dumb dragon take over. Actually, no, wait, *do* let your dragon take over," Harper yelled. "The dumb thing is right this time—this is *real* danger and a bit of adrenaline-boosted strength to get me out of here would be great right now!"

The creature had Callan at its mouth, a swarm of tongues lashing at him. He yelped, wolflike, thrashing to try to free himself.

Every instinct inside Everly screamed at her to not let her dragon take over.

It was wrong, went against every thread of her being, to let panic take control. But she could feel it raging inside her, wanting to burst free.

Maybe if she let it, if she gave in, stopped trying to hold it back, maybe her adrenaline would work how it was supposed to.

With a gulp, she let her barriers down.

Energy surged through her. Every part of her throbbed and seared with the riotous heartbeat tearing through her veins. She felt she would pass out entirely from the overwhelming intensity of the extreme panic attack.

Instead, she *lit up*.

At first, Everly thought the light filling her vision was her consciousness fading, a symptom of fainting, that she'd lost control entirely, but she quickly became more aware, the energy making everything clear.

A white glow filled the theater as sparkling tendrils emerged like lightning from her flesh, lifting her from the ground and carrying her toward the monster. An immense hunger washed over her, seeping deep into her bones.

She wanted ... needed ...

She surged forward down the aisle.

She couldn't control it—where she went, what she did. The light had taken over. The same scintillating, brilliant ribbons of luminance that had appeared the night Rylan was attacked.

It was real. All of it.

The blazing wisps lashed out toward the void-black monster, and it let out a heart-chilling, gurgling scream.

It flung werewolf-Callan free from its grasp. It moved so fast, it skidded on the spot in its attempt to flee.

Then it was nothing but a black flash. It smashed its way out through an exit too small for it, not even that slowing it down.

Callan rolled to a stop beneath Everly.

The hungry tendrils tried to reach for him, and Everly recoiled. She forced every scrap of control she had over herself into action.

An aching need to consume left her rattled to her core, and she battled against it, pushing it down, inch by inch.

The light faded and Everly drifted down onto her feet. Her legs wobbled and she fell backward onto her butt. Her vision swam, then cleared, and her breathing returned to almost normal. Her heart still pounded a rapid rhythm.

And she still felt *hungry*.

There was a clatter of debris as the werewolf who was Cherry slid down from above and thumped to the ground behind her.

He growled through his snout, "What the fuck was that?"

From where he still lay on the ground, Callan looked up at Everly with wide, bewildered animal eyes. "What the fuck are you?"

"What am I? What the fuck are *you*?"

Harper smacked her hands on the ground and cried, "What in all the fucks is going on?"

Chapter Twenty

What am I? Everly remained still where she was sitting, but her mind raced.

That happened. That wasn't normal. That wasn't human.

What am I?

Callan raised himself up in front of her, looming high above in his hairy, wolflike form. Everly shivered, still unsure if she should be afraid of whatever he and Cherry were. Or of what *she* was.

Callan prowled over to Harper, his paw-steps soft and silent for his size. He reached for her with a huge claw and Harper cowered back. He carefully lifted away the beam that had her trapped.

"Uh, thanks?" Harper gingerly got to her feet, then scooted over beside Everly. "You okay?"

"I have no idea."

Cherry stepped past them and bumped a clawed fist against Callan's shoulder. "Close one."

"Right?"

Everly gaped at the two of them. They both seemed to be themselves, on the inside, perfectly in control of their actions and emotions and speech, just changed on the outside. Callan turned to her, taking in her expression.

"It's okay. The weroth's gone." His voice was rough and not all the sounds were clear as he spoke through his snout-shaped mouth.

He wasn't what Everly expected a werewolf to be. If that's what they were.

And what was a weroth? Did he mean the other creature?

"Okay?" Harper squealed. "What is okay about any of this?"

"I don't understand anything right now," Everly said in a low voice. "Are you a werewolf?"

Callan crouched on his animal haunches in front of them. "No."

Harper eyed him up and down, gesturing at all of him. "But, I mean ..."

"I know what it looks like," Callan growled wolfishly. "Just wait here a minute."

He tapped Cherry's shoulder. "Come on."

With elegant, animal strength, Callan pounced across the rows of seating and into the upper level, Cherry right behind him, then they disappeared through an exit.

Harper and Everly turned to each other and spoke as one. "Let's get out of here."

After scrambling to their feet, they walked briskly out the way they'd come, Everly supporting Harper who had a slight limp, Harper supporting Everly who was shaking violently.

Everly caught Harper shooting her concerned sideways glances, but she didn't say anything. They were making their way across the foyer when movement froze them in their tracks.

Callan landed silently right in front of them, a snarl baring his teeth. Another thump sounded from right behind them.

"Wait," Callan growled.

Then he was surrounded by the spark-filled black haze, his body silhouetted within as it distorted and shrunk. As the shadowy mist faded away, he was himself again.

His clothes had been ripped badly, singed and dissolved, and he stuck a finger through a big tear in his jeans, pouting. "Aw, man, these were my favorites."

Still looking like a werewolf, Cherry stood next to him and dangled his racer jacket from one claw. "At least I saved this baby."

Harper and Everly just stared at them both, saucer-eyed.

"Normally, I'd strip off any good clothes I was wearing before dealing with a weroth. I just didn't have time."

"This isn't really the main explanation we'd like right now, but okay," Harper said.

Callan rubbed the back of his head and cringed at Cherry. "Yeah ... right ... I guess we have to explain."

Harper huffed. "You think?"

"Couldn't possibly be more busted than we are." Cherry shrugged a furry shoulder.

Harper looked him up and down. "Why are you still a werewolf? Could you stop being a werewolf, please?"

"Not a werewolf, and also, not all of us are as perfect as the Howell boys. Give me a few minutes, okay?" He rolled his wolflike eyes, a sight Everly never thought in her life she would see.

Callan started walking and tipped his head at them as a gesture to follow. Harper raised her eyebrows questioningly at Everly, and Everly shrugged.

He seemed like the regular Callan she knew—he seemed safe—but based on this whole new world of monsters and people not being what they seemed to be, Everly couldn't be sure. Still, Callan looked like he was heading to the exit which meant they'd be going the same way regardless, so she followed.

He led the way, speaking over his shoulder. "That thing

back there, it was a weroth."

"One of a group of monsters called eidolghasts," Cherry added.

Callan shot back, "I'm trying to keep it simple. Don't overwhelm them."

"Expanding my vocabulary is the least of my overwhelm problems right now," Everly mumbled.

"Okay, eidolghasts are the monsters, and we"—Callan gestured between himself and Cherry—"are shadyrs. A kind of shapeshifter, I suppose. But we don't change into just one thing. We have a bunch of forms."

"Right." Harper nodded along, her face twisting with the effort to understand. "Monsters are real. Monsters are eidolghasts. A weroth is a kind of eidolghast. These are all words that don't come close to describing the full-blown brain-breaker happening right now."

Cherry put a hand on his barrel-sized monster chest sincerely. "I know. It's a lot to take in."

"Nah, nah, it's cool. Just the whole world not being what I thought it was."

Everly eyed the still hairy man. "So you, a *shadyr*, can become like a werewolf and other things too?"

"Yeah. What we become depends on what eidolghast is nearby. Weroths give us a form like what you'd call a werewolf." Cherry put both hands behind his head, tilted his hips, and did a shockingly model-perfect pose.

Callan gave a dramatic sigh. "Vasmires—big tentacle-y things, like the fleshy chunks back in the theatre—give us a vampire-like form. Those two are the most common eidolghasts, but there are others too."

Harper pouted. "So there really were no vampires?"

"Didn't lie about that." Callan turned back and grinned.

Everly folded her arms, frustrated. "But also, there kind of *are* because you basically become one sometimes."

"A technicality," Callan replied.

Harper asked, "So you're like, what, a monster hunter who turns into monsters?"

Callan frowned at the term *monster*. "We turn into something that gives us the weapons we need to fight a particular eidolghast type."

Cherry gestured to their ruined clothing. "You saw all the acid flying around back there. That's why we get thick fur when weroths are around, to protect us. Vasmires exude a kind of knockout gas, so our heart and breathing rates slow drastically, and our skin turns hard and cold to protect us from their mouths."

Everly's jaw dropped, remembering the strange gas from the night Rylan had disappeared, how she had fallen unconscious so quickly.

That was a vasmire, then.

Callan took over the explanation again. "So we don't

turn *into* werewolves or vampires really. It's more like what most people consider a werewolf or vampire to be is some mash-up of sightings and legends about shadyrs."

"No one's ever realized we're all the same thing," Cherry said. His snout crinkled up, and he grumbled, "Yes, finally."

Smoky magic swirled up around him, cloaking his body in a spray of embers and darkness.

The other three waited with an awkward, polite patience as he changed. When the mist cleared, he was Cherry again, shirt hanging in ribbons from the stretched-out collar and pants ragged from the thighs down.

Callan offered a fist and Cherry bumped it. "Good work, that was quick."

Harper rubbed her head. "Wow. This is not how I thought my day would go."

"You didn't have seeing your new friends change into wolfy-beasts scheduled into your calendar?" Cherry smirked.

"This is going to take some processing." Everly bit her lip, also trying to absorb all the new information.

She couldn't dispute that it was real after everything she'd seen. As outlandish as it sounded, it made a whole lot of things come together in her head. Including Rylan's vampire appearance the night he went missing.

Everly remembered the moment Rylan had gone still in her hands, how his skin had turned hard and cold so quickly. Too quickly for normal rigor mortis.

"Rylan is like you too, isn't he? A ... shadyr?"

"Yeah, him, Mom, lots of people in Shroudhaven."

Just how vampire-like did a shadyr's form make them? All the legends about immortality gave Everly some hope. Could Rylan have survived those horrible wounds?

"Oh, Darkfrey Estate must be full of shadyrs, right?" Harper asked.

Callan nodded and gestured for them to get moving again, herded them toward the exit. "Shadyr central. Kind of a shadyr school, boarding home—"

"And despotic military hellhole of bigots rolled into one," Cherry finished cheerily as he pulled his red-and-white jacket back on and fixed his hair.

"Is this shadyr thing like something you catch from a monstery love bite?" Harper flicked her hair, revealing her neck with a wink.

Callan gave it a longing look, then coughed. "Genetic inheritance, sorry. Okay, now it's my turn to ask the questions. What are you?"

"I'm a hella gorgeous influencer who is feeling a bit out of her depth right now," Harper replied.

"I think he meant me." Everly smiled wryly. "But I don't know. I thought I was human. I didn't even know there were alternative options."

Harper glanced sidelong at Everly. "She's not a

shadyr-thingy too?"

Callan grabbed a fifties-style smoking jacket off a mannequin, shook the dust off it, and put it on over his shredded shirt. "Nope. What she did, I've never seen that before. How long have you been able to do that?"

"It's never happened before ..." Everly hesitated, traumatic memories churning, trying to breach the surface. "Before this week. I think it happened when Rylan was fighting the thing outside my house—"

"Probably a vasmire," Callan clarified.

"Okay, that. Well, I think that's how I survived, scared the *vasmire* off or maybe ... maybe killed it?"

"Even the best shadyr would struggle to take down an eidolghast on their own. No offense," Callan said. "You saw how that weroth back there hammered the two of us."

Everly lifted her hands in a shrug. "I don't know. And I don't know where Rylan went after that, except for ... well, kind of, *inside* me."

"I wish I was drinking so I could do a spit-take right now," Harper said.

Cherry snorted. "I will also refrain from what are totally inappropriate replies and just ask what that even means."

They reached the exit, and Everly stopped, squinting out at the glary light of the overcast day that felt so foreign to the world they'd just experienced.

A low blanket of clouds shone silver with blocked sunlight.

The sounds of cars and birdsong drifted in the cool air, undisturbed by the monstrous showdown in the theater.

The world seemed so normal out there, but Everly could already tell nothing would be normal again. "I mean, I've been dreaming about Rylan ever since that night, but very real dreams."

She turned back and looked at the theater. "It was Rylan who told me to come here. I had no reason to think anything would be here, but *he* knew. I think he, or some part of him, is really talking to me in my dreams."

"But he wasn't here, was he?" Harper asked, also looking back the way they'd come. "Should we have finished searching?"

Callan stepped out into the alley before turning on the spot and squinting back at the building. "He's not here. We checked the whole place while still in werewolf form—it has a nice speed-and-senses boost. I took apart that weird construction of black bones on the way out too, just in case."

"That was something, though, some proof that what Rylan told me in my dream means something?" Everly hated the pleading sound in her voice.

"I really don't know. I'm out of my depth here too now. We're going to need help." He paused, swore, and kicked an old can. "I'm going to have to tell Mom. Come on. Let's head back to Howell House."

Harper said, "Will you be in any trouble for letting the crazy out of the bag on your secret supernatural club?"

"I think we can be pretty sure you guys saw enough that you weren't going to blow this off as a trick of the light."

"Or *animatronics*?" Harper poked. "That place was haunted as all get out."

Callan raised his hands innocently. "Also, there's Everly probably fitting into the whole supernatural thing too, somehow."

"Yeah, somehow." Everly was still aware of the deep hunger within her that had stirred when the light emerged.

The shape of the light felt so familiar. As though her dragon was so much more real than she'd ever imagined. So much more monstrous than she'd ever thought.

Callan's eyebrows furrowed as he stared at her, and Everly noticed fear in his eyes. "Well, whatever you are, the weroth was scared of *you*."

Chapter Twenty-One

Everly and Harper sat staring blankly, shock catching up as Callan drove them up the tree-lined drive to Howell House. Cherry sat in the front seat beside him, muttering about how much trouble they were in.

Harper had pulled the crocheted throw blanket off the prop storage bed area and wrapped it over her and Everly's shaking shoulders. Every time Everly looked over at Harper, she was staring at her and she'd give a small, supportive smile that made Everly feel worse.

Each one a reminder that she had done something unnatural, unexplainable. And she didn't know what that meant.

They had barely pulled up and unsteadily gotten out when Lian came through the front door to meet them.

She took one look over the four of them and her lips grew thin. "What's happened?"

Callan cringed. "There was a bit of an incident."

"I can see that. These two look like they've seen things that knocked the color right out of them."

"Monster tea spilled *everywhere*," Cherry said.

Everly and Lian locked eyes, and the silent apology and guilt Everly saw there made hot tears well up. She turned away, her own guilt over kept secrets stinging even more.

She should have known about Rylan already. I should have told her before.

Callan walked over beside Lian. She looked him up and down, frowning at the singed and torn clothing. She placed a hand on his cheek. "Weroth?"

"Yup. And there's more. There's ... a lot. Can you call everyone?"

"Rush, Tammy! Team meeting, kitchen, now!" Lian called out.

The door to the RV around the side clattered open.

"What's up?" Denny asked, beer can fixed in his grip.

"Did I call you?" Lian grumbled.

"I'm sure I heard my name. Team meeting, huh?" He winked at Harper as he swaggered in, cheap cologne overwhelming the area. "Don't worry, girls. Daddy is here to explain things to you."

"I'm not sure whether to be more traumatized by what

we saw earlier or by that," Harper deadpanned.

Everly tried to smile, but the muscles in her face were too busy trying not to cry. Emotions overwhelmed her, swirling too fast to identify any one individually. She only wanted to weep and sleep.

And eat.

Denny headed inside first, and the rest of them followed. As Callan walked past Lian, she grabbed his shoulder. "What were you thinking getting Everly into this trouble?"

Everly's voice came out shaky. "The whole thing was my fault—"

"Nonsense," Lian interrupted. "How can it be your fault when you didn't even know what you could have been getting into?"

She shook her head at Callan. "I'm not happy about this."

Callan winced and pushed his hand through his long hair. "Then you're really going to be pissed about the rest of it."

In the kitchen, Rushelle already had the kettle going as everyone filed in and took a seat around the farmhouse table. When she found out that Everly and Harper were now privy to their shadyr secret, she gave them both enthusiastic bear hugs.

"Welcome to the dark side, girlies!"

Tammy was apparently the goth teen with the black hands. She sat away from the table, off to one side, silent and hidden by her hood, and had refused to shake anyone's hand on introduction. Obviously not a hugger like Rushelle.

Cherry slipped into the seat next to Harper before Denny could. When Everly sat on the other side, Denny grunted and raced around to get the seat directly across from Bellsy.

The skitter of tiny paws dancing around under the table drew Everly's attention, and she helped the elderly dog onto her lap.

"Hey, Birdie," she whispered and cuddled her close.

Callan laid out everything that had happened, from Everly seeing Rylan's encounter with a vasmire, to their visit to the estate, to the search of the theater and what they found there.

He hadn't yet gotten to how the fight with the weroth played out. Everly shook with nerves.

What were these people going to think when they found out she wasn't a normal human? Although they weren't exactly human either—all shadyrs, like Callan. Like Rylan.

Rushelle bustled about, clip-clopping on bright-yellow stilettos, bringing out hot drinks, biscuits, a cheese plate, and reheated pie, placing them in front of Everly and Harper.

"Comfort food time," she whispered with a wink.

Everly was ravenous, but no matter how much she picked at the food in front of her, the hunger didn't fade. Birdie whined, and she shared some small tidbits with the old pup.

Lian paced and fumed. "My son has been missing for days and you didn't tell me?"

Everly looked down at the table.

Callan's voice was low. "We only knew for sure last night, and even then, it was sketchy. The Darkfreys didn't give us much."

Almost everyone in the room scowled when he said Darkfrey. "We only ended up at the theater out of luck really. Everly can explain that part."

Everly gulped as every eye in the room turned to her. Birdie lifted her head and gave her a lick as though in encouragement.

"I ... Rylan told me to go there, in a dream."

"Ooh, fascinating!" Rushelle gushed.

Lian raised her eyebrows at Everly.

"Bet that's not all he did in the dream." Denny lifted a hand to high-five and everyone ignored him.

Callan continued with the story. "So she dreamed it, and there was definitely something there, some weird ritual bone thing, and a dead vasmire. Then the weroth attacked."

"Strange to get two different eidolghasts in the same

place so soon," Lian said.

"There was one of those bone things at my place too, that first night back. But it was gone the next day." Everly was sure of it now.

Sure what she'd seen that night had been real.

"I think the ritual thing, I think it was made to attract eidolghasts," Callan said.

"Well, that's deeply troubling," Rushelle replied.

"How do you know?" Denny mocked, leaning back and swigging his beer. "Suddenly some shadyr black magic scholar? That shit isn't real anymore. Shadyr magic hasn't worked since they did the nasty with humans way back when."

He made a lewd gesture with his fingers.

"I think Rylan was investigating something too, and I think it has to do with those creepy bones," Everly said.

"And now my son is missing." Lian shook her head and pulled out her chair at the head of the table before dumping herself into it.

"There's also this son here who feels like he's not being cared about right now, despite having almost been eaten by a weroth." Callan gestured to his shredded clothing.

Lian sighed. "You're still here, barely a scratch on you, so I'm relieved enough to be angry about it."

"Love you too, Mom." Callan grinned.

Tammy spoke up from across the room, her voice dull,

as though she didn't even care about the question she asked. "How did you even manage to survive? Just you two against a weroth?"

Cherry scoffed. "Is it really that unbelievable that Callan and I could take one down?"

Rushelle leaned over and patted him on his bright-red hair. "Aw, honey."

Callan tilted his head toward Everly. "So that's the next big thing. It wasn't just us."

Harper brought her hands up and waved them around beside Everly as though displaying a prize on a game show.

"Everly's a shadyr?" Rushelle gasped dramatically and flashed a huge smile.

"She can't be," Lian said without a hint of doubt.

"She's not," Callan agreed. "She's something else. Something I've never seen or heard of before. Something that the weroth ran screaming away from like a terrified bunny."

Silence fell around the room as everyone looked at Everly, expecting her to give some explanation or demonstration. She smiled awkwardly and shrugged.

Callan explained to them what he saw Everly do. The floating, the light—he made it all sound glamorous and not at all as freaky and horrible as it had been.

The mix of concerned and awed expressions pointed her way made her stomach churn. There she was, in a room full of shapeshifters with terrifying powers, who battled nightmarish monsters, and they were treating her as the oddity.

"She doesn't have a clue what she is." Callan spoke for her. "This has only been happening to her since this week."

"You haven't been back long enough to have been beshadowed." Lian took a slow sip from her mug and watched Everly through narrowed eyes.

Everly looked around for more of an explanation but it didn't come. "I haven't been back long enough yet to know what that means. What is being beshadowed?"

"Ah, blivs. So cute," Tammy muttered, sarcasm clear in her voice.

"That blonde at the estate called us the same thing!" Harper said. "And now I'm guessing it's not a nice thing."

Rushelle placed another plate in front of them, filled with hot oven-baked fries. She perched on one hip on the table beside them. "When an eidolghast settles into one territory for too long, the area and anyone in it becomes changed, possessed, and *weird*. Sort of like a haunting, all kinds of wacky things happen!"

She laughed like she was remembering a hilarious in-joke. "That's a beshadowing. Let it go on for too long and it can become permanent, including breaching a brand-spanking-new hole through to the Everdark."

"Oh hey, Everdark, another new term I had no idea

about." Harper's eyes widened and she let out a single, "*Ha*. Blivs! Like oblivious, right?"

"Not just a pretty face," Denny said, reaching over and taking a whole handful of chips. "Bet you can cook too."

Harper cringed. "Why are you even here?"

"To be the sexiest man in the room. You're welcome."

"Just ignore him," Cherry said. "He thrives on any attention, especially negative."

Denny stuffed chips into his mouth. "He's right. Even your disgust fuels my ego."

"Ugh," Harper grunted.

"Mm, yeah, that's the stuff."

Lian pointed a finger at Denny, a chilling warning in her expression bringing the whole room to silence. With a long sigh, she turned slowly back to Everly and Harper.

"I think it goes without saying, but I'm going to say it anyway. The things you've learned today about shadyrs and our world must remain secret."

"Especially you." Cherry tapped Harper on the shoulder. "No sharing with your adoring cyber army."

"Her what?" Lian asked.

"I'll explain later," Cherry said.

"Yeah, of course. Lips and selfies sealed," Harper agreed, and Everly nodded along.

"Well, whatever is happening with Everly, she seems okay for now, other than being a bit shaken up," Lian said.

"We need to focus first on finding Rylan. If he has some kind of dream connection with her, maybe he can also help us work out the rest, give us some more clues to find him."

If he's still alive.

Everly couldn't say that though. After the initial surprise, no one in the room seemed too worried about what she was, and she was letting that relief bring what little calm it could to her.

Maybe with beshadowings and eidolghasts and whatever else she still didn't know about their world, they were used to dealing with things a lot weirder than a woman with her own built-in light show.

There was more she should tell them—about her dragon, about how it had taken control, about how hard she had worked to rein it back in. About how scared she was that they wouldn't find Rylan alive. But Everly felt woozy under the weight of it all.

Lian stood up, prompting Birdie to yap and jump off Everly's lap to go and join her. "I'm going to give Mordan a call." She marched over to an old-fashioned phone on the kitchen counter.

"I still have so many questions. Do you guys have like, an introductory pamphlet or something?" Harper looked around as she tapped her fingernails on the table.

"You want the quick version of shadyr one-oh-one?" Cherry offered.

"Just, you know, the basics of why the entire world and reality isn't what I thought, yeah."

Rushelle and Cherry took turns running the no-longer-oblivious through a brief history of shadyrs while Lian talked on the phone.

"Lian, Lian Howell. You know who I am. Put me through to Mordan."

There was a whole other dimension, a place called the Everdark, where a race of shapeshifting beings once lived.

The dimension had been taken over by eidolghasts and the shapeshifters had to flee. They managed to break through a portal to the human world, right into what became Shroudhaven.

"No, I want to talk to him right now."

That was thousands of years ago. They took on human form to blend in and interbred ever since. Their descendants were shadyrs—mostly human, but still with some shapeshifting powers.

"Where is *Master Darkfrey*, then?"

The portal that brought the shapeshifters to the human world couldn't be closed, and eidolghasts followed them. Shadyrs considered it their duty to fight them back, to stop the eidolghasts from taking over this world as well.

"That's not soon enough."

Back in the dark ages, the eidolghasts had spread far beyond Shroudhaven and shadyrs fought them across the world, creating many of the sightings and tales of werewolves, vampires, and other monsters humans believed in to this day.

"I don't want an appointment. I want to know where my son is!"

And in those tales, the vampires and werewolves being hunted by humans were actually shadyrs.

Many times throughout history, shadyrs had been considered the monsters, rather than the ones fighting the true monsters, so they kept themselves and their powers secret.

"He is still my son. I don't care what you made your lackeys in the courts say."

Most of the shroudpools—the portals to the Everdark— were underground in Shroudhaven, with a few in protected areas aboveground too. There were also several shroudpools across the rest of the world, guarded by other shadyr groups.

"If you don't—"

There were shadyrs who chose to live elsewhere as normal humans, and many out in the world who didn't know what they were, and never would unless they came across an eidolghast.

But often they felt drawn back to Shroudhaven, as though feeling a sense of belonging for somewhere they hadn't found yet.

Most of them ended up at Darkfrey Estate, home to

shadyrs and their lore from the very beginning.

"No. I understand."

Everly stared at Rushelle, Cherry, and the others around the room. The secret history they'd shared changed her entire understanding of the world.

Is every monster story I've ever heard true, but got it completely wrong?

"Fine, *fine*. Tomorrow." Lian hung up the old corded handset violently. "Those ... *people*."

"Right?" Cherry woofed in agreement.

Lian looked over the room, settling her worried glance over Everly and Harper. She smoothed back her gray hair where fine strands had escaped from her bun.

"You two have had a big day and need some rest. You should stay here where you'll be safe."

Will we be safe here?

Knowing monsters were real, having just seen one, made nowhere feel safe. But Everly was exhausted.

The sun was only just setting outside, warm orange rays shooting in low through the back screen door. She was too tired to even try to argue about where they would stay that night. She trusted Lian, so she just nodded.

That seemed to signal the end of the meeting and everyone started moving around, clearing up the table. Tammy remained still, like a gargoyle in the corner.

Harper got up and stretched. She looked back at Everly

with laughter in her eyes. "And we thought our little car accident was going to be the biggest excitement on this trip."

Lian bent over and picked up Birdie, cradling the furball in one arm. "Everly can have Rylan's room. Callan, Harper can have yours. You take the couch."

"She could bunk in my RV with me," Denny volunteered.

"Never in a million years." Harper scooted over closer to Callan and away from Denny.

"Leave her alone," Everly said firmly.

He sidled up next to her. "You're just jealous. Don't worry. I like chubby girls too."

"Get out!" Lian ordered.

"Aw, come on. I'm being nice." He waved dismissively at them and marched away. "Forget it. None of you deserve me. Best damn shadyr in this house of runts and what respect do I get?"

Everyone was silent as he stormed out and slammed the front door behind him, still ranting and cursing.

Callan grimaced. "Sorry about him. He's the worst."

"You could call the police to get him to stop squatting on your property," Rushelle told Lian.

Lian sighed. "I know, I know."

"Then why don't you?" Everly cringed at the snap in her tone.

Lian brought Birdie closer to her face, looking into the

little dog's eyes as though she were talking to her. "He has nowhere else to go. A place to stay is something everyone deserves, no matter how big of an asshat they are."

"Even the biggest asshat ever, doing nothing to dress up the even more mammoth ass underneath," Cherry said as he moved away from the table, narrowing his eyes at where Denny had exited.

"Plus, shadyrs are safest going up against eidolghasts in groups of four or more. We kind of need him." Callan sighed as though hating the admission.

Everly glanced around the room. Assuming Lian wasn't out hunting monsters, they still had Callan, Cherry, Tammy, and Rushelle. As her eyes settled on the sunny woman, Rushelle waved both hands in front of her.

"Oh no, I'm not a field girlie unless it's absolutely life or death."

Harper took a big step, winced, and wobbled. Callan reached out and grabbed her before she went down. "Your leg still hurt?"

She laughed, putting an arm over his shoulder. "Just a human here, remember? No fancy healing powers or whatever you guys get."

From the side of the room there was a soft grunt, and Everly turned just in time to see Tammy disappear into thin air.

Chapter Twenty-Two

Everly gaped wide eyed at the empty space where the goth girl had just been. "What …? *What*?"

"Aw, poor duck," Rushelle crooned. She snatched up a jangly set of keys from a bowl on the kitchen counter. "I'll go and fetch her."

"From *where*?" Everly choked.

"Did Tammy just *disappear*?" Harper asked.

"Don't worry. It's normal. For her." Callan helped Harper back to a seat and went to the freezer, pulling out an ice pack.

"Normal. Right," Everly murmured.

She and Harper shared shrugs and 'what the fuck' looks with each other.

Rushelle passed Everly on the way out and patted her

on the shoulder boisterously, a friendly grin brightening her face. "See, there are plenty of weirdos in Shroudhaven, not just you."

"Okay then. I think I'm done for the night." Everly pushed her chair back, standing up slowly and carefully in case she fell back down again.

Anxiety ran high through her system and she did her best to appear to be functioning normally. As normally as someone who had just learned that day that monsters were real, at least.

She knew where Rylan's room was and started heading out of the kitchen. Lian put a hand on her back and gave it a sympathetic rub. "How are you holding up?"

Tears filled her eyes again. "You know. A bit overwhelmed. Tired."

Hungry.

Lian nodded. "Understandably. Get some rest, but also ... if you see my son tonight, tell him I miss him and he better be okay. Let him know we're all trying to find him now."

Everly offered a smiling nod, but fear clogged her throat. She'd tell Rylan. She'd keep searching.

As long as it wasn't too late.

Everly made her way along a pathway of heartbreaking memories. Up the steps to the second floor of Howell house, she ran her hand along the time-smoothed banister, remembering the days when she and Rylan used to drag a mattress from his bedroom and ride it like a toboggan down those stairs.

The last time they'd ever done that she was thirteen. It had been years since they had played the game, and they'd revisited the childish activity on a nostalgic whim.

When Rylan sat behind her on the mattress and put his hands on her waist after pushing off, all new sensations had rushed through Everly. She'd known she was feeling differently about him, that she wanted to be more than just friends.

That had been about a month before his father died.

Rylan's bedroom was down the end of the hall, and she peeked inside each of the other bedrooms as she walked by.

The first was fairly bare, still very guest-room like, but there were some punk-style red-and-white clothes hanging in the open cupboard that Everly guessed were Cherry's.

Callan's room was next, looking as though it had recently been stripped of boyhood decorations but not yet adorned in any new way. The bed was made with military precision.

Lian's door was closed, and the next room had black block-out curtains, black bedspreads, and black clothes flung across every surface. Tammy's for sure. It had once been a guest room Everly used when she had slept over some nights as a kid.

Everly exhaled as she reached Rylan's closed door. She turned the handle and swung it open. She stood in the doorway, as though crossing that threshold would be stepping onto sacred ground.

It was almost exactly how she remembered it.

Everly ran her fingers over the glow-in-the-dark stars stuck all over the walls and the boxy old retro gaming console. She had been so jealous when he got that, in his own room no less.

He hadn't even taken it when he left for the estate. It looked like he'd taken nothing of his childhood with him.

Still on the wall was the poster showing an anime man in a space fighter uniform shifting into a purple lion. It matched the one Everly once had on her bedroom door. Their favorite cartoon she and Rylan used to watch together. It was a sci-fi adventure where the people used to turn into magical animals.

Did Rylan like it because he felt like them? How long has he known what he is?

Everly wondered if she would be second-guessing every part of their history now, both hers and Rylan's, and the world in general.

The bed had been stripped and covered in a mattress protector, and a thin covering of dust lay over the flat surfaces, only as much as a few months might have collected though.

In the middle of the room was an open cardboard storage box, half-filled with toys and books, next to a small stack of additional flattened-down boxes, also filmed with dust, as though someone had begun packing away and never finished.

There was some shuffling behind Everly, and Callan appeared with some clean sheets and blankets. "Bit of a flashback, hey?"

"It hasn't changed at all."

But everything else has.

"Mine was the same when I got back. Mom let me change it up however I wanted since then, but I think, you know, without us here, this was her only way of keeping us near."

Everly's mouth twisted, thinking of what had become of her own bedroom. Had anyone ever cared about her the way Lian cared for her sons?

"You left for the Darkfreys to learn about being shadyrs?" Everly asked, trying to make sense of a past that had changed all context.

"Pretty much."

"Your mom didn't teach you?"

"She's not all about the monster-hunting thing. More into living a balanced life. The Darkfreys ... dealing with eidolghasts is their entire mission. Rylan thought we needed that." Callan put the bedding on the desk and started shaking out the fitted sheet.

"That's okay. I can do it," Everly said, taking over from him.

"Thanks. I really need to go and spend a few minutes making sure there's nothing mortifyingly embarrassing in my room before Bellsy steps into it."

"I think I saw a dirty sock on the floor," Everly teased.

Callan's smile dropped. "Really?"

"Right next to the neck high stack of pornographic material."

His grin returned. "It's good having you back, Everly. I bet Rylan would think so too, will think so, once we've found him."

Everly's small smirk faded as Callan jogged away back to his room.

She closed the door behind him and brought the sheet close to her face. Lian must still be using the same fabric softener she always had. It smelled of springtime flowers, childhood games, and early awakenings of love.

It smelled of home.

But it was never really the home she'd thought it was. It was a place full of shadyrs, people who knew the world wasn't what she thought it was, people who kept that secret from her.

Not that she was what she thought she was either.

Everly stared at her hands, wondering if she could make

the light emerge from her again. But the only way she could think to do that would mean dropping her barriers of control. She had no idea yet what that would mean, what the consequences could be of letting her dragon take over.

Especially when it felt so hungry.

Everly finished making the bed and then sat there, staring at the poster on the opposite wall as her mind rolled all the new information she'd acquired over and over.

A vehicle rumbled outside and Everly pushed the curtain aside to watch Rushelle and Tammy get out of a yellow vintage sports car.

Tammy, arms folded tight and head low, marched into the house away from Rushelle. Seeing Tammy vanish into nothing being treated as a normal occurrence was one of the weirder things that had happened that day.

And in a day like the one she'd just had, that was saying something.

Tomorrow would be her fifth day in Shroudhaven, and her last full day before she had to get back or risk losing her job.

Can I just leave Shroudhaven, knowing everything I know now?

Through her sleepy thoughts, Everly could hear echoes of Rylan telling her to go. This dangerous world of shadyrs and eidolghasts and the Everdark was what he'd known all along.

What he wanted to keep her away from. Maybe she should just leave, turn tail, and go back to her normal life.

But how could she do that until she knew what had happened to Rylan?

Rylan awoke to darkness. It was still strange to him, waking up into dreams that belonged to someone else. He steadied himself, wondering what weird world he'd be faced with this time. He'd seen dragons made of light, grass-hut day spas, and tsunamis so far.

It felt like being caught in a beshadowing, twisting his mind. He didn't care though. As long as Everly was still dreaming, it meant she was still alive.

Though it would be nice to know I was still alive.

As the setting grew clearer around him, it seemed strangely, distantly familiar. Like a place he'd only been once or twice when he was very young.

Dim lighting shone through a single high window, revealing the floorboard ceiling, the stairs leading up to a closed door. Shelves were stacked with torn, overflowing cardboard boxes, old sporting gear, and tools. This was a basement.

Everly's basement?

Seeking her, he heard her before he saw her. Sobbing shrieks and gasps came from a dark corner. A small figure huddled into it, swatting and cowering away from swarms of rats.

Rylan strode over, then scooped the young version of Everly up and away from the rodents, kicking them with impunity.

They're just dream rats.

They puffed into clouds of dust where they landed.

Everly, appearing around eight years old, wailed and clung to him. Her pale hair was stuck by tears to puffy red cheeks.

"Hey, hey, it's okay. You're okay. I'm here." He placed her onto her feet and kneeled so he was eye level with her.

She wiped her face furiously. Rylan wasn't sure if this was really *her* or just part of the dream. Either way, every fiber of him wanted to protect her.

"I hate rats. I hate them!" Young Everly balled her hands into fists, then grew before his eyes into the woman she was now.

I'm asleep. This is a dream.

Whispered words echoed around them. She took a deep breath and relaxed her hands, shaking them out. She didn't look him in the eye. "Sorry about that. Sometimes it takes me a while to know where I am."

Rylan was amazed Everly had as much conscious control

over the dreams as she did. He'd heard of lucid dreaming before, but it was a whole other thing to experience it firsthand in someone else's mind.

Everly's face was still wet and red with fury. Rylan stood back up. He wanted to reach out and wipe her tears, but instead, he put his hands in his pockets.

"This actually happened, didn't it? You told me about it afterward. Is this what it was really like?"

Everly looked toward the corner she'd been saved from. "He thought it was funny. A funny way to punish a kid for interrupting his and Mom's private time. He rubbed peanut butter all over my clothes and then locked me down here. For hours."

One of her mom's many male visitors. Calling them boyfriends or even lovers was probably elevating their position. Rylan remembered this one in particular, although he wasn't the only cruel jerk Rylan had secretly chased away.

By that age, he'd already known he was a shadyr. His mom had been upfront about it all—it would have been impossible not to explain after the first time he changed— yet she had refused to train him to fight, to use his shadyr forms to go up against eidolghasts.

But there were some monsters he learned he could use his powers on.

The scene shifted into something straight from his memory. His eight-year-old self in vampire form—skin paled, eyes darkened, teeth long and pointed—chased the man through dark rooms in Everly's home.

Everly watched it with a frown. "Is this real? Is this from you?"

Rylan shook his head. He hadn't meant to take control of the dream, hadn't known he could.

"It's you, isn't it?" Everly demanded.

"Yeah, that was me. I was ... wearing a costume." His voice came out bashful.

He'd never wanted Everly to see the side of him he'd always felt was monstrous.

Everly eyed him for a long moment. "That man, he left Mom, not long after I told you about the rats. Yelling about how he wouldn't stay in a haunted house. You did that?"

For me? The final words echoed in the air despite Everly's lips remaining still.

Rylan shrugged. "I guess I always felt protective of you. I mean, anyone would have chased a scumbag like that away though."

"Except my own mom," Everly whispered.

"Maybe she was the scumbag I should have scared away. I don't know. I was young. I didn't know so much back then."

Everly looked into his eyes. "Even after you moved to the estate, the worst of the men never lasted long."

Rylan drew his lips tightly together.

"I thought you'd abandoned me, but you were always around, weren't you?" Everly's full lips were parted and glossy.

Rylan stared at them for too long before replying. "Sometimes. You didn't need my help that often though. You were always so independent, how you grew up looking after yourself."

"I had to. I didn't have any choice." Everly's voice was laced with bitterness.

"Still, you thrived despite all that. You were strong enough to get away, to live your life."

"If I thrived or turned out good in any way, it was what I learned from you and your mom and your family. It was you ... all who showed me what family was meant to be, what love was meant to be."

Unable to control the impulse, Rylan reached out and took the very tips of Everly's fingers into his own. His voice came out rough. "I missed you, when I left for the estate. But I only ever wanted you to be safe."

Everly's nose twitched and she sniffed, then took her fingers back. "I didn't feel safe. I felt alone. I felt like I had ruined everything."

How did she ruin anything?

Rylan was about to ask when light shimmered above them, and the strange fractalized, slithering thing that Everly called her anxiety drifted through the ceiling and rushed at him.

Everly stepped between them, and power surged all around them in a battle of wills so strong, it made the hair stand up on Rylan's arms.

"Stop it. Go away!" Everly commanded, and the thing shimmered and rolled in the air before swimming through a wall. "Sorry about that. It's ... hungry."

"Your anxiety is hungry?"

"I'm not sure that's all it is anymore. A lot has happened today. I need to fill you in." Everly gestured for him to follow.

She walked up the basement steps, and when she opened the door at the top, bright light spilled in and they emerged on the main stage of Rook's Theater.

Only it wasn't run-down or destroyed. Everything was pristine, with stage lights shining over them. The cougar which showed up a lot stalked between the backstage curtains.

Rylan glared at Everly. "You went? I told you not to go."

"I'm sorry. But I had to know."

"And what *do* you know now?"

Everly ticked the items off on her fingers. "Shadyrs. Eidolghasts. The Everdark. Shroudpools. Weroths. Vasmires. All of that. But we still haven't been able to find you."

Rylan ran his hands over his head, huffing and stalking

away from Everly. She knew. She knew all of it—a world he'd worked for years to keep her away from, safe from.

He wished he could have stopped her from finding out. But he was useless while trapped in this dream world.

Why hadn't he woken up? Why couldn't he?

Everly called out from across the stage, "Lian said to tell you she misses you. I'm there now, at your old place."

Rylan stopped his pacing and his shoulders sagged. He had a complicated relationship with his mom, but he didn't want to hurt her. Not any more than when he'd already ripped her heart out by leaving her and taking Callan with him.

"What if I'm really dead?" he asked softly. "I don't want to do that to her."

"Then we need to find you. You need to start telling me everything, anything that could help. And I need to tell you everything too." Everly walked over to him, a spotlight following her all the way, making her white hair glow bright against the black backdrop.

She told him again about the night he disappeared, how light had come out of her then and saved her from the vasmire.

And how it had happened again in the theater, chasing away the weroth. When she finished, she waited, a look of anxious expectation curling her eyebrows.

"That's ... new."

"Maybe. My dragon has been with me as long as I can remember. Maybe if you hadn't done such a good job of protecting me, it would have come out sooner."

She turned to look at it, swimming through the rows of seats. She narrowed her eyes as though giving it a warning to keep its distance. "I have no idea why your consciousness is here, and we still don't know where your body is. What really happened that night?"

Rylan stared out into the space, remembering his last night outside of Everly's dreams. "I was on my own. Usually, Darkfrey shadyrs travel in a brace when hunting—a group of four is considered the minimum safe number for dealing with an eidolghast. But I was investigating something and wasn't sure who I could trust."

"The weird bone statues?" Everly asked.

She knows about those?

"Yeah. I'd noticed some strange things with the Darkfreys. A shadyr grave being robbed, talk of other missing bodies and ghast remains. I managed to follow someone and came across a room full of bones and weird artifacts hidden at the estate."

"Do you know who it was?"

Rylan winced and shook his head. "I got caught snooping around, and someone blindsided me, knocked me out, and cleared up the evidence. I didn't know at first why they didn't finish me off then, but maybe it would have been too obvious. They wanted it to look like I was taken out in an eidolghast attack."

"This place?" Rylan swept his hand around the theater, and it changed to the decayed and trashed state it was currently in. "It was a trap, and I fell for it."

"But you killed the monster. You made it to my house."

"Do you know how hard it is to kill an eidolghast on your own? It was a miracle. I'm lucky it was a vasmire. The form we get has a small amount of regenerative healing. It was enough to keep me going, but I was wrecked after killing the one in the theater. And I couldn't go back to the estate, knowing someone had it in for me. I'd only hoped at that point I could drag myself to Howell House and beg them to take me back and help me."

Rylan put his hand to his chest, remembering the pain of being broken apart. "I was halfway there when I sensed another vasmire, heading to your place. I had to stop it. I had to. But I was too worn down at that point."

Everly inhaled shakily. "The bone statues—Callan thinks they attract the eidolghasts. There was one in my garden that night."

"They must have known—that I have a connection to you. They must have set it as another trap." Ice filled Rylan's veins. It was his fault. Just him knowing Everly had put her in danger. He should have stayed away, never even gone near her old home.

Everly's voice was barely a whisper. "Whoever it is that set the bone statues up, if they were also the grave robbers, could they have stolen your body?"

"Maybe? It doesn't help us much though, because I don't know who it is."

Everly had grown very still, a terrified look in her eyes.

Rylan opened his mouth to ask why, when his brain started catching up.

Everly had always been smarter than he was. She'd already connected dots that were still forming in his head.

That the people who made the statues, had made them from shadyr bones.

And what they might have done with his body.

Chapter Twenty-Three

Somebody bad could have taken Rylan's body, taken his body for horrible things.

Everly awoke with a start, the realization she'd made in her dream shocking her into consciousness. She hugged the pillow around her head, willing herself to return to sleep, to be with Rylan again.

She couldn't sleep. She wanted to tear the whole town down searching for Rylan. But she didn't even know where to start.

They would be meeting with the Darkfrey's leader today. That had to get them somewhere. They would help find Rylan, wouldn't they?

Everly pushed out of bed and rubbed her face. She tiptoed by the other bedrooms, down the stairs, and past

Callan sprawled and snoring on the couch, his long legs sticking out over the end.

In the kitchen she found Lian pacing, a steaming mug held under her nose. She looked like she hadn't slept at all.

"Tea?" she offered, moving toward the range and clicking on the burner under the kettle.

"Thanks." Everly finger-combed her hair and braided the white strands. She felt dried up and crumpled from a bad sleep in yesterday's clothes. Tea might help with that, but it couldn't help the ache in her heart or the burning worry for Rylan.

"Did you ... dream about my son?"

Everly blushed. "Yeah. And I'm worried."

Lian nodded and handed her a warm mug of tea. They each took a seat at the table. Everly explained everything Rylan had told her that night, from what he'd been investigating to his battle at the theater and again at her place.

"My boy," Lian whispered. "He always was a strong one. Strong and stubborn. Not many shadyrs could take on an eidolghast on their own."

"Almost two of them." Everly's nose twitched, and she sniffed the threatening tears away. "He'd almost beaten the one at my place too, before it ... It looked so bad, what it did to him."

Lian reached over, plucked a tissue from a cabinet

behind her, and handed it to Everly. "Shadyrs are tough. Especially in vampire form. It gives us stonelike skin and regenerative healing. And Rylan's one of the toughest."

She pulled out a tissue for herself too and blew into it fiercely. "I just wish he'd come to me sooner."

"What do you think it means? Being able to talk to Rylan in my dreams?"

Lian sipped her drink and shook her head. "All kinds of oddities can come from beshadowings. Dream connections aren't unheard of. The circumstances of this one are strange though, especially the apparent lack of an actual beshadowing. Sometimes, just a certain kind of exposure to an eidolghast or shroudpool can lead to a person ... changing."

"Like Tammy disappearing? What happened to her?" Everly asked.

Lian blinked sad eyes and spoke softly. "Stuck her hands right into a shroudpool a few years back. Ever since then she's had the bad habit of popping right out of existence. Luckily, she reappears in the same place every time so we know where to find her."

"Oh," Everly said, unsure what else she could possibly say.

Lian rubbed a thumb over her chin. "Your light powers, though, they're different."

Almost on cue, Everly's hunger manifested in a loud

rumble from her stomach.

Lian chuckled. "Want me to put on some breakfast?"

Everly shook her head and finished the last of her tea. "I have more work I need to do at home. I should head back and do what I can until everyone else is up. I'm a bit behind, what with everything that's happened."

"I'm sorry, love. You don't need to be a part of all this. You shouldn't have been pulled into it. Best you finish up with your old house and get back to your life outside this town."

Everly nodded weakly. This was meant to be her last day in Shroudhaven. She and Harper weren't supposed to be part of the shadyr world.

It would be the right idea for them to just leave, try to go back to normal—pretend that this never happened. Would that even be possible?

Lian cleared up the mugs and started making herself another tea. "You don't have to come along today. We can handle things from here."

"No. I saw things about Rylan that no one else did. I need to be there."

Lian paused by the sink. "Won't be till midday that we can get into the estate. I don't want you alone all that time."

"Need a chaperone?" Rushelle popped her head into the kitchen, her platinum hair pinned back in retro curls. "I can keep an eye on the little duck."

"You don't have to, I'm sure it will be fine."

"It's really no trouble. I'm a morning person," Rushelle sang, as though it was possible she'd be anything else.

Lian nodded once. "Midday. We'll pick you up then."

Everly rose to her feet and gave Lian a quick hug. "Let Harper know where I am when she wakes up?"

"Of course." Lian stepped back, wrapping her woolen coat tight around her as she walked Everly to the door.

Rushelle gathered up her laptop and a few jangling items into a yellow purse and followed.

Everly was down the front steps and halfway through the yard when Lian called out, "You could have told me, when you came by the other day. You could have told me you needed help."

Everly stood out front, looking up at the old Boderleth building, wondering what else she could do in the short time she had left. The whole place needed repainting, but that wasn't going to happen.

Working that morning was more of a distraction than anything, an attempt to keep busy and keep nerves at bay.

Rushelle kept her distance, finding a spot where she could sit and tap away on her laptop, keeping the level of awkwardness at a bare minimum.

Everly finished up a few jobs and had a shower by midday, then Harper arrived in her van, bringing Lian and Callan with her. Everly wiped damp, nervous palms on her jeans and hopped in with them.

"Sorry I didn't come back sooner to help. Man, I was wiped!" Harper leaned around from the driver's seat as Everly took a spot on the bench beside Callan. "I guess redefining the structure of your whole world and seeing monsters for the first time deserves a big sleep in."

Everly nodded blearily.

Rushelle grabbed a seat as well, and Harper rumbled the camper on its way.

The drive across the river and up the hill to Darkfrey Estate didn't take long. It was agreed Harper would wait in the van.

There wasn't any point in letting the Darkfreys know more than one bliv had been let in on shadyr business. She parked out front and waved cheerily as Everly, Lian, and Callan got out.

Rushelle stayed with Harper. "Just in case. Never a good idea to be alone in Shroudhaven."

Harper called through her open window as they left. "Good luck!"

When they reached the ominous gate, Lian pressed a few buttons on the keypad, muttered her name, and the gates clunked and squealed as they rattled open.

Everly had to admit to a small amount of excitement as they walked up the steep drive and the first glimpses of the estate came into view. She'd always daydreamed about what was hidden up there.

What the place that Rylan and Callan had run away to was really like. Whether it was a luxurious palace or a haunted house.

It turned out to be a bit of both.

As they reached the peak of the hill, the dark woods around them fell away and the grounds opened up into formal gardens and sporting areas.

Clusters of grand buildings with crenellated towers, spires, and balconies of gray and white stone were joined with covered walkways and spread along the cliffside, looking down over all of Shroudhaven.

"I can't believe you lived here," Everly said in a hush to Callan.

"It's not as exciting as it looks."

"Really? Because it looks like a castle full of magic and adventure."

"The only thing true about both the appearance of this place and the reality of it is how old-fashioned it is."

A group of tweens jogged by, all in matching gray and maroon sportswear. They were led by an older man and ran in step with military precision. A few other groups of four, of mixed adult ages, also ran exercises around the grounds, from Tai Chi to fencing.

As they drew closer, a number of gardeners and cleaners became clear too. Everly couldn't help but notice a distinct divide between those training and those working. A divide of skin color.

Upper management and those in braces were distinctly paler than those in service roles. Only the cardigan-wearing shadyr Everly had dreamed of as part of Rylan's team stood out with his slightly darker skin.

"Is everyone here a shadyr?"

"Yep. Everyone except you." One of them waved at Callan and he nodded back. "Not everyone does hunting duties though. There are a lot of other jobs in the shadyr world and estate."

"And how are the jobs allocated?"

Lian snorted. "It's *supposed* to be on merit."

Everly didn't miss the emphasis on *supposed*. She knew Callan had left because of disagreements over how things worked here, and she wondered just how deeply their 'old-fashionedness' ran.

"Callan?" a voice called out, and a young woman with rich red hair jogged over to them.

She wore tight maroon leggings and the same plated undershirt that Rylan had showing under her loose singlet.

"Hey, Annabeth," he replied.

"What's going on? Is there news about Rylan?" She looked at him eagerly.

Lian answered, "Sort of. Going to see Mordan now."

Annabeth's eyes pleaded with them. "I wanted to be out looking, really. Master Darkfrey grounded our whole brace up until this morning. Rylan has to be okay though, hasn't he?"

No one answered, and they left Annabeth standing and staring at them in their wake.

They walked the rest of the way to Mordan Darkfrey's office in silence. Callan and Lian clearly knew exactly where they were going as they entered the largest of the buildings and marched along lengthy hallways lined with suits of armor from every era.

They rose a few floors in a Victorian-style caged elevator that barely fit the three of them inside and faced imposing double doors made from carved black wood.

The Darkfrey name and coat of arms—with crescent moon, twin fang-like blades, and three skulls—was detailed in high relief and well-polished.

Lian spoke through an intercom on the side and the doors swung open.

"Come in," Mordan's deep voice called. It sounded tired, although not unfriendly. "Finally come to return the artifact you stole when you left, Lian?"

"I certainly don't know what you're talking about or

that anyone here would be able to do anything with it anyway," Lian muttered.

Everly shot Lian a sideways look, shocked. Who knew she had such a rebellious streak?

Mordan, in his glossy black and maroon suit, bent over the huge desk, signing paperwork. His office walls were covered in aged hunting trophies of a mundane variety—moose, lions, rhinoceros—and Everly wondered if there were any trophies of less mundane types hidden elsewhere.

The gold and maroon office looked like it could have belonged to a king from an earlier century.

Another person, or shadyr, stood at Mordan's shoulder. A slab of soldierly man with a face like a cinderblock, he wore body armor with no shirt over the top and a distasteful grimace.

Mordan Darkfrey glanced up at Everly as they entered. "I didn't realize you were bringing an *outsider* with you."

"This is Everly Boderleth. She's become aware," Callan answered with a level of formality Everly hadn't heard in his voice before.

His normally loose shirt had been tucked in, and he even stood at attention.

"Nilson." He nodded once to the shadyr behind Mordan, then leaned and whispered to Everly, "Mordan's son."

Nilson didn't offer a greeting in return. There wasn't

a lot of family resemblance except for height and obvious annoyance at those they were meeting with.

Lian dragged out one of the seats across the desk from Mordan and dropped into it, gesturing at Everly to take the other. "Everly is an old family friend and can be trusted. She came to know most of what she does now on her own. And it involves Rylan."

Mordan clicked the cap onto his very fine pen. "Yes, Rylan. You have some information?"

Lian gestured to Everly to share what they knew. She gulped and stuttered her way through the night of Rylan's disappearance, her confusion, and the statue in her yard, right through to finding the other statue and facing the creature in the theater.

Callan helped fill in parts with what he knew and his theory about the statues summoning the eidolghasts. Everly left out any mention of her light or her dreams, as instructed by Lian, who had felt it best the Darkfreys didn't know about that yet.

When they'd finished, Mordan stared for a moment and then snorted a laugh through his nose. "You think there is some conspiracy? All based on the ravings of a hysterical bliv?"

Everly's hackles rose. "I know what I saw. I mean ..." *Do I?* "Others saw it as well."

"Where's your proof? Where are these bone structures?"

"The one at my place was gone the next day. Someone must have taken it away. But the one at the theater is still there," Everly said.

Callan shook his head, his lips tight. "I went back there this morning. It's all been cleaned up."

"It wasn't logged by our cleaning crews," Mordan noted, tapping one of the sheets in front of him. "Are you even sure that's what you saw? You know how areas on the cusp of beshadowing can trick your mind. It was probably just a pile of trash some kids were playing with."

Callan looked over at Everly, his jaw twitching. Her mouth moved weakly but she didn't know what to say.

Mordan continued. "Even if it was some ritual formation, shadyr magics don't work anymore. Only pure-blood shadyrs could use magic before they came to this world and interbred. This is all nonsense."

"What's nonsense, is that my son is missing and you're doing nothing about it," Lian snapped.

"Of course we're doing something. I have teams out searching even now. It's being treated very seriously. Rylan is one of our best and is like a son to me."

Lian shot forward in her chair, a scowl on her face.

A nasty sneer rose on Nilson's lips as well.

Mordan didn't flinch, just lectured on. "But he chose to leave his brace and go off on his own, which is a dangerous move. Shadyrs don't last as long when they don't have people they trust to look out for them."

Callan hung his head.

"I think you need to prepare yourself for the possibility that he won't be found alive. Not due to some conspiracy or foul play, but due to the dangers of *his* job and the stupid risk *he* took. The simplest explanation is often the right one."

"Then where's his body?" Lian demanded, her eyes glossy and furious.

"Given the activity being logged around your area, it's not impossible his remains could have been taken by wild animals. There do seem to be a high number of sightings, possibly even a beshadowing behind the growth in numbers and aggression."

Nilson gave a sharp nod and stepped forward. "Which my team are looking into. Let us Darkfreys handle shadyr business. We don't need a mob of misfits and blivs getting in our way."

Mordan waved a dismissive hand at him, and he took a step back again, scowling at Callan and Everly.

Lian pointed a finger across the desk at him. "You can't stop us looking for my son."

Mordan's expression grew dark. He straightened up in his chair with a threatening slowness.

"You know it's only your Pimey bloodline that affords you the privilege of staying on my good side, Lian. That means I let you play-act as shadyrs with your little team of runts instead of putting an end to it. So I wouldn't be pushing my luck."

He leaned back in his chair again, eyeing Lian.

The longer she gave him no reply, the larger his smile grew. "Now, you know the way out? Or should I have Nilson escort you?"

Lian stood up, dragging the chair harshly across the floor. "I know exactly how to get out of this place."

That was it?

Everly glanced around from Callan to Lian to Mordan. The looks on all their faces said they were done.

Everly felt humiliated, left with nothing. She wanted to scream her lungs out at Mordan Darkfrey as though somehow that could bring Rylan back, but she swallowed the urge and stood as well before following the Howells from the office.

"Oh, and Lian?" Mordan called when they reached the door. "Do be careful bringing blivs into shadyr business. It didn't work out so well last time with that husband of yours."

"Is that a threat?"

"It's reality."

Everly fought tears all the way out of the estate.

This couldn't be it.

Maybe she should have stayed home, just kept working

there. Maybe if she, the hysterical bliv, hadn't gone into the meeting, Mordan Darkfrey might have taken it more seriously.

He'd said they already were. That they'd been looking. And if a whole estate of army-like supernatural monster hunters hadn't been able to find Rylan, what hope did she have?

Chapter Twenty-Four

The mood in the van was as gloomy as the weather as they drove down the hill away from Darkfrey Estate with nothing.

"We should go and see Crow. Maybe she has some insight," Rushelle suggested.

"You know she's hit and miss." Lian sighed. "And I hate sage."

Callan rolled his shoulders, a darkness clouding his expression. "Yeah, but if all else fails, at least we can have a drink. I for one could do with something strong."

Lian shot him the look of a mother not yet come to terms with her son having grown up.

"Crow, as in Crow's Nest?" Everly asked.

She knew the bar. It had been a local establishment

as long as she remembered. But she'd left Shroudhaven before she was old enough to drink legally.

Not that it was the bar most kids wanted to go to. It was the dark, seedy bar everyone joked about as being the place only weirdos went. Everly was already starting to guess what those weirdos really were before Callan confirmed it.

"It's a bit of a shadyr hangout. Crowea, she's kind of the town witch. Not that anyone except for her believes in all the wiccan stuff she gets her kicks from, but she does have some powers."

"Worth a shot?" Rushelle encouraged.

"It's only two o'clock?" Harper said like a question.

Rushelle batted a hand at the air. "Shadyrs keep weird schedules. Crow's Nest is open all hours."

"What do you think?" Harper half turned to Everly, keeping her eyes on the road.

"I don't know. I guess. Sure." The way the others were talking made Everly feel like this was a last resort. A heavy pressure built behind her eyes, making them burn.

Callan gave Harper directions. They pulled up in front of a plain, flat-faced building with a dungeon-style door as an entrance. The bar's name glittered in small gold lettering across the front of the aged wood.

From across the road, Cardboard Box Barry watched them all exit the baby-blue van. A trash can clattered down a nearby alleyway, making Everly jump. A small creature scurried out of the toppled over bin. Just a raccoon.

Lian grabbed her bag and from it pulled a strange sword scabbard on a belt and buckled it on under her long coat. "I'm going to go and look around on my own. See if I can find anything. You kids have fun."

Rushelle stepped beside her. "Right, I'll go with you."

"You know you don't have to."

Rushelle beamed sunnily. "I know."

"We'll let you know if we find out anything." Callan leaned on the door, pushing it open with his back as he waved.

Everly turned to say goodbye as well, but the raccoon caught her eye again.

It watched her, eyes glinting moonlight blue in the shadows. The headlights of a passing car shone over it for a brief second. Its fur was ragged, patches of the wrong colors in the wrong places. It hissed at the light and ran.

"Come on." Harper jiggled with excitement, dragging Everly by the hand into the bar.

The inside of the Crow's Nest looked nothing like the outside but lived up to the name far more. Trinkets and lamps, colorful scarfs and throws, fantasy paintings and figurines filled every space, making it seem more like a new age store than a bar.

The furniture was eclectic, not a single armchair or table matching another. About half the seats were occupied, and a low murmur of conversation mixed in with the tune of the mermaid in the lighthouse song playing in the background.

Every eye was on them as they stepped inside, and Everly got the impression they weren't entirely welcome.

Callan led them to the large timber bar that looked like something out of a western. A tall woman with massive, wild blonde curls shot through with gray streaks turned to greet them. Her bright, flowing hippy dress swayed and she wore tie-dyed silk gloves that covered her to her elbows.

Her peachy skin was a cobweb of wrinkles, and one of her eyes was covered by what seemed to be a large, broken fang protruding from it, surrounded by scarring.

Taking in the sight of them, she crooned, "Hello, babies. Look at these new faces."

Callan leaned on the bar. "Hey, Crow. This is Everly and Harper."

She reached toward his arm, but didn't touch. "I've been hearing talk of a missing face too, hearing it was your brother. I'm sorry that's all I've heard though, if you've come looking for more than a drink."

Everly couldn't hide the disappointment on her face, but Callan still seemed hopeful.

Crow leaned away from them. "Oh, you've come for a bit of Crow magic, haven't you?"

Callan nodded, and to Everly, he said, "Crowea has a

sort of psychometry skill. She can sense information from things she touches. I thought maybe she could touch you, find out—"

"Oh no. I'm not touching that. I can feel her from here. I don't know what is happening there but it's not something I want to get close to." She bent down behind the bar and returned with what looked like a fat, pale-gray, loosely wrapped cigar.

Using a lighter from her skirt pocket, she lit the end, and once it started smoldering, she waved the smoke around each of them. Then she pushed it into Callan's hands.

"Sage for cleansing. Best you keep that." She gestured at him to keep smoking Everly.

Everly coughed.

Callan pleaded, "Couldn't you—"

"No means no. You want to use my visions but don't trust my other senses? You get sage, and you can all have a drink on the house because you are clearly in dire need of it."

It was as though frigid water had been injected into Everly's veins. It was unclear how real whatever Crowea had sensed was, but the fact she refused to come near her didn't feel good. She felt broken, at a dead end, unable to fix anything.

Crowea didn't stop to ask them what they wanted to drink, just started mixing a large share jug with spices, herbs, flowers, blessings from the goddess, and generous splashes of alcohol.

She lit her lighter again and waved it over the top, invoking the elements, before pushing it over the bar to them, along with a stack of four highball glasses, then shooed them away.

Harper carried the jug and glasses and led them toward a free circle of armchairs in a corner.

As they crossed the floor, Cherry stepped out in front of them. "Oh! Hey, what are you all doing here?"

"Things didn't go great with Mordan, so this seemed like the next logical place to go," Callan replied.

"I can relate to that."

"You here alone?" Everly asked.

"Yeah, well, I guess it's solo-day-drinking kind of weather."

"Join us." Harper grinned. "We have a share jug of who-the-heck-knows-what."

"Ah, one of Crowea's signature cocktails," Cherry said.

"She even gave us four glasses. Ooh, that's spooky!"

Everly sunk into a vintage armchair and Harper poured the drinks. Cherry tapped away on his phone, keeping the screen close to his chest.

"Is she really a witch? Is that a thing too?" Harper asked.

Callan chuckled and snuffed the sage stick out on a

used plate at the table across from them. "Jury is still out on the wiccan stuff, but the psychometry has proven real in the past. You probably noticed her eye?"

"No!? Was there something in her eye?" Cherry cried, looking aghast.

Harper snorted her first mouthful of drink back into her glass.

Callan smiled around a sip of his drink. "It's an eidolghast tooth. From a dislimner, I've heard people say. Super rare. I've never seen one myself. She's had the psychometry power ever since it got stuck in there."

"Cool, cool, cool. So cool. Cool and normal." Harper nodded, then attempted again to take a drink. "This, however, is not bad at all."

Cherry tossed back a few mouthfuls of his drink, wiped his mouth, and checked his hair on his phone camera. "BRB, friends."

Everly tended to avoid alcohol, having seen the path her mom took to her early grave, but tried a small sip out of curiosity. It had a rich, honey flavor with a sharp, spicy bite that warmed her throat, but didn't warm her heart.

They were no closer to finding Rylan. It didn't feel like the time for social drinks.

"What are we going to do?" she asked quietly. "Rylan could be anywhere, and we're meant to be leaving first thing tomorrow."

Harper pouted. "You're going to find Rylan. Because you're amazing and can fix anything."

"I can't." Everly shook her head.

I'm not enough.

It felt over. Time to go back to their regular lives and forget all this ever happened.

"You don't understand."

I think he's dead. Either wild animals or bone-stealing grave robbers got to his body and ...

"I didn't do enough and it could be too late."

"This woman," Harper began, pointing at Everly and talking to Callan. "You know how we met?"

"I'd love to know," Callan said, leaning in.

"So, my malicious man-child ex doxed me."

"I remember when that happened. So wrong."

Harper took a swig of her drink and continued. "Everly was the superintendent in my building, and I was *flipping out*, trying to get her to install new locks for me and everything. When I explained why, without a moment's hesitation, she offered her own apartment to me if I needed somewhere to hide out. My first response was 'how weird' and 'should I be scared of *her*,' right?"

Callan sipped his drink, eyebrows raised at the turn in conversation.

Everly half smiled. "I'm sorry. It was weird."

"It was damned beautiful is what it was. Because when

some creep started messaging photos of our building to me in the middle of the night and I ran to Ev's doorstep, she just let me in. Just straight up let a stranger who needed help inside and even gave me her bed. And still this woman thinks she's not good enough."

Everly remembered that night, how shaken up Harper had been. She hated to think what might have happened if she had sent Harper away.

Even without the close call, she hated to imagine a world where they hadn't become friends that night.

Harper looked at Everly, a fiery adoration in her eyes. "People see us and expect Everly tags along with me, but I'm the one clinging to this absolute goddess here."

Everly bit her wobbling lip. Harper leaned in and put an arm over her round shoulders and bumped her forehead to hers.

"She always was amazing," Callan agreed.

Everly sniffed self-consciously. "Please stop, it sounds like you're both eulogizing me."

Callan leaned forward in his chair and put a hand on her knee. "Really, you've been incredible through all this, and done everything you could have. We wouldn't even know about Rylan's disappearance if it weren't for you."

"And now we know just enough to know he's gone and we have no idea where and we can't help him." Everly gulped back a sob and stood up quickly to hide the broaching tears. "I'm going to the bathroom."

Harper popped to her feet. "I'm coming too."

Everly marched away, but Harper caught up. She spotted one sign and tried to follow it, but the back area of the bar was a maze of small rooms and curtained-off private areas.

Harper hurried to keep beside her. "You okay?"

"No, not really," Everly croaked.

"I'm sorry. I was just trying to cheer you up."

"It's not your fault."

Everly hit a dead end and tugged aside a curtain, hoping it led the way to the bathroom, and instead revealed a small storage area with Cherry and the cardigan-wearing shadyr from the estate neck-deep in each other.

Harper squealed.

"Whoa!" Cherry jumped away and put his hand on his mouth.

"Sorry!" Everly said, backing up and letting the curtain drop closed again.

From behind the curtain came the hiss of whispered arguing. "I told you we shouldn't."

"Ghast damn it."

The curtain opened again and Cherry grabbed Everly's arm. "Wait, listen, umm ... You can't tell anyone about this. *Anyone.*"

"It's okay. No big deal."

"No, really, big deal," Cherry said.

Jasper stepped beside him, smoothing back his hair. His forehead remaining creased.

Cherry said, "No one can know. Not even Callan knows. Or at least he pretends not to for our sakes."

"Oh." Everly's eyes widened. "He said the estate was old-fashioned. Is it really that bad around here?"

Cherry rolled his head in a large, sarcastic nod. "Me being *me*, is what got me kicked out of Darkfrey Estate. Jasper is only still there because no one knows that he is who I was being *me* with. And for some ghast-forsaken reason, he wants to stay there. So no one can know."

Jasper gave Cherry a gentle, suffering look as though they'd had plenty of long conversations about exactly what his reasons were for staying at the Darkfreys.

"I'm riled up, okay? I know it's hard to leave. I know," Cherry said.

Jasper's eyes softened, and under his breath in a tone Everly expected was just for Cherry, he said, "And often it's also arduously difficult to stay."

Cherry reached for his hand, and Jasper's fingers squeezed around his for a second before he pulled away and straightened his cardigan.

Harper mimed padlocking her lips. "We will treat it as an even higher-level secret than our supernatural underworld knowledge."

Cherry gave her a quick hug. "Bellsy, you are the best."

"We won't tell a soul," Everly agreed.

Jasper cleared his throat. "Nice to meet you both again. I'm going to leave now before anyone else discovers our forbidden romance."

He gave Cherry a pointed look, and Cherry stole a peck on his cheek before he strode away.

"You weren't really here for solo day-drinking after all." Harper grinned. "How long have you two been together?"

"Almost a year," Cherry gushed proudly. "I know he comes across a bit stuffy, but he's ... he's amazing. I was so high on love for him after a few months together that I came right out to the whole world. Didn't take long for the Darkfreys to find a reason to boot me out after that."

"Was that around when Callan left?" Everly asked.

"Uh-huh. He fought so hard to make them let me stay, but when they wouldn't change their mind, he left too. I think we're better off away from there now."

Harper's tone was soft. "Jasper didn't leave with you, though?"

Cherry shrugged. "He has this whole internalized-shame deal going. Totally get it. Stuff he has to work through. Plus, he's super proud for ranking into one of the Darkfreys' best braces, considering he's not the most lily-white. That's hard for him to let go of."

"I did notice that about the Darkfreys," Everly

mentioned, and Harper frowned.

"Still, Jasper doesn't want to lose that. And I'm okay with supporting him and sneaking around for now."

"Sorry we busted you," Everly offered.

Cherry waved the apology away. "Honestly, it's kind of nice to finally have someone who knows! But I could do with going back and finishing off that jug now. Phew!"

Harper asked Everly, "You still need the bathroom?"

"Never did really. I could do with heading back home soon though."

"Yeah, of course. Home it is. Whatever you need."

The need to sit in a corner and cry had subsided for now, and Everly thought she could probably make it home before it took over again.

It's not home, she reminded herself. She was leaving tomorrow to return to her real home. The one she'd made for herself outside of this place of shadows and grief.

Even if it tore her heart apart to leave with so many questions left unanswered.

They remained at Crow's Nest long enough to finish the share jug between them, then piled into Harper's van for the short drive home.

Except Harper insisted they take the scenic route back. "Just one final tour around town to say goodbye, yeah?"

Everly nodded, but she knew Harper was just trying to hold on to hope for her sake, that they might still find something. Everly leaned her face against the glass of the passenger-side window and stared, watching the quaint town pass by as Harper cruised around.

The red-and-white awnings of Pimey's Diner had faded, but the warm glow of the interior stirred a homesickness inside Everly.

Cardboard Box Barry stood his vigil on a blustery street corner. The way the mountains rose up behind the rooftops, framing the town with their dark slopes, and the soft roar of the river and falls in the distance all felt almost like home.

She would miss it, a little. But she'd said goodbye to it once and could do it again.

Callan sat in the middle seat up front and Cherry leaned over from the bench behind them, offering Harper directions for streets to drive down and things to see, statues of town founders he provided the sordid backstories for, shadyr ruins mislabeled for the public eye, places he'd had his most epic battles against eidolghasts.

It was a side of the town that had been invisible to Everly, that made it feel less like home.

It was obvious that Harper was circling around every

block between the theater, the Boderleth house, and the fringes of the woods that reached the edges of town.

The sky was a thick soup of low clouds, blocking any sign of the approaching sunset. Harper had been driving for over an hour, when they headed along a side street a couple of blocks from Everly's old home which looped around between the woods and the main road.

"I think we should probably go back now," Everly murmured.

Harper smiled, but her eyebrows twisted. "I just thought, you know, you might want to see a bit more of town. It's no problem."

Everly sighed. "We're not going to ..."

Up ahead on the side of the road, Everly noticed a familiar figure—silhouetted, human-shaped, hunchbacked, dragging something.

The night of Rylan's disappearance, when her mind swirled into unconsciousness, hadn't she seen the same thing? In the aftermath of all that chaos, she'd forgotten. There had been so much else to try to work out.

But now that she saw them again, she was sure.

The same person had been there that night.

Maybe they had seen something. Maybe they knew something.

"Stop the car!"

Harper slammed on the brakes. "What is it?"

Everly jumped out her door and ran toward the hunched figure. As she drew closer, she could see it was an old woman wearing a ragged, muddy coat. She bent over, picking something off the road and putting it into a large canvas sack.

"Hey," Everly called out. "Excuse me?"

The woman startled and dropped the sack.

"Sorry, could I ask you a few questions?"

The woman shied away and was reaching for the sack when Harper, Callan, and Cherry got out of the van too, rushing across the road to join Everly. The old woman spooked and bolted, dashing off into the forest faster than her age suggested she'd be able.

"I just want to talk," Everly called after her. The woman flitted between the dark trees.

Everly frowned. *Like I saw just before the car accident.*

"Who was that?" Harper asked.

"I don't know. But I saw her the night Rylan disappeared, and before our car accident."

"What's in the bag?" Cherry sniffed and kicked the corner of it.

Callan lifted the opening and glanced in. He inhaled sharply and his jaw dropped, tongue out and gagging. "That is messed up."

Everly braved a look. The smell hit her first—the overwhelming stench of death and rot. In the gloom and shadow of the sack, she could make out pieces of fur, messes of bloody gore, and bent and broken creatures.

Everly fought the urge to vomit. There was a stain on the side of the road from where the woman had just added another piece of roadkill to her sack.

Harper moved closer.

Everly blocked her view. "Better not. Can't be unseen."

"It's full of dead things. Animals, and I think maybe some bits of eidolghast," Callan told her and Cherry.

Harper frowned. "Little old lady has been collecting animal bodies?"

Cherry shuddered. "What for? Wait, do I even want to know?"

Everly's mind raced. If that woman had been there the night Rylan had fallen, if she had seen his body lying shattered on the road ...

"Do you think there's a chance she might have collected a *larger* body?"

Chapter Twenty-Five

Everly sprinted toward the tree line, crashing through the long grass and undergrowth on the verge of the forest where the old woman disappeared.

"Hello? Are you out there? Come back, please!"

There was no reply. Everly pushed further into the woods.

I have to find her. She could have seen what happened to Rylan. She could know.

She could be our last chance.

In the low light, under the thick canopy of green-black leaves and twisting branches, it grew dark quickly.

Panicked, Everly blinked, trying to force her eyes to see better. "Which way did she go?"

Callan caught up first, his eyes massively dilated and

sparkling in the dark. "You really think the old woman knows something?"

"She was *there*," Everly pleaded.

Callan squinted through the trees. "This way."

Harper and Cherry arrived just as Callan took off, leading the way.

Everly hesitated, frowning at Harper.

"Don't even think about warning me off. We're sticking together," Harper said, putting her hand out.

Everly nodded and took it. She held tight as they chased after Callan.

Within the woods it was dark as night, and the temperature dropped sharply. Harper took her phone in her free hand and switched the flashlight on, but it only cast light over the next few steps in front of them.

At the speed they ran, it barely gave them enough warning of when to jump a fallen log or duck a low branch. They each stumbled a few times, but when one did, the other caught her with their joined hands.

Callan raced ahead, clearly more concerned with not losing their target than not losing those behind him. Cherry made up the in-between, helping the women keep course, his shadyr eyes sparkling in the dark.

The tree trunks were densely packed and mazelike. Everything was moist, slimy, and mossy, and muddy leaves squelched beneath their feet. Crooked branches and thorny vines seemed to reach out, tangling and tearing at them as they ran.

Everly lost track of their shadyr guides. "Which way did they go?"

Harper shone the light around. "That way."

Everly was sure she would have lost Harper out there too if they hadn't remained holding hands.

This isn't a forest I want any of us to get lost in.

Locals avoided going into the woods, and many of those who entered never came back. It was considered an unsafe place even without the truth of what could be creeping in the dark.

They sped forward again, and almost ran headfirst into Callan and Cherry, who had stopped beside a massive oak, its branches drooping, umbrella-like around them.

"Where is she?" Everly asked between gasping breaths.

"I'm sorry. I lost her." Callan pulled his long hair back, twisting it in his hands before tying it away from his face.

"I hope you haven't lost us, too," Cherry said, staring up at the obscured sky.

"No, I think we're pretty close to the main road still."

Everly frowned, thinking about where they had started and the direction they'd run. "That would mean we're pretty close to where we had the car accident."

Where another body may have disappeared from. Everly had been so sure she'd heard the car hit the cougar that day, and then there was nothing.

Her mind whirled. "We have to find her."

She turned on the spot, staring out into the twisted forest. Sounds of things moving in the distance, owls hooting and twigs snapping, came from all around. Two bright, reflective eyes peered straight at her.

Cherry gasped and hissed, "Is that a *cougar*?"

Harper looked at Everly, wide-eyed.

Everly could barely make out its silhouette against the shadows. But it was a shape she knew well from her dreams. Her skin tingled with goose bumps and a deep feeling of connection.

The creature turned and bounded away.

"Follow it," Everly whispered, rushing after the big cat.

It kept an easy pace, weaving between trees and skirting puddles, always just ahead of them as they sprinted behind it.

Deeper into the woods again, the cougar hesitated and looked back at Everly before springing up a tree trunk with its powerful claws and disappearing.

"No, come back!" Everly cried out, as though it would listen.

What had she thought would come from following it? It was nothing more than a wild animal. She was getting all mixed up, her need for some final hope in finding Rylan making her chase wild geese—or wild cougars.

Harper caught her breath. "Did we lose it?"

Callan frowned at Cherry. "Maybe not. You feel that?"

"Yup."

"Feel what?" Everly asked.

"Eidolghast," Callan said.

"When they're near, we get this tingly kind of 'I'm about to self-combust and change form entirely' feeling," Cherry added.

"A vasmire, maybe?" Callan frowned, turning his head and rolling his shoulders. "But dull, like the dead one at the theater. Come on."

Callan took the lead again, moving slower this time, letting his shadyr senses guide him. Each of them had a try calling Howell House on their phones as they went, just in case they needed backup, but there was no coverage.

Callan seemed sure they weren't walking toward a full, living monster and tried to comfort them. But the idea that they were walking toward pieces of monster didn't make Everly feel any better.

Up ahead, the trees parted, revealing a log cabin perched on the swirling buttress roots of an ancient fig.

Smaller rooms and lean-tos of recycled doors and planks had been hodgepodged onto the sides, and an uncountable number of bowls were strewn around the ground surrounding the hut.

Most were empty, but a few held rotting remains,

crawling with maggots.

The smell of rank meat filled the air. In the tree line surrounding the clearing, things of all shapes and sizes moved in the dark.

The old woman stood awkwardly near the front door, as though they'd caught her just arriving home. She stared at them with terror in her eyes.

Everly stepped forward quickly. "We want to talk. Just talk. It's okay."

The woman hunched over, as though it would make her invisible.

"Go away!" she pleaded, her voice gravelly and high.

"Please." Everly edged closer, reaching out a hand. "We don't mean any harm. We're looking for a friend of ours who is missing."

The woman turned hesitantly their way. Wiry copper-gray hair jutted out all around her face from under the hood of her ragged coat. Scars cut through the leathery skin on her face, cross-hatching her deep wrinkles. As her gaze passed over Callan, her expression drooped sympathetically, and then hardened again.

"You won't hurt me or my animals?"

Everly eyed the bowls and the shifting shapes in the trees, wondering what kind of animals the woman was talking about.

"Of course not." Harper joined them near the front

door, smiling cheerily. "We love animals."

The woman's face brightened. "Not all people do. They can be so cruel. I'm Nell. Missing friend, huh?"

Everly nodded and introduced herself and the others.

"Come on, then." Nell gestured to them with a blood-stained hand to follow her inside, but thankfully didn't extend it to shake.

The four of them warily went through the cabin door after her. On the way, Callan whispered, "There's definitely a vasmire here, but not a strong source. Can you keep yourself from changing?"

Cherry nodded.

Inside, Nell took off her coat and hung it near a stone fireplace. It was the only light source in the room, down to just a scattering of red coals. Everly had to step carefully between the bowls on the floor, and the odd small creature dashed past her feet.

Please don't be rats. Doorways hung with tattered fabric led off into a couple of other rooms.

"You have a lot of pets?" Everly asked.

"I'm a wildlife carer. I'm just trying to help the poor creatures people have hurt so much." Nell's clothes were a bundle of layered odds and ends, knitted woolens and tattered skirts over thick pants and gumboots.

There was a hand-knitted pouch slung around her chest, resting against her belly, where something squirmed and mewled.

There were two shredded armchairs. Nell took one, and Harper insisted Everly take the facing one.

Cherry and Callan stood behind the armchairs. They kept glancing at each other as though communicating silently, their muscles visibly tense.

"I've been running my little animal sanctuary out here for a while now. We take in all the animals we can."

"Is that what the roadkill is for? To feed them?" Callan asked.

The old woman squinted at him but didn't reply.

"We?" asked Everly.

"Me and Hubby." She smiled, eyes crinkling, and waved toward one of the doorways.

A dark figure meandered by within the other room, obscured by the threadbare curtain.

A low groaning sound came from him that resembled a "Hi."

Something the size of a small dog skittered across the ground, right past Everly, making her squeak and pull her feet in closer.

Its fur was ragged and its shape strange, making it hard to tell what it was in the low light. Callan put a hand on her shoulder, his eyes wide. What was he seeing that she wasn't?

"Honey? Can you bring in some firewood?" Nell called.

"Yeaaahh," Hubby moaned and continued to wander

around the side room.

The corners of the room crawled with small shapes.

Everly shivered and swallowed her fear. "Where do you find the animals that you help? On roads?"

"Mostly. I help the ones that need my help the most. That no one else cares to help. That no one else *can* help," Nell said, pride in her tone.

Callan bent close to Everly's ear and whispered, "These animals ..."

"I think it's wonderful. I've sometimes thought about being a wildlife carer myself," Harper gushed, although Everly caught a wariness in her tone.

Nell smiled sweetly at her.

Callan hissed, "These animals are all *dead*."

Chapter Twenty-Six

"What do you mean dead? They're moving," Everly whispered at Callan.

Her eyes darted around, unable to see whatever it was Callan could see in the low light. How could all these animals be dead? The place smelled of death, but that had to be from the roadkill the woman collected.

"I mean this is zombieville and we are surrounded by franken-animals."

Was Callan making some kind of sick joke?

Zombie animals? Is that even possible? She wasn't sure in this disturbing new world of monsters she'd fallen into.

Then something pounced onto Everly's lap.

A small black cat. But not just a cat—careful stitching held its patchy coat together, mixed with fur that clearly hadn't originally belonged to it, and sections that looked like the sickly gray flesh of a vasmire.

Lips that had rotted away exposed broken teeth. It stared up at Everly with milky-white eyes.

She gasped, freezing in place.

"See what I've been able to do?" Nell leaned forward, enthusiasm sparkling in her eyes. "I discovered things in Shroudhaven, amazing things, that I could never have done in all my years as a veterinary surgeon elsewhere. The countless lives I've saved with my new techniques."

Everly remained frozen, eyes on the zombie-like cat on her lap.

Its head whipped around, and Everly jolted, thrusting a hand between herself and the animal. The cat had begun to clean itself, but was startled by Everly's reaction, hissing. It lunged, jagged maw aimed at Everly's raised hand.

She shot to her feet, dropping the cat. It dashed off into a sooty corner.

"Sorry about Mittens. You know how cats can be when they are frightened." Nell chuckled.

Standing now, Everly could see out the window, could see all the shapes creeping around them. Like a sickly puppet show, silhouettes of big cats, bears, wolves, and more shambled around the cottage.

This was madness. This woman was stitching together roadkill with monster parts and keeping a menagerie of undead animals.

Everly looked at the small creatures skittering in the shadows underfoot. Were they dangerous?

The increased reports of animal attacks around Shroudhaven made her think yes. She almost laughed. It really had been animal attacks all along.

Undead animals.

But maybe not all of them were dangerous. Everly and Mittens had just scared each other equally, but the cat didn't actively try to eat her brains.

It was now sprawled in front of the fireplace, purring a disjointed rumble. A shaggy raccoon trotted over and curled up next to Mittens as though they were old friends. None of the other small animals scurrying around were trying to feed on their flesh.

Nell seemed proud of how she helped these beasts. How she could bring them back from the brink of death—or even beyond.

As horrifying as the concept was, Nell did seem to be doing a good thing for the animals. If the number of food bowls was an indication, she'd given a lot of creatures a second chance at life.

Okay, just try to ignore the zombie animals for now, Everly told herself, in a sentence she never thought she'd think.

She had to get herself under control and ask the question she came here for. Because she could only hope this old woman had saved more than just animals.

Callan and Cherry were on edge, as though ready to attack, and Harper was still smiling at Nell, but cuddled herself, the fear in her eyes clear.

Nell shifted in her seat, eyeing them suspiciously.

"Sorry, the cat startled me too." Everly settled back into her armchair again and nodded to her friends. "It's okay."

From over Nell's shoulder, Cherry gave Everly a sarcastic look that said, 'Really?'

Just to make sure she and her friends weren't about to become Mitten's dinner, Everly asked, "Your animals, they're ... friendly?"

"Friendly? Oh no. They are ... how do I say it?"

Everly gripped the armrests and waited.

"Not *domesticated*, mostly. Lots of wild animals in rehab out there, so don't go riling them up or trying to pat them or something."

Everly blinked a few times, glancing at the Frankensteined cat and raccoon sharing the last bit of warmth of the dying fire, then back at Nell. "Of course. We'll leave them alone, they'll leave us alone, right?"

Nell gave her an appreciative smile. "Exactly. Now, we don't often have guests, but would you like a cup of tea? Hubby can brew some."

"Teeeeeaaa," he groaned.

Everly eyed the curtain blocking the view of him. She

fought off a shiver and shook her head.

"No, that's okay. The reason we're here ... a few nights back, out in front of the old Boderleth Antiques store, a friend of ours got badly hurt and has been missing ever since. I was knocked down in the garden. I don't think you saw me, but I saw you."

Nell's eyes narrowed. "So that's why you were chasing after me. I try not to be seen, when I'm out working."

Everly leaned forward in her seat, holding Nell's gaze. "Do you know what happened to our friend? Or maybe, did you help him too?"

Nell broke eye contact and looked down, her puckered mouth twisting. "I wondered if someone would come looking for him."

Everly's heart leaped into a gallop. "Is he here?"

Harper put her hands over her mouth. Callan crouched beside Everly, waiting for an answer.

Nell nodded slowly. "I saw the poor boy, all broken up like that. I don't normally work on humans, but I had to do something. Hubby helped carry him and what remained of the other creature back here."

"Heeerrre," came a grumble from the next room.

"I didn't see you, love. Otherwise, I would have tried to help you, too." Nell leaned forward and patted Everly on the knee with fingers stained in dried blood.

Everly found herself very grateful then to have been

hidden by the rosebush.

"Where is he? Is he ..." Everly choked on the word *alive*.

Callan had turned very pale.

Nell pursed her lips, eyeing them as though weighing her answer.

Harper kneeled beside Nell. She asked gently, "Did you manage to save him?"

Nell shrugged, her lips turned down. "No."

The word hit Everly like a bullet, but then Nell continued. "Not really. His body just ... healed itself. I didn't even need to do any surgery. But he just won't wake up for some reason."

The breath that had caught in Everly's throat was chased free by a sob of relief. Rylan was alive.

Nell's shoulders slumped, and the creature in her pouch gurgled and hissed. "Sorry. I'm not good with people like I am with animals."

Hubby pawed at the fabric door hanging. "Goooood."

"Thank you for helping my brother," Callan said, his voice tight and hard. "But we need to take him home now. Where is he?"

"He's safely hidden away. I was worried someone would come and think the wrong thing. Can't be too careful when you have a human body lying around." Nell rose creakily to her feet and stretched out. "I'll take you—"

Something clattered and clanged outside, the sound

of metal pet bowls being thrown around.

A man's voice followed. "What is this stinking mess?"

"I think we found our beshadowing," replied a woman.

Nell turned on Everly, eyes wide and fierce. "Who else did you bring here?"

Callan looked out the window. "It's the Darkfreys. Two braces. This isn't good."

"Why are they here?" Harper asked.

Her question was answered by a growl, then a loud thump and a whimper.

"What are they doing?" Nell howled and charged to the front door, Everly and the others close behind.

Outside stood what appeared to be a group of vampires. One, built like a soldier action figure with a blond crew cut, had a ragged fox pinned under his boot.

Everly recognized him from earlier that day. Nilson Darkfrey.

The young redhead who knew Rylan still appeared human for a moment before being engulfed in black smoke and sparks. When she emerged, she had the same long fangs, white skin, and sharp claws as the others.

"Monsters," Nell gasped.

"What are the Howell runts doing here?" Nilson bellowed.

Another shrugged and rolled up his sleeves. "Who cares? Clear off, kiddos. This is Darkfrey business. We have a beshadowing to eliminate."

Callan stepped in front of Nell. "I don't think there *is* a beshadowing."

Annabeth barked a laugh. "You're kidding, right? Have you seen this place?"

In her changed form, her features were sharper, less human. Everly could only identify her because she'd seen her change.

One of the others might have been Jasper, based on the cardigan, but she didn't recognize the rest. They all wore military-style jackets similar to the one Rylan wore, with their hoods up, shadowing their faces so only their sharp-fanged mouths showed, glinting in the low light.

"Vonny, get your brace onto finding the ghast. We'll take care of the collateral." Nilson twisted his foot, grinding down the fox pinned under his boot. There was a sickening sound of bones cracking.

Nell shrieked. "No, no, what are you doing?"

Harper looked like she was about to vomit. She marched forward, fury shaking her fists. "Stop it!"

"The beshadowed animals are dangerous and can't be allowed to remain," the one likely to be Jasper said bluntly.

Cherry moved closer to them. "It's not like that. Just wait, there has to be another way."

Jasper stepped back and looked down his nose. "It's our duty to keep the darkness from taking over."

Spooked by the shouting, a ferret sped out of the cabin between their legs, making a run for the tree line. It moved so fast it was just a small furry blur. But the shadyrs were just as quick.

In a flash, Nilson snatched out an arm and grabbed it. He held it up by its neck. "Look at this abomination."

Nell cried, "No, don't hurt it! The animals haven't done anything wrong. They deserve to live."

Around the clearing, glowing blue eyes surrounded them, from tiny squirrel-sized to ones at bear height. The beasts clung to the shadows, weaving through the trees, keeping their distance.

"Leave it alone," Harper cried. "The animals are ... okay, maybe they're a little undead, but they're just animals. You don't have to kill them."

"Shut it, bliv. You don't know what you're talking about."

Everly thought she did. The animals weren't attacking any of them, and if Nell could be believed, they weren't any more dangerous than regular wild animals. There had been more animal attacks, but if anything, it was the concentration of so many animals in one place that was getting dangerous, not the undead state of them.

Callan stepped forward. "Nilson, listen, man, there's more going on here—"

"Enough. Undead critters, eidolghast, and crazy,

beshadowed old ladies all have to go." Nilson clenched his grip and broke the ferret's neck.

Nell flung herself at him—a flurry of shrieks and wild hair and clawing fingernails. He swiped his arm through the air, throwing her back to the steps of the cabin.

A deep growl cut through the air. A huge half-wolf, half-Labrador bounded into the clearing, landing in front of Nell. With its back to her, it roared ferociously at the Darkfreys.

And then from the shadows of the trees, chaos erupted.

Creatures of all shapes and sizes poured forward, a surging current of fur, feathers, and claws, launching themselves at the Darkfreys. Those people had hurt the woman who fed them, cared for them, who had healed them.

The animals didn't seem happy about that. Nell's warning about riling them up rung through Everly's mind.

Shouts went up from the shadyrs as creatures from massive stags to swarms of lizards charged at them, tearing through the clearing.

The beasts created a living wall between the shadyrs and Nell. Everly had remained near Nell, but Callan, Cherry, and Harper were on the other side. Bodies scattered in every direction, human and shadyr versus animal. Hisses and howls and the crunch of impacts filled the air.

"Harper!" Everly screamed.

Everly tried to run for her friends, but hands grabbed at her, clutching fistfuls of her shirt and hair.

Nell was on her feet again, her face wild with anguish. "You led them here! They're killing everything!"

"I'm sorry. They aren't with us. Please, we just came for our friend."

Nell's fingernails dug into Everly's skin as she forced her backward into the cabin. "You'll never find him! Never!"

CHAPTER TWENTY-SEVEN

Everly grabbed at Nell's hands, trying to release herself from the terrifyingly strong grip.

They wrestled, back and forward, Everly trying to use her weight to her advantage, to push past the crone-like woman.

But Nell was much stronger than she appeared. She roared, lunging forward, and tackled Everly into the cabin, landing on top of her. Food bowls smashed and clanged around them. Others, caught under Everly's back, jabbed into her.

Ragged, bloody nails flashed in front of Everly's eyes.

"I'm sorry. We didn't want the animals to be hurt," Everly cried. She brought her arms up to cover her face as Nell pounded at her with gnarled fists.

"You're all monsters!" Nell screamed, her fingernails scraping across Everly's neck.

Everly rolled to the side, throwing the woman off her. She crawled backward to get to her feet. Nell landed on all fours and scrambled at Everly like a wild creature.

Everly dodged behind an armchair. "Please, stop. I don't want to fight you."

One of the Darkfreys burst through the front door, wrestling the Labrador-wolf. Its slobbering maw snapped close to his face. He put his foot into the animal's belly and kicked it back out of the cabin. There was a thud and yelp from where it fell.

Nell howled and rushed, banshee-like, at the man, flying across the room. She latched onto his back, hands clawing at his eyes and face from behind.

The shadyr swore and swatted at her, trying to shake her off.

Freed from Nells' wrath, Everly took her chance to dodge away from the grappling pair. Harper and the others were out there, somewhere amid the cacophony of animal and human cries, and she had to get to them and help.

She ducked to the side, under the man's swinging arms, and reached the front door. On the porch, she froze, trying to make sense of the scene.

It was a roaring tornado of animals. Tattered eagles, owls, and crows dive-bombed into the fray. Dogs, cats, foxes, and badgers dashed about, and in the center, three shadyrs fought to bring down the biggest bear Everly had ever seen.

One Darkfrey shadyr writhed on the ground, overwhelmed by a layer of smaller animals, smothering them. Everly's eyes widened as a streak of orange flashed through the clearing.

Was that a tiger?

The battle had kicked up the bowls of rotting food and forest litter and the air had a rank, earthy odor like blood and dust.

Across the clearing, bright red caught Everly's eye. Cherry was there, changed into his vampire-like form, but recognizable by his vivid hair and matching red-and-white jacket. Back to back with him was Harper.

She'd picked up a couple of large steel food bowls and was using them as shields, holding her own against the rabid creatures.

A few animals nipped and chased them, but their defensive behavior wasn't drawing nearly as much attention as the Darkfrey's aggression.

Everly couldn't identify Callan in the messy battle. The undead animals were striking out at everyone who wasn't Nell. Anything human-shaped was their enemy.

Before Everly could make it out the door, the tangle of shadyr and Nell smashed toward her. The man tripped on a steel bowl, and Everly had to jump out of the way as the two of them came tumbling down.

They crashed through some shelving and upturned the armchair Everly had sat in earlier. From underneath it, a pulsating swarm of fur squirmed. Everly's stomach squelched and backflipped. Dozens of tiny bright-blue eyes stared at her from the swarm. Startled from their sanctuary, they rushed toward Everly.

Rats. RATS.

Everly's brain shorted out, overtaken by panic. Her skin crawled and her breath caught. She tumbled backward on pure primal instinct. Her back came up against the cabin wall, scraping against the rough wood.

The rats swarmed over the furniture, hopping across the room like speeding arrows, a flood of fur, coming her way.

Everly screamed and rushed to escape them, herded away from the exit, toward the other doorway. The tattered cloth curtain tore away as she pushed through it and she stumbled into the dark space beyond, barely able to see.

She ran into a bench, spilling plates and pans off it. They clattered and broke on the floor around her.

I have to get out of here, have to get back to the others.

She couldn't go back the way she'd come. She physically couldn't force her body to move back toward the teeming rodents.

A little light came through a window to Everly's side. She grasped at the latch, pushing and wrenching, but it wouldn't open.

There has to be another way out.

She squinted into the darkness. And inhaled a scream.

The rats, undead or otherwise, ran in, pouring through the door, and dashed under her feet. Then they *climbed up her.*

Everly felt their sharp claws as they scurried over her clothing, using her as a bridge from the floor to the sanctuary of the cupboards behind her.

Her whole body froze, completely petrified except for the uncontrollable shaking. Her dragon roiled within her like food poisoning, making her nauseous, wanting escape. She fought it back with everything she had. Her breathing had become staccato, faltering.

Go. Get out of here, she pleaded with herself.

She regained enough control to take one shaky step.

Movement flashed outside the window, then with the clash of thunder it caved in, the entire wall coming with it. The giant bear's back filled the space, twisting and swinging at the shadyrs trying to end it. Glass and splinters showered across the room.

Overhead cupboards tore from the walls and collapsed, smashing over Everly, bringing her down with them.

Her head hit something hard.

Everly twisted to the side, thrashing her arms out to push away the avalanche of timber and crockery that covered her. But there was nothing there.

There was nothing anywhere. Only inky darkness, only the barest sense of firm ground beneath where she lay.

Oh no. No. Wake up. Wake up!

"Hey, it's okay. You're dreaming." Rylan appeared in front of her.

He crouched down, hands on her shoulders to comfort her as she slowed her breathing enough to speak.

"No, I don't think I am." Everly held one of his arms for support and he helped her to her feet.

He frowned at her response. His warm green eyes met hers, stared right through her.

"I mean, it is ... different than usual," he said, looking around into the empty void. "Normally there'd be more imminent terror manifesting around us."

Still clutching Rylan's arm, Everly tried again to wake up, but nothing happened.

Her voice trembled as she said, "I'm not dreaming. I think I got knocked out."

"You *what*?" Rylan growled.

Everly winced away from his anger. "We were so close. I thought we'd found you, but then everything went wrong."

"What hurt you out there? Are you still in danger?" Rylan demanded.

Everly just shook her head. She didn't know how to answer. Couldn't bear that Rylan was only worried about her and not whether they were going to be able to save him.

Nell's curse haunted Everly: *You'll never find him! Never!*

Rylan squeezed her hand. "Was it an eidolghast?"

"No."

She remembered the rats, the bear, the fighting, and destruction. She had no idea how badly she was hurt. Getting knocked out was not great though.

She wanted to wake up, go back out there, help her friends, find Rylan, but even when conscious, she hadn't been able to fix things.

"I couldn't do anything. I couldn't help anyone. I couldn't find you. I failed everyone." Everly covered her face with her hands, tears shaking loose from her eyes.

Everly felt Rylan's fingers over the top of hers, over her cheek. "You haven't. It's not your fault."

"You don't know what's happening!"

"But I know you." His voice came from close beside her ear. "And I know the world is cruel and dark, and terrible things happen, and that *isn't your fault*. You do the one thing that matters."

Rylan coaxed her fingers away from her face, and she looked up into his golden ocean eyes.

"You *try*."

Their hands remained locked together, fingers entwined.

"You always try so hard to help, to fix everything. And not everything is able to be fixed, but it's the trying that matters. It's the caring. In this dark, screwed-up world, compassion like yours is the one thing that can make the world brighter."

Everly's whole body convulsed, shaken by sobs. "It's not enough."

Rylan leaned in close, resting his forehead on hers. "You can't blame yourself for the darkness. You can't blame the sun for not chasing away every shadow. Believe in yourself, Evie. You *are* the light. And before you, the dark *will fall*."

Everly's sense of gravity lurched, tugging at her from within.

Am I waking up? Or am I dying?

She wanted to stay there with Rylan, with his hand in hers, with his face so close the temptation to kiss him was unbearable.

The pull was too strong, and she was dragged away, screaming, to face her fate.

Chapter Twenty-Eight

"Ow." Everly groaned.

Her eyes cracked open. Splintered wood fell off her as she sat up. Gingerly, she touched the back of her head. Not bleeding, but tender. Alive. Awake.

Rylan ...

She'd woken up again so quickly. But this wasn't a situation where she could linger in dreams. Animals and shadyrs still roared in battle nearby.

Everly still felt Rylan's touch on her hands and face, longed to have him with her. And his real body was somewhere nearby.

She had to find him.

I am going to find him.

The fight with the bear had moved outside again, but

another large shape stalked toward her, pale eyes glowing like small moons in the gloom.

Cat. Big cat.

The cougar. She had seen it enough in her dreams to know it right away.

It bared its sharp teeth, a growl low in its throat.

Things moved in the broken timber and kitchenware around her. Rats—panicked and fleeing around the room, around her. Everly held her breath, cringing away.

The cougar approached and Everly was sure it was the one from their car accident. Not yet full grown, it was big enough to be terrifying, but some spots from infancy hadn't yet faded to its plain adult coat, and its feet were too big for its body.

Rough sutures tracked across one of its shoulders and its eyes were milky blue.

It was Nell Everly had seen in the woods that day before the accident. Nell and Hubby must have taken the cougar. Healed it.

Poor thing. We did hit it after all.

"I'm so sorry," Everly whispered as it reached her. She flinched back, waiting for it to enact its revenge.

Jaws snapped, and there was a shrill squeak. The cougar snapped up a rat that had been crawling along Everly's arm, then flung it away. It swiped its paw at another on her leg.

Everly exhaled in vibrato and stared at the young

cougar, unsure yet if it was helping her deliberately or if it just hated rats as much as she did.

"Here's another one! I'll get it," a burly voice grunted the words. The big, cruel shadyr, Nilson, stepped in from outside, over the rubble, stalking toward the cougar.

"What? No!" Everly gasped, jumping to her feet and placing herself between him and the cat. "Stay away from it."

Nilson grinned, white lips spreading and baring razor-sharp teeth. "Or what? Have to go through you, will I? That's not much of a challenge, bliv."

The man towered over her and was built like a machine. Everly doubted she'd be able to match him. But she had to do something.

You try, Rylan's voice still echoed in her memory.

She had to try. She couldn't fight every darkness and shadow in the world, but even if she could save just one life—unlife?—it was worth doing.

"I won't let you hurt it."

He lowered his head and swayed it side to side as though thinking. When he looked up again, his grin dripped pure malice. "I think I see what's going on here. You're clearly beshadowed as well. Just a bit more collateral damage in the cleanup."

The man lashed out, faster than Everly could even react against. He grabbed her around the neck, his hands cold and hard as stone. Everly gagged.

A loud *clung* boomed through her ears, and the shadyr's grip released. His eyes rolled back into his head and he went down like a landslide into the jumble of shattered kitchen.

Behind him, a stout, elderly man stood, milky-eyed and slack-jawed. A large cast-iron frying pan still swung in his grip.

His shirt was too big for him, bulging out around suspenders, the sleeves rolled up to the elbows, revealing scarred hands and sallow skin. Another large scar puckered the side of his mouth, leading to his ear.

"Goooooood," he moaned.

"Umm, thanks?" Everly rubbed her neck.

Behind her, the cougar had vanished, hopefully finding safety. Hubby tilted his head in Everly's direction, but it was impossible to tell where he was looking or what he was seeing with his white-washed eyes.

He grunted loudly and Everly flinched. Then he raised an arm crookedly and beckoned her to follow him, shuffling into the main room. "Coooome."

Everly stepped in after him, finding the room completely trashed. There was no sign of Nell. Sounds of scuffling came from outside, and Everly heard her friends calling her name. She headed for the front door.

Hubby smacked his hand against the doorframe leading into a different room, flicking his head for her to follow him. "Boooy."

Rylan? It might be my only chance to find him.

Everly turned from the exit to the undead man before following him into the shadowy bedroom.

An overturned LED lamp cast a pale light over the area. A double bed was lovingly covered in embroidered pillows and crocheted throws. A framed photo of Nell and her husband in their youth, standing outside the gates of a zoo, sat on the bedside table.

The bed was off angle, pushed to the side and revealing a trap door that had been violently flung open, the wood cracked to pieces around the latch.

"Dooown." Hubby hobbled into the hole beneath the room.

Reaching out a shaking hand, Everly grabbed the lamp, took a few deep breaths, and followed him down.

The wooden steps creaked. They were slick with black ooze, sticking under her boots. The rough-hewn dirt walls of the stairwell gave off a peaty smell, which didn't quite cover the pungently sweet scent of rot coming from ahead.

Everly pulled her sleeve over her hand and covered her nose. She hurried after Hubby, along the short tunnel that brought them lower beneath the earth, and into a wide cavern. Hubby wobbled to the side, giving Everly a clear view into the space.

The dim light of the small LED lamp wasn't strong

enough to breach all the darkness before her. But she could see in the center of the cave a makeshift operating theater.

Dozens of unlit lamps of all shapes and sizes hung from the ceiling, cables running in a spaghetti tangle to a generator on the side. An operating table stood beneath those lamps.

On it lay a human body.

Beside it was a Darkfrey shadyr, bent over the body.

At first, Everly thought they were attempting to revive the person, but then she saw their clawed hands, wrapped around the body's neck.

"No!" Everly boomed. "What are you doing?"

The shadyr turned. She couldn't make out who it was in the dark, with their distorted form and hood covering their head.

Everly flung the LED lamp down and charged the shadyr. She knew they were in vampire form. They were probably stronger, faster, and any blow she landed on them would magically heal.

She didn't care. She was just *angry*.

So much death, so much violence.

What is wrong with these people?

She bellowed wordlessly, coming in swinging. The shadyr dodged back, hissing. Everly's fist glanced over their Darkfrey jacket.

From beneath their hood, the shadyr growled, wilder

than any of the animals up above, then pushed Everly back with both palms, cracking against her shoulders and sending her tumbling across the rocky ground.

She rolled, hands scraping as she brought herself to a stop.

The shadyr turned their back on Everly as though she didn't even matter. Their head turned, seeking, and they picked up a large stone from near their feet. They raised it high above the lifeless body on the slab.

"Stop it! Why are you doing this?" Lightning seemed to flash behind Everly's eyes, the storm of her fury breaking.

She'd been trying to control herself, trying to reason with them. Now she just wanted to make it all stop.

And screw the consequences.

Something inside Everly cracked open. And she didn't fight it.

Roaring and rushing, gleeful in its hunger, light surged freely from her.

Brightness filled the cavern, stinging her eyes.

She soared above the ground toward the shadyr, a seething star of power and wrath. Tendrils drifted out of her skin, then struck forward.

The shadyr dodged and swatted at the starry strands, moving in a fast blur. They leaped away, taking cover behind shelves and stalagmites. The tendrils chased, whipping after them, relentless, ravenous.

The hunger in Everly rose. The shadyr seemed like nothing more than prey, than food. She wanted to eat them all up. She yearned for it.

No. This isn't right.

Everly tried to reel the light back into herself. The tendrils held still for the barest moment before extending again, swirling like the stingers of a jellyfish, out of her control.

In the brief pause of reprieve, the shadyr dashed to the side, making a run for it. Everly's body turned against her will, tracking her prey. She floated across the room, dragged along in the swell of voracious light.

The shadyr reached the exit, disappearing up the dark stairs.

Just let them go. That's enough, Everly pleaded with whatever was inside her, whatever this power was. Her dragon, taking over.

But it was hungry. Too hungry. It demanded sacrifice.

The wisps spread through the cavern, seeking, and found another victim.

"No," Everly gasped.

Hubby moved too slowly, hobbling away into a dead-end corner. A low, heavy wheeze came from his throat. The sparkling streams shot out at him like lightning, wrapping him entirely.

Everly could feel the life being sucked from him, drawn

along those long strings of light, feeding her dragon.

No! Everly fought against it, struggling to make it stop. Her heart raged, searing light and pain coursing through her as she tried to force herself under control.

The hunger was too strong. Until it wasn't.

The tendrils detached, slithering slowly away. The glow faded.

Her dragon was satiated.

The old man's body slumped onto the ground. Everly stumbled over to him, her knees cracking as she fell in front of him. Glassy eyes stared emptily. Whatever essence, whatever life he'd had was gone entirely.

"No. *No.* What have I done?"

I've killed him.

Bile rose in Everly's throat. She tried to bargain, to justify. He was already dead, wasn't he? Undead? But he'd helped her. He'd been kind. He'd been loved. And now he was no more, and she'd done that.

The dragon inside her had done that.

The LED lamp still rocked slightly where it was discarded earlier, its glow obscured behind loose stones. The low angle made the shadows on Hubby's wrinkles and scars stark and strange, his face frozen in a mask of fear.

Rylan had been wrong. She wasn't the light. She was darkness.

She turned slowly, tearing her gaze away from the fallen

soul. Only one hope kept her going, kept her moving. The body lying on the operating table. Her feet dragged, numb and heavy, as she edged toward it. In the low light, Everly tried to gather what she could see.

The body seemed whole. A tall man with short buzz-cut hair. His upper body was bare, a dark shape of a tattoo on his shoulder.

"Rylan?" Everly stumbled forward, tears blurring her vision.

It's him. It's him.

Please be alive.

Chapter Twenty-Nine

Everly collapsed over Rylan's body, clung to his chest, and wept.

"Everly?" Harper's voice reached through the sounds of sobbing. "Are you down there?"

Everly lifted her head slightly.

She called out, her voice cracking, "I'm here."

Footsteps galloped down the wooden stairs and across the stone floor toward her. She turned to find two shadyrs, still in vampire form, and Harper following behind, holding a bright lamp. With more light, Everly could identify the two shadyrs as Callan and Cherry, mostly based on their hair and clothing.

"Oh, thank everything you're okay!" Harper wrapped Everly in a strong hug, the lamp banging into Everly's back.

"It's Rylan—you found him," Callan gasped.

"Oh, wow," Harper said in a hush.

She let go of Everly and held the lamp over Rylan. He lay still, completely unaffected by the noise around him. His skin was pale and firm, although not as white as the shadyrs in their full vampire form. Everly wondered if beneath his closed lips she would find fangs.

"Is he alive?" Cherry asked softly.

Everly nodded. She had heard a slow, soft heartbeat as she'd pressed her face to his chest and felt the barest rise and fall of breath. He seemed to be sleeping peacefully.

Harper turned back to Everly. "I was so worried when we lost track of you. That was craziness!"

"I was worried about you too."

Cherry snorted. "No need to worry about Bellsy—she was fierce."

"For a human," she added bashfully. "We came to find you as soon as it was clear enough. The Darkfreys, they killed just about everything."

The horror and fury in Harper's eyes made Everly's own sting.

Harper must have seen her expression darken, because she added, "We tried our best not to hurt any of the animals. Managed to chase some away. I'm sure some survived."

"They should have listened to us. None of that had to happen." Callan's pale face grew stern, and he squeezed his hands into fists.

Black mist surrounded him, and he returned to his normal self.

Cherry pouted over vampire teeth. "Show-off. Way too much vasmire ... bits ... nearby for me to change back now."

The extra light in the room showed the full extent of Nell's laboratory. Around the varying levels of the rocky floor, wooden shelves had been constructed to fit the spaces. They held body parts of all shapes and sizes, white labels hanging off them, black ooze dripping between them.

There were a lot of tentacles.

"You'll get there soon," Callan encouraged. "It just takes practice."

"Takes more than practice, runts."

Four Darkfrey shadyrs stepped out from the stairway passage. Nilson, Annabeth, Jasper, and another Everly didn't know.

Could one of them be the shadyr who tried to hurt Rylan? Everly clenched her teeth so hard they ached.

Nilson continued his sneering words. "Which is why you should leave it to us. Where's the vasmire?"

Cherry pointed at the shelves. "There. There. A bit over there. And also there."

"What in the Everdark is going on down here?" Annabeth asked.

"No vasmire?" the fourth shadyr asked. "Just bits? No

wonder I felt weaker than usual."

Callan watched them warily. "Like I told you before, there wasn't a beshadowing here. Not really."

"So we could have avoided all of this mess if you'd listened for once instead of following orders blindly." Cherry glared at Jasper. Their gaze met for the barest of moments before Jasper turned away.

Nilson walked over to a shelf and kicked a tub of gore. "Alive or not, the eidolghast parts were affecting this area, the animals, and the crazy old witch."

"Where is Nell?" Everly demanded.

His pale teeth twisted into a dark grin. "The old hag? With her dead pets."

Everly's heart closed in on itself, and she spoke through clenched teeth. "You didn't have to do that! You're murderers!"

"She was ghast-twisted. She attacked us and had to be put down." In a puff of black mist and sparks, he shifted back into his regular form.

The other three followed, suddenly a lot less threatening, but no less monstrous.

Everly's voice grew loud. "You attacked her animals first. If you'd listened, you'd know she was only trying to help."

"You're just a bunch of bleeding hearts. That's why you shouldn't be messing around in our business. You're not strong enough to do what needs to be done."

Everly wanted to rage and fight and consume them whole. They were monsters and murderers.

But so was she. And if she gave in to that again, she didn't know what the consequences would be.

"Oh, is that Rylan?" Annabeth squeaked, running toward them.

"Yeah, it is." Callan stepped into Annabeth's path, blocking her before she could reach him. "That's why we were here in the first place."

"Is he alive?" Annabeth froze, her mouth open.

"Nell saved him," Everly spat, her words a weapon of guilt. "Nell saved him like she saved all those animals. And you murdered them all."

Annabeth seemed to shrink a little, taking a step back.

Nilson strolled over to Everly and poked a hard finger into her collarbone. "They weren't animals anymore. They were atrocities, and we did our job."

"Get your disgusting hand off me," Everly growled.

Harper, Callan, and Cherry pressed in by her side, staring him down.

Neither Annabeth nor Jasper moved up beside Nilson to match them, only the unknown shadyr, part of his brace, joined him.

Nilson cricked his neck and stepped back, his chin lifted, jutting out. "You shouldn't even be here. You're lucky we came along to put an end to this nightmare. Don't forget that."

"That's enough. It's over and done," Annabeth said. "We need to take Rylan home now."

The vision of one of the shadyrs trying to end Rylan's life flashed through Everly's mind again, nearly overcoming her control.

The cavern became almost imperceivably brighter, and Everly clamped it down. No longer hungry, the light was easier to contain, quickly fading again.

She exhaled her words through clenched teeth. "No. He's not going with you."

"Of course he is. He's one of us. He's part of my brace." Annabeth shook her head in confusion, her red hair, held back in a ponytail, swinging.

The remaining three Darkfrey shadyrs entered the cavern. When they saw everyone else, they shook off their vampire form as well, revealing Vonny and two strangers, the remains of Nilson's brace.

"What's going on in here?" Vonny snapped.

"They found Rylan, but they don't want us to take him."

"Found him? Alive?" She peered skeptically over their shoulders at his body on the table. "What's wrong with him?"

Everly glanced back as well. No matter the yelling and

commotion, Rylan hadn't stirred at all.

Callan watched Everly, frowning. "We don't know."

Jasper tilted his head, looking at the body. "Then we should transfer him back to the estate for medical aid."

"Not a chance. Not after what I've seen." Everly shook her head.

Vonny narrowed her eyes. "What are you talking about? What did you see?"

Everly wished she knew, wished she could point out the shadyr who stood in front of her now as the one who'd attempted to take Rylan's life. But she couldn't.

"I saw enough to know there's no way I'm going to trust any of you with keeping him alive."

Vonny laughed her off. "He's a Darkfrey and he comes with us."

"He's a Howell and stays with us," Callan said, stepping in front of her.

"These guys are out of their ghast-damned minds," Nilson said.

Vonny huffed. "Fine, you know what? Keep him, then. He's been more trouble than he's worth lately anyway— running off on his own and ending up in whatever mess this is, leaving us to take the blame."

"Vonny, no. He's one of us. He's our brace leader," Annabeth argued.

"*He* made the decision to not be part of our brace

anymore. And he can be replaced." Vonny marched away, out of the cavern, and Annabeth scuttled after her, still arguing and pleading.

"Looks like you guys have won yourself a vegetable." Nilson snickered. He turned to leave too, talking on his way. "Good luck with that. Whatever you do with him, better do it before the cleanup crew arrives. 'Cause he looks like he should go in the trash with the rest of the corpses."

The rest of the Darkfreys followed him.

Jasper frowned at the Howell team, opened his mouth, closed it, then left as well.

"I can't believe they did that. All that killing, like it was nothing." Harper's eyes were narrow and glossy. "And poor Nell ..."

Cherry sighed. "It's what they are trained to do—destroy a beshadowing, at any cost."

Harper said, "It's like they enjoyed it!"

Callan and Cherry nodded, sharing a sad look with each other. Everly wondered if they had seen far worse.

Harper cuddled her arms around herself. "At least we got Rylan back."

Everly's chest tightened. "At what cost?"

Callan said, "None of what happened here is our fault. They would have come out to deal with this whether we found the place or not. It was just bad luck we were here at the same time."

Or good luck. They'd saved a few animals and Rylan. A few moments later, and Rylan would have been nothing but more body parts.

Everly's traumatized mind was still trying to turn back time, replaying every choice she'd made, every hesitation, pointing fingers at where she'd gone wrong.

If only she'd done this, if only she'd said that, if only she'd done better, been stronger, maybe there wouldn't have been so much tragedy. But she *couldn't* turn back time. She couldn't fix what she'd done.

She couldn't give back the life she'd taken.

Harper grunted. "How can they get away with this?"

"The Darkfreys own Shroudhaven. The cops, the courts. They do as they please and clean up the mess afterward." Callan looked around the room at the mutilated monster pieces. "Speaking of which, they're right. They'll have a cleanup crew out here soon. We should get moving."

"Whoa." Cherry spotted the crumpled body of the old man in the corner and pointed at him. "Who is that?"

Everly's mouth opened but was clogged by guilt.

"Is that Nell's husband?" Callan guessed. "What happened to him?"

Everly shook her head. Her voice broke over the words. "He's dead."

"Those horrible Darkfreys," Harper snarled.

Tears washed hot over Everly's eyes. She couldn't tell

them, couldn't speak what she'd done. What would Harper think of her?

Harper turned away from the body to the two men. "You guys made the right decision getting out of that place."

Callan nodded slowly, his gaze on his brother. "I just wish Rylan had gotten out sooner too. Then maybe this wouldn't have happened."

They all turned toward Rylan, lying still on the table.

"He hasn't moved a muscle. Is he in a coma or something?" Cherry asked.

"He's so pale," Harper said.

"It's like he's only partly in vampire form, half and half," Cherry said, still in full vampire form himself.

Everly found her voice again. "He looked human, like this, the last time I saw him. In part of the fight he seemed more vampire-like, then he seemed human, then at the end he turned cold again."

"He must have changed back so you didn't see what he was. If his injuries were that bad, maybe he couldn't change again fully. But even like this, with all the vasmire parts around, he must have had just enough regeneration to heal himself," Callan whispered.

"What do we do now?" Harper asked.

Callan shrugged. "Try to wake him up, get him out of here?"

Despite it being what Everly desperately wanted the

most, her hope of Rylan waking up had fallen low.

Still, she bent over him, speaking close to his ear, "Rylan? Can you hear us?"

Everyone seemed to hold their breath, but nothing happened.

"Hey, come on, man. Wake up," Callan said, patting his cheeks.

Nothing.

Cherry checked Rylan's pulse and rubbed his sternum with his knuckles.

Harper tried yelling and clapping her hands loudly in front of his face.

Nothing made any difference. Rylan remained as still as death.

Chapter Thirty

Everly hauled a plastic tub of monster gore into her old bedroom, while Harper smoothed out the new sheets on the single bed.

Who would've thought this is where we'd end up today?

They'd found Rylan, but it didn't feel like a win.

Callan and Cherry carried his body into the room and laid him carefully on the mattress.

Since finding him, they'd made sure to never let his body be separated from the dead monster bits.

After making their way out of the woods, they had emptied out some tubs of props and photography gear from Harper's van and returned to Nell's laboratory to fill them with random chunks of vasmire anatomy off the shelves.

They assumed that as long as there were vasmire pieces nearby, Rylan's body would continue to renew itself enough to stay alive. That was about all they had to go on for now.

In the days he'd been missing, Rylan hadn't seemed to have lost any muscle mass or become dehydrated. It was like he was in a kind of stasis.

Given that he wasn't strictly human, and the remaining weirdness surrounding the situation, they all decided that a hospital wasn't the best idea.

Everly got checked over by Callan and Cherry, who both had medical training from their time with the Darkfreys, and they thought that despite briefly being unconscious, she didn't need a hospital either unless she started showing any other symptoms of concussion.

Everly and Harper had also cleaned up their minor scratches with some hand sanitizer from the van. It stung violently, but they were desperate to remove anything left by the filthy claws and nails that had made the marks. Callan and Cherry's vampire-tinted skin showed no wounds, completely healed already.

The vasmire parts helped Rylan, but they also presented a challenge, because not all the Howell House shadyrs had trained enough to have full control over their bodies in the presence of eidolghasts. Even dead ones.

Cherry, and Tammy too, Callan had thought, would be resigned to vampire form all the time if the vasmire parts were kept near them.

So they'd ended up at the Boderleth house.

Callan had allowed his vampire form to return to help carry his heavy brother up the stairs but went back to human again once the job was done.

"I can't believe we're doing this." Harper's voice had an edge of hysteria to it.

Cherry grinned over his still pointy teeth at Harper. "You didn't think to yourself this morning, gosh, it would really end the day well if we brought home an unconscious man and a few boxes of monster tentacles?"

"Maybe I did, but that's my own private business," Harper replied.

Everly leaned over and tucked the blanket up to Rylan's shoulders. She wasn't sure whether he could feel the cold, or anything at all, but it made him look more comfortable.

We found you. Please wake up. Wake up so everything can be okay.

"He's going to be all right," Harper offered, rubbing Everly's shoulder.

"Yeah, for now," Callan said, shaking his head as he stared at his brother. "I have no idea how long the vasmire parts will keep working. Those look pretty fresh, but I imagine they won't last long."

Faces turned grim, then Callan shook his head, smiling wryly at Harper and Everly. "We'll work something out. How about you two? Handling?"

Harper waved both hands in front of her, gesturing to

the tufts of fur and splatters of blood across her clothes. "This, you mean? How am I handling *this*? I'm going to hold off on an answer until after I take the longest shower ever in an attempt to wash off all of *this*."

Cherry shrugged. "I'd tell you guys that tonight was crazy-out-of-the-ordinary, but I'd be lying."

Harper just stared at him for a long moment, then shuddered. "Okay, I'm going to hit that shower now."

She fluttered a hand and left. The sound of the bathroom door closing and shower turning on came faintly through the wall beside them.

"I want to get out of here too. I'd really like to have my own skin back." Cherry flexed his pale fingers. "You guys all right?"

Everly and Callan nodded, and Cherry headed for the door. "Good teamwork tonight. Including honorary members."

Everly tried to smile a goodbye, but her face fell. It didn't feel like the night had gone well. They'd found Rylan, but in every other way it had been a disaster.

I killed someone.

In brief moments of distraction, she managed to forget, but that weight crept into the forefront of her mind as often as it could, bringing cold chills and a stuttering heart.

"I'm sorry. I know that was all really hard, with the animals and Nell. I don't agree with what the Darkfreys did either," Callan said, his frown matching hers. "Beshadowings are tricky. Even partial ones. Nell had been working with eidolghast parts for who knows how long. It would have changed her. She wasn't really human anymore."

"And what are we?" Everly countered, tears in her eyes.

"We're not beshadowed," Callan said firmly. "Although Nell was doing the right thing now, beshadowings never end well. I'm not saying the Darkfreys handled it the right way, but if nothing changed, things would have only gotten darker."

It didn't end well.

Everly screwed her eyes shut. Then, worried, she opened them, staring at the semitransparent plastic tubs and the mess of flesh within. "Is that going to be a problem here? Is that going to affect Harper and me?"

Callan put his hands into his pockets and winced. "Maybe? We won't leave it long enough to find out. This is temporary, okay? We're going to get this worked out as soon as we can."

A soft knocking came from the bedroom door. Everly turned to find Lian there. "Cherry let me in on his way out. Thank you for calling me."

"Of course," Everly said. She moved out of the way, letting Rylan's mother come into the small space.

Lian stepped in and slowly walked to the bedside.

Gingerly reaching out, she placed one hand on Rylan's chest and another over her mouth.

A moment passed as she stood frozen there, and Everly wondered if she was feeling for the dull beat of Rylan's heart, needing to feel that proof of life herself.

Then she turned around and hugged Callan. "You found him."

Callan returned the embrace. "It was Everly who worked it out."

They briefly explained Nell's animal sanctuary to Lian, her eyebrows rising at every new detail.

"Everly saw a Darkfrey shadyr trying to kill Rylan when she found him," Callan told his mom in a low voice. "She wasn't sure who. They ran as soon as Everly called them out."

That was the story Everly had told the others, anyway. She still couldn't put into words what she'd done to Nell's husband. She couldn't tell anyone what had happened. She could barely understand it herself.

Her mind swirled with confusing feelings of how much she'd been in control, or not in control, and she wasn't sure which option was scarier.

Lian sighed. "Whatever Rylan was looking into, it made him a serious enemy. I'll sort out shifts with our lot, make sure there's always someone keeping an eye on this place."

"I was thinking the same thing," Callan said.

"You really think they might try to come after him again?" Everly asked.

Lian shrugged and avoided eye contact. "Better to be safe, either way. We'll work out the rest later. For now, we have Rylan back. That's what matters."

The three of them looked at his body, and Everly knew they were all thinking the same thing. That he was only half back. And what really mattered was making him whole again.

"We'd better go, let you get cleaned up and rest after all of that," Lian said. "But we won't be far away if you need anything."

Callan followed Lian to the bedroom door, then turned back.

"Sure you're okay with this?" he asked, tilting his head to Rylan's still body.

"It's the least I can do. I'll look after him," she said. *Just like he always looked after me.*

Everly followed them downstairs and said goodbye.

"You done with this?" Lian asked, wrapping her hand around the weed trimmer that rested on the back porch.

"Yeah, thank you." Everly had never gotten to clearing the backyard, but it didn't seem important anymore. Her time limit in Shroudhaven had run out. But she wasn't going anywhere.

"You can borrow it again any time you like. Anything

you need. You're family."

Everly swallowed. After the week she'd had, thoughts of her own mother's death had vanished entirely, especially in the face of the pragmatic, salt-and-pepper-haired woman who stood before her now. The woman who raised her more than Janey Boderleth ever had.

Everly felt her heart warming and breaking simultaneously. "Thank you, for letting me be part of your family. I'm sorry I was part of everything falling apart."

"Nonsense. What you are, is part of bringing it all back together again." Lian was already walking away, garden tool resting over her shoulder. She turned back briefly, her eyes full of emotion. "Thank you for bringing my son home."

Everly stood at the back door as Callan and Lian disappeared around the corner of the house, then she remained there a while afterward, hugging herself against the cold and staring out into the dark night. The murky shadows seemed so different now that she knew what could be creeping within them.

And something was creeping in her backyard. Everly startled as a blurry shape moved beside the garden shed, down near the broken fencing. She held her breath, hoping it was just her bad eyesight or her imagination and not some new horror.

The shape moved again, and Everly was sure she recognized it.

Moving slowly, on quiet feet, she stepped inside to the kitchen. She grabbed an old breakfast bowl off a shelf and put in some raw beef mince that had been intended as part of their dinner that night. A dinner that had never happened due to other adventures.

Taking it outside, Everly placed the bowl in the long grass at the center of the yard, then quickly backed away again to the porch. She wasn't exactly sure what an undead cougar would eat, but she figured meat was good for both cats and zombies.

The grass shivered in a trail as the cougar prowled through it toward the bowl. As the grass cleared, it hesitated, milky blue eyes flashing toward Everly. Then it chomped the mince up in one gulp and pounced away.

Everly watched the darkness and found a small smile growing on her face. She had done that. She had saved the young cat's life. It was a small consolation, after all the carnage that night. But it was something—something she hoped was good.

"Hey." Harper stepped outside, patting the ends of her hair with a towel and yawning. "Everyone's gone?"

"Yep. Just us, Rylan, and the monster chunks now."

"So fun."

"I'm sorry about all this. I mean, when we came here, I knew Shroudhaven wasn't great, but I honestly had no idea this is where things would be five days later."

Harper put an arm over Everly's shoulders and they headed back inside. "Well, we did get you reunited with Rylan at least. You know. In a way."

"So fun," Everly muttered, echoing Harper's tone.

They both giggled, more in a shaky expression of relief than with any humor. Back in the kitchen, Harper got the kettle boiling and dropped a couple of teabags into mugs.

"Sooo ... I guess we're not heading home tomorrow?" Harper said.

Everly picked up a mug and slowly dunked the teabag up and down. The scent of chamomile filled the air. "I don't think I can. The dreams are too real. I'm sure there's some connection there, something that could help Rylan wake up. I can't leave him like this without trying. But you don't have to stay."

"Oh no, I'm sticking around. You can't have all the fun without me." Harper pouted. "Plus, I haven't even had a chance to do anything with the antiques yet."

Everly laughed through her nose.

Harper took a sip of her tea, regarding Everly. "What about your job?"

"It's okay. I'll work something out." Everly wasn't sure what a solution would look like.

Her savings were already almost gone due to cleanup expenses. And with Rylan's situation, she couldn't exactly rent out a spare room here.

"I can always try to sell off any of the intact antiques to get by until we move home again. Or there must be some repair work available around Shroudhaven."

"I bet." Harper yawned again. "My offer's still open too. I could really do with a partner in my work. Someone I trust."

Can you really trust me? Everly wondered. She didn't feel as though she even trusted herself anymore. "Thank you. I should be okay though. This is temporary. Just until Rylan wakes up."

Harper smiled and shrugged noncommittally.

They finished their tea and headed up the stairs. After peeking in to check on Rylan—still unmoving, still stable—Harper brought Everly into a tight hug. "We'll work things out. One day at a time, until he wakes up."

Everly stood at the doorway to her old bedroom for some time after Harper had gone to bed, staring at Rylan.

In the low light of the dimmed desk lamp she'd placed beside him, the lines of his still face seemed so familiar. It wasn't the face of the boy she remembered, but it was the face of the man she knew from her dreams.

She wondered how much she really knew him though. He'd lived and grown and trained with the Darkfreys for years.

Was he like them now? Did he share their attitudes? Their violence? Had he become a mindless soldier, or worse, one who relished in the spill of blood? Or did he still have the same kind heart from childhood somewhere beneath his Darkfrey tattoo?

Maybe she would find out when he woke up.

If he ever wakes up.

Chapter Thirty-One

"Evie? What's happened? Are you okay?" Rylan's tone was frantic and deep with concern.

Everly heard him calling to her through the darkness before she could see anything.

The world shifted and turned. Petal-shaped fragments of scenery fell into place like puzzle pieces around Everly. Wherever she turned, reality blossomed to meet her observation.

A crinkling ground of autumn leaves beneath her. A night sky swirled with cotton-candy galaxies above. She sat on the edge of a sheer cliff, a dark forest at her back and an endless universe before her.

Rylan's shape emerged, crouched on one knee beside her. "Are you—?"

"I'm asleep. This is a dream." Everly spoke the words as she always did in her dreams, helping to ground herself, to take control.

Rylan dragged a hand over his mouth, eyes still stormy. "Asleep where? Are you safe? What was happening before?"

"It's okay. I'm fine." Everly looked up at him from under her eyelashes, her eyelids still puffy and tired despite being asleep. "And you're okay too. We found you."

Rylan moved slowly into a sitting position, his knees bent in front of him and his elbows on them.

His voice was barely a whisper. "You found me? Am I ..."

"You're alive. Healthy even, except that you won't wake up. In a semi-vampire sort of state, it seems, which is keeping your body going."

"What in the Everdark has been going on? When you were here before ... what happened? Where were you? You were so upset and *unconscious*!"

Everly gave him the quick version of what had happened with Nell. Her lips wavered and eyes stung. She didn't mention Nell's husband, what she had done to him. She looked around, half expecting him to haunt her dreams as well, but he was nowhere to be seen.

"You did it. You saved me. I told you, you're the light."

He gave her a soft smile, but his words only brought a dark chill creeping through Everly's bones.

She knew now that the light within her was nothing to revere. It felt as monstrous as anything she'd seen since returning to Shroudhaven. What would Rylan do if he knew what she'd done? Would his Darkfrey training require him to treat her as a monster too?

In the nebulous sky above, her dragon spun its body in glowing wheels, and the cougar stalked in the shadows behind them. At her side, nestled into the leaves and stringy golden grass, was a playset of plastic zoo animals.

Rylan grunted. "I can't stand this. Whenever you're awake, it's like I've fallen asleep. I don't know anything that's happening. I can't do *anything*. You're going off into all this danger and I'm completely useless."

"I'm sorry. I don't know why you're trapped here. We'll do everything we can to wake you up."

Rylan shook his head fiercely, then turned and held her gaze. "That's not what I mean. You're not even supposed to be here. You're not supposed to know any of this. You're supposed to be somewhere safe, away from nightmares like the one you were just in because you were trying to help me."

Everly drew in a shaky breath and looked away. Beside her, the plastic animals came to life. Miniature lions and bears pounced over leaves, hunting. Tiny shadyr action figures emerged and rushed in terrified circles. In her dream, they were no match for the animals and were gobbled up, one by one.

Tears spilled from Everly's eyes as tremors shook her whole body. "It all went wrong. What I did ... you don't understand. I have to—"

"Shh, it's okay. It's over now." Rylan shifted closer to her and put his arms around her shoulders.

The arms she'd longed to have around her for her whole life. She felt their strength, their warmth, but it did little to comfort her. Sobs rattled the embrace.

He was only trying to comfort her, be the protective big brother like he'd always been, until he'd just want her gone so he wouldn't have to keep protecting her. She knew he still wanted her gone.

Everly swallowed away her feelings. "I'm going to make things right."

Rylan shook his head against her shoulder. "You've done enough. You found me, despite everything. You found me and you saved me," he whispered.

"Then why are you still here, in my dreams?"

Rylan's hold on her tightened ever so slightly. "Even if I'm not whole, you're keeping all of me safe—my body and my soul."

"Like you always kept me safe," Everly whispered. She sniffed and wiped her eyes. "It's my turn now."

Something nudged Everly's other side, and she turned to see the cougar nuzzling against her knee. It was only half there, shimmering and translucent, a gray mirror of its true self.

It settled down like a sphinx, belly squashing the plastic action figures and toys at war. They could be seen squirming through the cougar's ghostly body.

Everly moved slowly, tentatively at first. She reached out her hand and touched the back of a finger to the cat's forehead. Its pale-blue eyes closed, so she ran her whole hand over the soft fur between its ears. It rumbled a single, soft purr, then was silent.

The dragon swooped low, illuminating them with its glow. It had been satiated, for now.

She could control it again. She could keep it away from Rylan and the cougar, whatever part of them she had here with her, inside her. She would keep them safe.

Everly turned back to Rylan and found her face so close to his that she felt his breath across her cheeks. He watched her intently. Everly's tears had slowed, and her sobbing had ceased.

The smile she gave him tasted of salt. "I'm staying. In Shroudhaven. Until we can wake you up."

He frowned at that but didn't argue. He did let her go though, moving out of the embrace. Everly shivered, missing his warmth.

"I just wish I could do more." He glanced at her from the side of his eyes, then turned away. "But I can't.

I can't have the people … around me be hurt when I can stop it."

"Sometimes we don't have that choice." Everly's heart fluttered, looking at him.

A rise of anxiety spiked through Everly, and her dragon seemed to relish watching her squirm.

Everly took a moment to ground herself.

Five things she could see: Rylan's green eyes, his eyes, looking into hers, his eyes, not turning away, his eyes, not shaming or blaming, his eyes.

Four things she could touch: the dreamlike fuzz of the cougar's neck, the silky strands of dream grass beneath her, the insubstantial press of dream clothes over her body, Rylan, if she only just reached out.

Three things she could hear: Rylan's breath, close to her ear, and her heartbeat, racing, driven thunderous by that breath. How loud it made her swallow.

Two things she could smell: Home, home. Howell house and Boderleth Antiques.

One thing she could taste: the saltwater of her tears.

The boy she'd loved as long as she could remember was gone. The man he was now was someone she was only just starting to get to know. But she could feel, deep within her, that he was still good.

It had been his words that had gotten her through the nightmare.

She repeated them out loud. "Sometimes the world is dark and cruel, and all we can do is try."

Everly raised her hand, as tentatively as she had with the wild creature beside her. She placed a single finger on Rylan's chin, then turned his face back toward her.

"Whatever happens next, we are in it together."

She had to get his consciousness back into his body. She had to wake him up.

No matter what dangers and horrors this town threw at her next.

Rylan's body has been found, but can Everly make him whole again?

Everly's entire life is upside down. She's not even sure if she's human anymore, and no one seems to know what she is.

Or whether it's good or evil.

The only thing she's sure of is she has to save the man she loves. And to do so, she's going to have to face up to Darkfrey Estate, crazy cultists, and a creature that is only tangible in the darkness. With the Howell team on her side, Everly uncovers dangerous secrets, ones that could break her apart.

Continue the adventure in Blood Bound, book two of the Beshadowed series by Selina A. Fenech.

More Books by Selina A Fenech

Shadow Dragon Saga

Into a haunted realm a creature unlike any is born, and must be protected. Diverse young adult epic fantasy with dragons and magic

Memory's Wake Trilogy

A modern girl lost in and hunted in a fairy tale world. An illustrated young adult portal fantasy with Arthurian and Victorian themes.

Empath Chronicles

Teenagers with superpowers fueled by emotions ... what could go wrong? A young adult superhero romance.

Fairy Tale Wishes

Romantic fairy tale retellings with a twist. Young adult, standalone paranormal romance in urban and epic fantasy settings

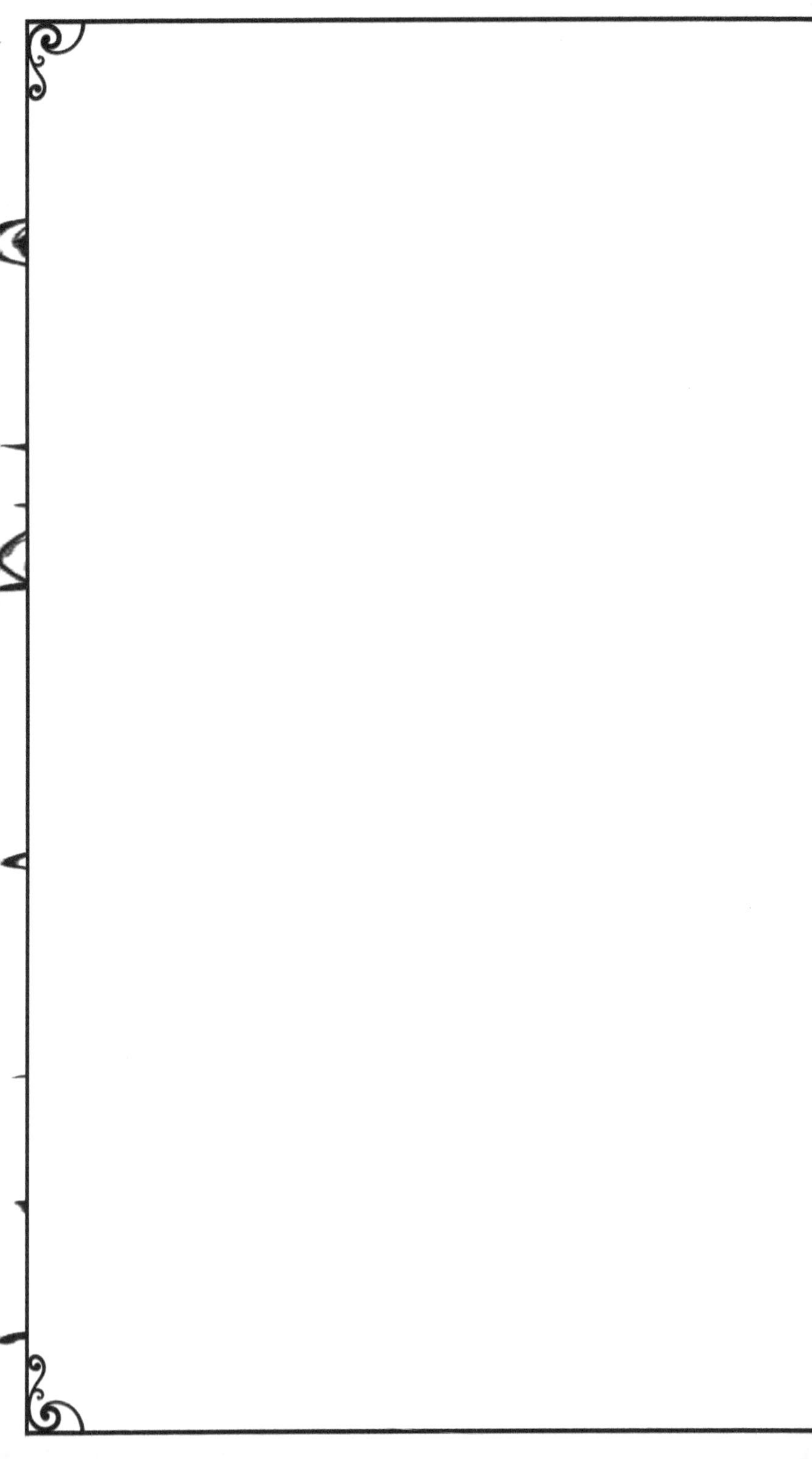

About the Author

Professional daydreamer, Selina A. Fenech writes "adorably dark" Epic and Urban Fantasy for teens and adults. Filled with sweet and quirky characters, laugh out loud moments, and perilous adventures, her magical worlds are perfect for readers who love daring twists and happily ever afters.

A cancer survivor determined to live life to the fullest, she is an escape room enthusiast, avid gardener, foodie and self-proclaimed geek, residing in Australia.

In addition to literature, Selina applies her unique take on the dichotomy of light and dark as a professional fantasy artist working under the name Selina Fenech and has published many illustrated books, oracle decks, and colouring books.

Find Out more About Selina

OFFICIAL WEBSITE:www.selinafenech.com